MW01121361

2008 05 29

DATE DUE	RETURNED	D
OCT 2 1 2009		
Feb. 2/15	OCT 1 4 2014	

3199 LAKE...
TORONTO, ONTARIO M8V 1N.

Greener than Eden

Greener than Eden *a novel*

Michael Kohn

Cormorant Books

**Canada Council
for the Arts** **Conseil des Arts
du Canada**

ONTARIO ARTS COUNCIL
CONSEIL DES ARTS DE L'ONTARIO

The publisher gratefully acknowledges the support of the
Canada Council for the Arts and the Ontario Arts Council
for its publishing program. We acknowledge the financial support
of the Government of Canada through the Book Publishing
Industry Development Program (BPIDP) for our publishing activities.

Printed and bound in Canada

LIBRARY AND ARCHIVES CANADA CATALOGUING IN PUBLICATION

Kohn, Michael S. (Michael Steven), 1965–
Greener than Eden / Michael Kohn.

ISBN 1-896951-99-6

I. Title.

PS8621.O46G74 2006   C813'.6   C2006-904377-9

Cover design: Angel Guerra/Archetype
Cover image: Angel Guerra/Archetype
Author photo: Tanya Norman
Interior design: Tannice Goddard
Printer: Friesens

CORMORANT BOOKS INC.
215 Spadina Avenue, Studio 230, Toronto, Ontario, Canada M5T 2C7
www.cormorantbooks.com

To Tanya and our son, Isaac

To my parents and sister Jen for believing

And to everyone who's ever stooped to plant a tree.

CHAPTER ONE

WHEN I GET off the Greyhound at Betty's truck stop in Upsala, he doesn't even ask me who I am. He just picks up my duffel bag and says, "My crummy's across the street."

"Your what?"

"Boy, you're green," he says. "My truck."

"The name's Noah. Bob, right?"

"Backwards and forwards, just the way I like my people." He squeezes my hand firmly as if he can't feel through his callouses. "Green palms, but you play guitar. Southpaw ..."

I suppose the list sent from Head Office told him, and that I'm not at all versed in his lingo only verifies it, but I can't help thinking that by *green* he means a whole lot more than never having planted before — that his eyes read *no dirt under his nails. Urban refugee. Virgin to more than the woods.* But maybe that's what he needs: X-ray vision, no surprises. From what I was told at the orientation, the weather up here is enough of a variable without a camp supervisor having to worry about the sanity of twenty-to-thirty-odd people.

We toss my gear into the back seat of his crapped-out white one-ton, jump into the cab, and roll westward along the Trans-Canada — briefly hitting highway speed before we slow for the fork of a logging road, the overloaded Prairie Schooner hitched to our ass-end swerving in and out of the sideviews. Northward across the tracks of the train I'd missed, and the woman I'd dreamed would be aboard it. Past a logging truck passing between two massive red corrugated drums to straighten out its load. Off the gravel and up a rainslick dirt road, rising with the rocks, falling with the dips, brooks, and swamps, sloshing through mud-filled ruts left by wheels so big I can't even begin to imagine the size of their machines. The sharp bends and crumbling shoulders, the bumps and blur of trees have made me carsick, so I close my eyes and listen to the last distant radio signal fade. Even the CBC's gone. Good.

Bob slides a tape into the cassette player, but every few words a bump, the sound blurs and it ejects. "Fuck. Two weeks and the damn thing's bit the dust — literally. This machine ate more road dust on our stint in Ear Falls than it did all last year."

"No spring rains back in Toronto either."

"I'd guess you've lived there all your life. The way you say it — *Trawna* — The accent's almost American."

He turns his eyes back to the road, and it's my turn to look. He's got a ski-bum's face. He's got a buzz-bomb lure — for fish too big for lakes — hanging from the rear-view mirror.

"I'd guess you're from the West Coast," I say. "Vancouver Island."

"Hornby," he says.

"Where's that?"

"An island off an island off Vancouver."

"City?"

"Island. But it's not as isolated as it sounds. ... You look tired. Want some chaw?" He reaches for a tin of chewing tobacco that's sitting on the dash. "I used it on the drive from B.C. — I had only three days to get to Ear Falls and had to go non-stop."

Yawning, I shake my head. Then I shut my eyes tight, trying to squeeze the rattling of the doors out of my head, long enough to sleep.

❧

"Jesus H. Christ!"

The brakes squeal. I wake up airborne in the cab, the crummy sliding back from under me. I see him whole for an instant, horned with the weathered branches of some great hardwood, neck well-hung with the weight of his dewlap. My head snaps forward as my seat belt locks; we jolt to a stop and I'm snapped back. Now he's a sea of tea-box figurines, fragmented as the glass.

I peer through a small triangle of uncracked windshield. He doesn't even flinch, his eye a white aura frozen around a pupil dilated big as a silver dollar and so glass-like you'd think he's been taxidermied. But he can't hide every twitch and pulse of life, so he runs. Off the shoulder into the thick woods.

Bob's leaning up against the steering wheel, staring straight ahead, eyes showing more white than the moose's.

"See the rack on him? That was one big fuckin' bull — musta weighed close to half a ton. Smoke?"

I don't usually smoke — I chain-smoked one of the two complimentary packs of Daily Mail I was given in jail, traded the other for two chocolate bars and quit when I got out. Now I take my first smoke since February in trembling fingers. Bob lights mine, then his.

Grimacing, he blows a jet of smoke. "So it was your head that fucked my windshield."

"What?"

"You're bleeding." He hands me a wad of napkins. "Feel dizzy?"

I daub at the warmth trickling down my forehead. The last time I really bled, I'd been bludgeoned from a Caterpillar bulldozer with a mounted-police baton, an armoured horse rearing up over my stunned, limp body, a stranger lying at my side slipping her hand into mine and mumbling *we shall live in peace* — or some other comforting lie — through her own blood. The windshield may have even reopened the same wound.

"I think I'd better dress that before we move on," Bob says. He hops down from the cab, reaches behind the seat, and pulls out a large unripe lime-coloured industrial first aid kit. "Hey, come on, we haven't got all day."

I get out and sit on the bumper. He shuffles the part through my hair as if grooming out lice. I wince where he stops, clenching my teeth as he trails a peroxide-soaked cotton ball through the wound.

"Damned flies," he says, fanning his hand over my head.

"They don't seem too bad."

"They will in a week or two, once they've chased the rest of the animal kingdom out to the road. Before the season's through, their great-great grandchildren will be hatching to get their fill. That's why you've got to plant fast. The instant you stop, you're history. So, what's drawn you up here — I mean, aside from the two greens?"

"The two greens?"

"Ma nature and money, or were you sent?"

I shrug. "The fishing."

"Oh I see. Natural wealth. ... You know, you're just about as thick as the forest. But ten springs ago I boated a kid almost as green 'n even quieter 'n you to a contract I was tree-runner on way up the Campbell River, and he's still with me now."

"And he still plants?"

"No, but he may be training you how. Lyndon's finally mellowed enough to make foreman. Man. ... He was so bottled up his first season, it's as if he ran on nothing but heat 'n steam. But the forest broke him eventually, and it's gonna break you too, sooner or later. My advice is, don't resist it."

He cocks his head as if listening to the sky, then paws a buzzing insect from the air. Holding it by the wings, he sorts through its kicking legs and plucks out its suckle shaft. "Disarmament," he smiles, dropping the mosquito to the road, and for a minute I'm left wondering if he knows more about my leanings than he lets on. But then he reaches into the first aid kit and tosses me two flat packages, each two inches square. One's a gauze compress for my head, the other's for my wallet, for my other head.

I look into his face, all a-grin.

"Thanks, but I don't think I'll be needing both of these."

"Gotta girlfriend back home?"

"No, and I plan on keeping it that way up here."

He laughs and shakes his head. "How many priests have I heard make that vow? The locals say it gets so lonely in the bush even the bears start to look good ..."

I toss the Shields back into his hands. "Ever done more than look?"

His face sours. "Never had to. Every camp I've ever run or been in has had its share of women. And I've had my own." He shuts the safe back into the first aid kit. "Well, at least you'll know where to find these when your mind's changed."

"If."

"Whatever." He swats a mosquito that has landed on his wrist. "Let's just hope that none of these flying fuckers can spread the fucking plague, or we're all history."

We get back into the crummy and tear off for camp, Bob hunched over the wheel, squinting through the tiny clear triangle of unshattered windshield, driving faster in spite of the moose to make up for lost time. Cresting a hill, we swerve left along an elevated ridge that twists and winds like a snake's spine through the forest. The spherical compass perched on the dash rolls around in its watery shell: west northwest, a few hills ahead, storm clouds piled up thickly and stalled, cast dark shadows and sheets of grey over the rocky, uneven landscape. Suddenly, the ground opens up into a vast stretch of stripped land, small logs felled and unclaimed forming a thatchwork over the yellow soil, quaking aspen left to grow in small clumps — solitary oases — and no other living tree in sight until the edge of paradise, wherever that is. Then I see the charred wood, signs of scorching.

"Forest fire?"

"Slashburned clear-cut — all ours."

"You mean we've got to plant that?"

Bob nods. "Looks like more than it is, though. Should only take us a couple of weeks with every crew in the camp in there ..." He eyes me for a very full second. "Looks like the Bomb was dropped, eh?"

Looks like the ground just opened up and swallowed the forest. Looks like a hurricane passed through, the biggest windfall. My stomach sinks with the crummy into the first spatters of rain.

Through the small triangle of uncracked windshield, a lone figure — too far off to tell if it's approaching or walking away from us — is kicking up puffs of dust through the dampening surface of the road.

"Probably a surveyor," Bob says. "Or prospector."

But there isn't a vehicle of any kind in sight.

Bob slows down. The figure is a woman. She is walking toward us, south, maybe for the highway; stumbling under the weight of an overstuffed backpack and dragging a duffel bag in the dirt. Her shock of dark hair is tangled and frosted with dust blown from the already bone-dry road. Rivulets of dried blood cut and criss-cross her dusted cheeks and mud-smeared neck.

"Well, well," Bob smirks. "There's your bride, Frankenstein."

I lean forward, squinting: her eyes are almost swollen shut. "She's been in an accident. Or beaten up."

"Beaten up, alright. By blackflies."

"I thought you said it's still too early for flies."

"Normally, it would be. But the temperature hit a hundred and five Fahrenheit, May first, broke the ice off all the lakes. The bugs might sense a drought coming, and they sure as hell smelled Miss Ten Rounds here. Shit. She looks like she's been on an all-night bush-crash."

Bob rolls down his window as we roll to a stop. "Need a lift somewhere?"

"A job," the strange woman says. She holds up the long-bladed shovel she's been dragging along with her other hand. "I had to leave my camp. ... They weren't feeding us very well."

"I'll have to talk it over with Head Office," Bob says. "I don't know if we can take you on but you're welcome to stay the night. Squeeze in."

The woman opens the rear door of the cab and jams her shovel between my gear and the seat back. Then she pokes her swollen face in through my window. "Got any more room in that trailer?"

Bob shakes his head. "Your shit'll have to ride with us up front. No matter. It's only another ten k."

I slide my saddle-sore ass out of the crummy and help her stack her overweight pack and duffel in the space behind the stick shift. Then I slide back in, shove up against her gear as tight as my frame will allow, squeeze my legs together, but can't make enough room.

"You'll have to sit on his lap," Bob says to the woman. She hesitates, then climbs in, hunching her head and back under the windshield as she sits on my kneecaps, just able to pull her toes in enough for me to close the door. The crummy jerks forward and up the next hill, and she half slides, half falls back into my chest, never moving the cool green warning iris from the corner of her slit eye.

As we're rolling to a stop, the woman, who's been perched on my lap for the last ten k's, opens the door and stumbles into a run for the boat launch at the bottom of the sloping grass road. Where she kneels to wash her face, the lake is so smooth I can see the rings and ripples of raindrops expand from their moments of impact, intersect and continue.

Bob rolls his eyes. "Long blade and overly concerned with cleanliness and godliness and god knows shaving her legs. She's greener than green, I tell ya. Probably why she didn't survive her last camp." He hops out and whistles to several wet figures huddled in the doorway of a small, square shack knocked together from two-by-fours and tarps. "I need a few strong bucks over here to help me unload the kitchen."

"I guess by buck you don't mean doe," a woman answers.

A tall man with short, fair hair ducks inside, the rest pretend not to hear. Bob links his thumbs through his belt loops and curses under his breath. "Jaegs! Aleron! Daniel! Stop fuckin' the dog or we'll never get camp up. And Mitra, you know I don't mean swinging dicks when I say bucks."

The tall man peaks out, grinning, then ambles toward us; a short, tanned man with tightly curled hair and a luxuriant moustache follows, a third, with long black hair braided down his back, drags along behind him.

Bob turns to me. "We're raising the mess soon. When you hear the horn, drop whatever you're doing and hustle back here."

"Where should I pitch my tent?"

"Anywhere in the woods is fine, only not too far from camp central. Lyndon doesn't like having to go tromping all over the bush every morning, dragging out the dog-fuckers who missed wake-up call."

The drizzle turns to rain. I slide into my Wetskins, grab my backpack and tent, and cut through the bustle of construction: two men in varsity jerseys, each in a hole he's dug about three feet into the ground, and a group of women unrolling a thick piece of vinyl — big, round and striped as a parachute. The rain starts hammering down, so I pull up my hood and hustle across the treeline, bogging down in the moss carpet that covers the forest floor. I won't be able to run here, but I won't need to waste my breath on my air mattress either: this bed will make a softer one than I've ever had.

The forest is a maze of tents, sleek cycling tents that sleep only one, geodesic domes of all sizes up to six-man and in various shades of blue, green and red, and two-man mountain tents — the kind advertised as "bomb-proof" for their ability to withstand hurricane-force winds, though I'd guess that the radioactive fallout of a distant blast, say in Thunder Bay, would make short work of such uv-sensitive nylon. I pitch mine, a Canadian Tire pup tent, on a small plateau overlooking the lake. I anchor the pegs, which don't hold well in moss, with rocks and fallen limbs. Finally, I lash the fly-strings around two saplings, toss my pack into the tent, crawl in after it to unroll my sleeping bag and organize the rest of my scant belongings: the rolled up air mattress I'll use as a pillow until the moss is too beaten down to cushion my back against the cold, hard ground (a process I hope to speed up with the help of a soft, warm woman); the maglite, which can be converted into an electric candle for reading books or the face of a lover; a candle that can be blown out in case the nights are cold and lonely; and my travel alarm. Until the very last moment before I was supposed to be boarding the train, this was the only time I carried with me because it could be folded up and slipped into a pocket where I wouldn't have to be faced with it.

The watch! I pull back the sleeve of my rain jacket to check for damage from our run-in with the moose; its unblemished black face and gold hands and intersecting golden dials stare back at me. A tiny dial at 9 o'clock to tick off the seconds, the measure of minutes at 3, and circling its entire Swiss-made face, a telemeter for gauging distances. A watch that, ironically, made me miss my train.

I was booting it down the long platform of Union Station, a steward urgently waving me on from the rear gate of the now-rolling train, and my father struggling to catch me.

"Noah — wait!" he gasped.

"Hurry," I said. "All I gave you to carry was my guitar and you can't keep up? You should cut back on those butts."

"I have something to give you."

"There's no time. The Trans-Canada runs once a day."

"Then you'll have to miss it."

"No way."

"Please, Noah, it's important. I'd meant to give it to you earlier, on your birthday, but —"

"But what?"

"I guess I wasn't quite ready to give it up. Besides, things were especially tense between us then, and I was waiting for the right moment."

"Now? You have my crew's post office box in Thunder Bay."

"Noah, it can't be mailed."

"Who says? For Chrissake, Dad — are you trying to make me miss the train or what?"

"You should know me better than to think that I'd stoop so low," he barked at my heels.

The train began to accelerate, but we'd just about pulled even with the last door.

"Let's go!" The steward gesticulated wildly.

"Just give me the guitar," I said, grabbing for the case.

Father hung on. "I hate to spoil a surprise, but I don't think you should trust your grandfather's watch to Canada Post."

I stopped dead in my tracks, watching as the train passed the end of the platform and receded down the rails.

Now I dig into the back pocket of my jeans for the note that accompanied Father's gift. Plain white paper. Blue ink. "A belated Happy 20th Noah. I hope this watch will see you through your storm as it saw me through mine."

I'm not sure he hadn't planned all along to derail my departure, or at least delay it. Once I was gone, there'd only be Mom and him in their cookie-cutter oversized suburban house in a cookie-cutter suburb of a suburb. Though he must have known that at this point in our lives, nothing could make up for his absences, I don't think he's beyond trying to hold onto an opportunity that has already passed. He's been enchanted with this watch from the time his father first showed him its golden hands and its one special function; passing it down must have been hard for him, as much for the new life it marked for each of us as for the giving up of a treasured heirloom, the only possession that he's truly coveted.

I wrap the watch in the note, tie it with an elastic band, and slip it into the waterproof map-pouch on my pack, where it will remain for the season. A horn blares: the mess will be ready for raising. ... I struggle to extract myself from the living form I've cast in the moss beneath my tent, and ponder the meaning behind my father's cryptic note, wondering why he never told me that story.

CHAPTER TWO

A DRAINAGE DITCH a foot wide and almost as deep has been dug, from the site for the mess all the way down to the lake. Jaegs, the lanky blonde with the hairless face, walks along the pile of dug-up earth, uncoiling a length of septic hose, which Aleron lays in the trench. Mitra kneels, sweeping the long, kinky wefts of her sun-red hair back from her freckled forehead, tucking them behind her ear. She seals the hose to the last length laid and reaches into her tool apron for another clasp. Behind her, two others are refilling the trench, patting down the earth with fire spades, maybe so it won't sink under the traffic of four crummies and twenty-five pairs of feet. The two holes I thought were being dug for kaibos now hold large plastic garbage cans, the earth packed firmly around them. I lift the lid on one: ten-pound blocks of cheddar and mozarella standing on end along the sides, four-litre bags of milk stacked up in the centre, butter and margarine overtop.

"Looking for something?" A woman with long wet locks of greying auburn hair is smiling down on me, about a dozen pallets of eggs stacked between her downward extended forearms and her chin.

"Just curious."

"Then would you mind opening that other Rubbermaid for me?" She thrusts forth the eggs slightly with her groin.

I pry off the lid. She crouches down, but her arms aren't long enough to reach the bottom, so she kneels and carefully lowers herself to her chest.

She stands, brushing herself off as I replace the lid. "I'm the cook, Rosemary, but everyone calls me Rose for short." She shakes my hand. "You must be Moses, hey?"

"Noah."

"I knew it was something biblical."

"A lot of names are, Rose."

"Well, Noah, if you need anything, just ask."

"The kaibo."

"The shitters." She points. "See the flagging tied around that big spruce bough?"

I scan the treeline, but no matter how much I squint, all I can see is green.

"It's a blue tape — it might be hard for you to see 'cause you don't have your eyes yet."

"There's nothing wrong with my eyes."

"No, I mean you don't have your planting eyes. After you've been working here awhile, you'll be able to distinguish similar shades at a glance." She points again. "The guy over there chopping wood. The path's to his left."

At the path, I break into a run.

The day of my release from prison, I ran to the university to drop all my courses, and on to the campus career and placement centre to look for a job that would take me to a place so far away that I wouldn't feel the urge to run anymore. I didn't even have to step inside: taped to the wired window in the door was a sign:

plant trees up north
8–10¢/Piece
Make $100+/day

I doubted that anyone could plant a hundred trees a day, let alone a thousand, but I went to the afternoon orientation session anyway — a briefing warning of bad bugs, bush fever, sudden snowstorms in June, tornadoes, and wildfire. Weeks spent away from the nearest town, in wilderness accessible only by 4x4, boat, floatplane or chopper. With every new threat of calamity, plague or deprivation, the crowd at the session thinned and dwindled some more, till fewer than a dozen of us remained.

When my interview came up, I told the company recruiter that I was looking for a challenge, and a chance to give something back to the earth. Isolation wouldn't be a hardship; it was what I sought.

"You'll be planting two-by-fours and t.p. for your grandchildren," he said, yawning.

"T.P.?"

"Bum wad. Camping experience?"

"Boy Scouts."

"Play any musical instruments?"

"A little guitar."

"Good," he said. "You'll be starting on a contract somewhere in Northwestern Ontario — on whose crew I'm not sure yet, but probably Bob Ferret's. The start date will depend on the thaw, but we can usually count on sometime in early May. Your crew's mustering point will likely be Thunder Bay or one of the small towns west of there. Any questions?"

I had many, but I saved them for the road map I picked up as I was leaving the campus for the last time.

Flying Dutchmen's recruiter had made the job sound so horrific that only a handful of students signed for a position, but three months and a thousand plus miles away from the Big Smoke sounded like paradise to me, and the way to paradise would be a bus or train ride up 69 and west across 17, then up or down some unnamed road, to the middle of nowhere.

I come to a fork and stop. Jesus — right, left, which way is it? I choose the left and twenty metres down the path I'm standing before a standard outhouse with a crescent moon ass-crack cut above the door for ventilation. Ladies. Segregated crappers. Shit. I start back for the fork but the sound of a car horn filters through the trees so I dive into ladies and wrestle my jeans to my ankles. The horn blares and blares. Thirteen hundred kilometres away from home and still no room to empty myself in peace. In my northern paradise, there would be no car horns, no cars, no car phones, no phones, no phone companies, no bathroom signs, no outhouses to pool our fly-riddled collective shit in a hole with a stinking half-life of a thousand years. I could simply go out into the woods, scoop a hole in the moss and shit; simultaneously passing words — all the city shit, all the civilization bile — out my mouth at the top of my cruddy lungs: "Gold fix, price fix, detox, nuclear free zone, expressway, deficit, beneficiary, cloning, credit card, pogey, Contras, contraband, New Age, Reaganomics, gastronomics, tender-cut, deep cuts, clear-cuts, budget cuts, Big Ben, Sudbury stack, CN Tower, Empire State, penis envy!" But I don't know if I could do without toilet paper, which this shitter is missing, especially when paradise is coniferous. A different horn blares — three louder, more impatient blasts. I yank up my pants, bolt through the door and run back down the path.

Almost everyone in the camp is standing around the parachute-like roof of the mess tent. Christ, the architecture says it all: a circus big top for a mess, and every circus has its strong man, its midgets, and bear wrestlers, its trapeze artists, contortionists, snake charmers, barkers and spielers — a troupe of nomadic freaks parading from place to place in the attempt to leave their pasts in the dust. Perhaps I should've gone someplace where they make everyone shave their heads and pray. Or practise martial arts and meditate. Perhaps I should've gone alone. But it's too late now.

Bob strolls up and purposefully pulls me aside. "We're waiting for Lyndon to cut a fresh pole for the tent-raising. Might be a good time for you to meet the rest of the crew." And with a slap on the back I'm sent around the circle like the bottles of beer being passed from hand to hand.

"Daniel Krantz," says the long-braids guy whose name sounds Jewish but who looks Asian. "You must be the greener Bob said we'd be getting from Toronto. So what brings you all the way up here?"

"I can't stand walls. They're like bad air to an asthmatic. I needed to breathe — right through my skin. You know?"

He nods. "I met Bob and Therese last summer on a nudist beach in Van. They made this place sound like paradise."

"Is it?"

"Bob has a real penchant for exaggeration, so I dunno if I'd call it a paradise but it's alright as a refuge. I'm a classical guitarist and I was looking for a place where I could hear my music speak to me again. And distance from the border. Seattle's my first home but I left the States so I wouldn't have to register for the draft."

"A rebel patriot."

He looks at me quizzically.

"You know — people who have to disobey or rebel against the cranks who've seized power in the effort to defend their country's true values, like the draft dodger profs I had who fled up here during the war in Vietnam."

"Not me. I'm no rebel; I just want to play music and live my life without unnecessarily getting into other people's faces. As for that Paul Revere patriot crap, the only things I stick by are who I love and what's in here." He slaps his heart. "My nation under God respects differences and territories without imposing borders. Know whose crew you're on?"

"Not yet. How many are there?"

"Clem's crew, Lyndon's crew, Therese's." He points out two men who've just emerged from the treeline carrying a freshly felled log. "The clear-cut blond one there, Clem, foremans the highballers — the high production, high dollar planters. That pumped mother with him, Lyndon, runs the lowballer crew — all the greeners and grunts and folks who've come for the scenery." Daniel waves them over.

Clem's handshake is polite, almost reserved, but Lyndon's —

The two return to their work. Legs spread over their log, knees locked, Lyndon raises a sledgehammer high above his head and swings down in a perfect arc, driving the pole's thick, squared-off base into a bracket hinged to the platform.

"Another two inches," Clem says. "Try to hit it square this time or it'll pop out of the base."

"I'd like to see you do better," Lyndon mutters. "Couldn't even lift a hoe-dad over yer head without falling on yer ass." He swings down on the log again, and again, each time more aggressively.

"Alright, damn it — that's enough," Clem says.

Lyndon tosses the sledgehammer aside, grinning toothlessly like the enforcer on a hockey squad. "Well what are you waiting for, man? Fetch me the fuckin' stakes. And tell that pantywaist Jack he'd better figure out where he stashed that polecap or I'll string him up for the flies."

Aleron drops a tub at Lyndon's feet. "Jack sends his love," he says in a rich Latino accent.

Lyndon reaches into the tub and pulls out a square-socketed iron ring that is fastened to a pulley and has four short steel suspension cables bolted around it. Bracing the log between his knees, he fits the ring over its squared-off tip, tapping it firmly into place with a small, rubber-coated mallet. He looks down the length of the pole to Aleron, who has clasped a winch about five feet from its base. Aleron runs the winch cable up the pole, threads it through the pulley, and hooks it to a steel hoop. After knotting endless yellow ropes to each of the suspension cables, they stake the pole's platform with iron rods. With each ringing blow, Aleron's black-as-cherry eyes flit nervously between his hands and Lyndon's sledgehammer.

Bob steps into our restless circle and blows two piercing blasts on a bear-scare whistle — the kind of noisemaker you're just as likely to see on a city woman's key chain as on a hiker's backpack. "The centrepole's ready to go up. I want a crew on each rope. Walter and the hardcores can take up the fourth line once it's erect. The rest of you can help me 'n Jack prop the pole while the others are hauling."

A woman with a beautifully weather-aged young face sidles up to me, a heavily armed tool belt hanging around her wide hips. She looks me up and down as if sizing up a piece of lumber. "So this is my new grunt." She shakes her head. "Dutch has obviously been out of the field too long to be much use as a recruiter."

My face grows hot. "You must be Therese."

She laughs. Her handshake could be as crushing as Lyndon's, but she quickly relaxes her grip. "We're on the far rope — the one that'll be bearing most of the weight. Let's see what you got."

I fall in behind Therese and Daniel and the rest of her crew, who have taken up the rope 6 o'clock from the pole's top. Lyndon's gang picks up the rope to our left, Clem's to our right. The hardcores wait by the rope directly across from us.

Bob blasts his whistle. Steve, Daniel and Therese grip the rope tightly and start pulling. Standing at the end, I wrap the slack around my butt and lean back.

The pole jerks from the ground and begins to rise. Bob and Jack move under it, pushing it up as they inch toward the base and we pull back, marvelling at its smooth ascent. It's as if we're resurrecting a totem.

A sudden, wild gust catches the top and the pole jerks down, yanking us forward. We lean back harder, digging our heels into the quaggy grass.

"*Tabernac!* Bob —" Therese yells. "Get some more bodies on our rope or we'll be catapulted clear across the lake!"

"We're the ones under the fuckin' log. Pull!"

"We're pulling, goddammit! We need more weight on our side."

Clem's and Lyndon's gangs close the gaps between their ropes and ours. The hardcores take up their rope and swing to one side to counter the crosswind.

"It's too blustery," Bob says. "We'll have to drop 'er, Jack."

Jack shakes his head. "Either we get it up now, or we go to bed cold, wet 'n hungry."

I glance back over my shoulder: deep billowing layers of grey cloud are bearing down on us, darkening to an angry purple as they drop closer to the ground.

The wind picks up, swaying the forest so violently that trunks creak and crack all around us. Veins bulging from our arms, faces flushed and coated in films of sweat, we lean back as if in a tug-of-war with a giant. But we just can't break inertia.

Shouldering the pole, Bob pulls off his baseball cap and tosses it into the dirt. "Shit."

A faint noise like the distant buzzing of a chainsaw penetrates the dense woods.

"It's Buzzard," Rose says. "That's Buzzard's Norton."

A giant, silver-helmeted figure in a black bomber and leather pants roars over the last slope on an ancient motorcycle, black with lots of chrome. He stops by Lyndon and lifts his visor. "Hey, Boss."

"Hey, Buzzard, you're late," Lyndon snaps. "Held up in paradise by your lady or just picking your beak? Get your ass under the pole!"

Buzzard revs his old Norton, races over to the Prairie Schooner, dismounts, sprints toward Jack, stops halfway, turns around, removes his helmet (revealing a long, matted mohawk), bowls it back to his bike, turns again for the centrepole.

Arms straining under the log, Bob and Jack shuffle back to admit Buzzard's broad frame. Seventy degrees, 60 degrees, 55, 50 — we begin to slide forward. But Buzzard ducks his shoulder underneath the pole, wraps his gargantuan hands around its two-foot girth and pushes it back up: several inches for every step he takes toward the platform. Once the pole has risen out of their reach, Bob and Jack move to his side and resume their merely mortal contributions.

The pole is grabbed by the wind again and held fast.

"Can't you push any harder 'n that?" Lyndon shouts.

"What the hell are you yelling at me for?" Buzzard shouts back. "The wind up there's like the hand of God, and if He don't want it up —"

"That's what we hired you for, dumbfuck."

The woman we'd picked up on the road steps down from the back of the Prairie Schooner, holding a bag of frozen peas against the more swollen side of her face. "Need a hand with that?"

Buzzard snorts. "You think you'll be the one to get it up?"

"You never know which branch might break the moose's back."

"There's two dozen — thirty counting me — pushing and pulling on this damn log."

"If you're really as strong as six men, you should be on a rope, where you'd do the most good. Here." She approaches him. "I'll take the log. You can pick up the slack behind that guy on the end of Therese's rope. He's looking tired."

"You look like you kissed the mouth of a beehive," Buzzard says. "I can't even see the whites of your eyes."

"The whites don't do the seeing and my eyes won't be doing the pushing — or the eating. I'm sure I'm not the only one here who could use a hot meal and a fire."

Reluctantly, Buzzard shifts the log from his shoulder to his hands, Bob and Jack straining to keep it up as the woman takes his place.

"That freak of nature yours?" Buzzard says, taking his newly assigned place behind me.

"No," I say, moving up the rope to give him more slack. "Bob picked her up from the side of the road."

"Looks like it too." He spits a gob into one hand and works it into his palms.

On the count of three, we start pulling back. As before, the log rises smoothly till the top catches in the wind, but instead of falling back it hiccups upward between the gusts. Bob, Jack and the woman combine for one last synchronized shove. The pole jumps forward the last few degrees and comes to a quivering stop on its hinge. The hardcores swing their rope back to stabilize it.

Bob drags his shirtsleeve across his forehead. "Alright, Lyndon. Stake 'er."

We raise a cheer, for ourselves, and for the woman at the pole. Some people are like that: they can walk into a strange place and draw together everyone in it and nobody feels usurped — well, almost nobody. How Buzzard might feel remains to be seen.

Lyndon and Clem stake our rope first, then quickly stake the other three.

Standing within the chimney hole in the vinyl big top, hugging the pole, Aleron starts winching. The orange-yellow-blue-striped top rises like a half-opened umbrella, swallowing his head as it edges skyward. As soon as it's up, Jack and Therese circle the top, wedging two-by-fours under its lip.

Bob and Lyndon have barely finished velcroing the Egyptian cotton siding around the edges of the top when the storm cloud explodes, blowing out the two-by-fours. Driven from our work by horizontal sheets of rain, we crowd into our shelter. Jack carries in an armload of firewood. The big top is unwinched until, at half mast, it sits on the ground like a giant teepee. Rosemary stacks the kindling. A fire is lit.

When Bob asked her to sign on, she said her name was Cass, and when he pressed her for her surname, "Just Cass." He insisted he needed a last name for all the paper-pusher's forms: TD1, Remote Worksite Allowance, the Union Dues list, the Company contract. Besides, he probably thought this woman, whose face was so bug-bitten that her nose was almost completely lost in the pulp of her cheeks, was doing her best to be untraceable. But when she produced her driver's licence, the only name on it was Cass. Jane Doe had proven she wasn't an escaped convict or loonie, but she left me wondering. Even Christ had a last name. She couldn't have been born and raised without one.

Scanning her application form, Bob had said: "I guess you must've disliked your name pretty bad to have it legally changed — uh, erased."

"No. Changed," she said. "First and last. I had a dream and that's what the dream named me."

I don't know why I believe her. Maybe because I want to believe that at least some of us still listen to our dreams.

CHAPTER THREE

"SUN'S UP IN the swamp!" a deep, gruff voice booms through the forest.

"Sun's up in the swamp, alright. It's still dark as hell down here," a second voice booms back.

"He must've meant the swamps of Borneo, or Peat Down," a third voice agrees.

"Buzzard! Bartram! You lazy sons of bitches — get the fuck up! Or am I gonna have to baptize you again?"

"Hey Lyn, give us a break. It took me a week to dry out my bag after the last time. Besides, if anyone needs baptizing, it's the new guy."

My nose and ears are numb. I can see my breath. The chilling call of a loon reminds me that the lake may still be edged with ice in the bay behind my tent, and the lake's what they mean by baptism.

The sound of feet plodding through the frozen underbrush draws near. Lyndon's shadow falls across my tent.

"Okay! I'm up."

He grunts. "Breakfast's at quarter to six."

Still in the bag, I slide into my dark green workpants, put on a denim shirt; both are cold and damp as the air. Then I worm out and, teeth chattering, put on two sweaters. As I'm tying the laces on my stiff new workboots, the horn blows — two short blasts, one long.

The forest is dusky, and even as I reach the clearing, the sun's still caught in its spiky canopy. Last night's storm clouds, red-edged and on their way east, are already at the horizon. I follow the smell of bacon smoke through the mouth of the big top.

Jack, the campee, is stoking the oil-drum stove, which we had added to the centrepole, along with an aluminum stovepipe, after last night's storm had blown over and we were able to winch the big top back up.

I cross the dirt floor to join the queue that's forming behind Rosemary, who is laying out the lunch spread. She drags two boxes of fruit from under the table and breaks them open. Then she dashes off to the kitchen Bob installed in the converted Prairie Schooner and heaves an aluminum soup pot onto her head.

"Three each, gorbies," she warns, squeezing between Jaegs and Daniel to lower the pot to a space behind the tuna salad.

"Cookies!" Jaegs says.

At once the orderly queue collapses into a crush of grabbing hands and poking elbows.

I stand back, waiting for the free-for-all to end. "Jesus, they're not gonna leave as much as a crumb. They're just like a school of piranhas."

"Except piranhas leave the bones."

I turn around: Aleron smiles in greeting, his almond-shaped eyes already fired for the day. From everything I heard around the oil drum last night, he's the rising star of the camp — the rookie who's got all the highballers, even the most seasoned, looking over their shoulders. Daniel told me that he's a refugee of the civil war in El Salvador who stole across the Rio Grande by night and gradually made his way up to Vancouver through a modern-day underground railroad, the stations and transit points, houses of holy. That has me wondering if he's still running, pushed farther and farther north like an animal trying to stay a step or two ahead of the advancing frontier. Yet, nothing about Aleron suggests he has been weighed down by such heavy matters, not even the beginning of a frown line or the faint reminder of a sun-faded scar.

"Don't worry, wanker," he says. "She always saves cookies for the sleepy heads. There is always plenty of food — all you can eat."

As others finish packing their lunches and flock toward the provisions shelf for mugs and plates and cutlery, space opens up at the table. I stick a knife into the margarine, but it's frozen. So I spread a thin layer of mayonnaise over four slices of rye bread and pile them high with corned beef, lettuce and tomato.

Aleron eyes my sandwiches and shakes his head. "If you eat like that, all your blood will go to your stomach and you will move like a snail. Fruit, nuts, cookies — that is all you should eat on a warm day on the block."

Rosemary returns, replacing the empty pot with a smaller one. "I saved these for you," she says. "Remember to save some for the foremen."

I tear two bags off a supermarket roll, stuff a handful of cookies into one, apples and oranges into the other and zip them into my knapsack, leaving my sandwiches to the late risers and the camp dogs or any scavengers who'll take them.

The breakfast spread outdoes any of the lumberjack specials I'd seen at the truck stops on the bus ride to Upsala. Aside from bacon and eggs, there's granola, oatmeal, orange and grapefruit juice, and steaming pans of freshly baked cornbread.

I load up a plate and turn to take one of the seats in the circle around the oil drum, but even Innuk, Walter the superballer's pup-sized husky, can't nose his way to warmth through the tight huddle of scruffy men and women standing there, rubbing their hands and holding them up to the faint glow. So I sit shivering at an empty table by the mouth of the big top, glad of each piping hot bite of food and every passing moment that turns our tiny patch of earth a little more toward the sun.

Bob ducks in, wearing an old, greying horsehide bomber and holding several scrolled-up papers under his arm. He takes the seat next to mine and unrolls a poster-sized aerial map on the gingham cloth. The way he taps his pen on the sunlit swamp reminds me of my father, hunched over his underlit scribing table, long ago, before the computers took over. But of all the maps he'd drawn, the lines and contours he'd caressed from his hand, I can't remember him drawn to a single one. Like the satellites that took the infrared photos he'd draw from, David Abramson remained in a fixed orbit, altering course only as mapping technology moved from paper to screen and removed him farther and farther from earth. Forestry, geological survey, demographics for area studies — he'd mapped them all. But it wasn't until I got enough distance from him to get an overview of his work that it dawned on me: maps were mainly records of what would or could be made to disappear — one long, scrolled-up history of navigating, boundary-laying, colonizing, totem-razing, terra-forming and tower-raising, all in the name of civilizing and corporatizing.

The horn blares again. Therese, in a light blue track suit, circles in behind Bob, affectionately pinching the inches bulging over his belt.

Bob jumps. "Aw shit — Therese." With his shirt sleeve he mops the coffee he's splashed all over the map.

"Lighten up. In another two weeks, your winter coat will be gone and I'll have to find other parts to pinch. Besides," she taps the tannin blur. "Isn't this the spot where that beaver dammed all the conduits and washed out the road?"

"Yeah, but two weeks more of this 'n all I'll be able to do with this map is sell it to the National Gallery."

Clem and Lyndon file into the mess, walk around to the far side of the table and huddle over the map. Bob starts giving directions, drawing fluorescent pink lines through the maze of logging roads, marking out the day's areas.

Rosemary feeds a tape to the boom-box sitting on the edge of the kitchen counter:

> *Drove the highway to the end of the road,*
> *rode the rails to the end of the line,*
> *hoofed the trail till I lost my way,*
> *followed a river right out to the sea.*
> *Well, I've been waiting for a long, hard rain,*
> *and I've been searching for a stake to claim ...*

Finally, Bob rises from the table and rolls up his map. "Better choke that down fast, Noah. We've gotta make tracks."

"Can I come?" It's Cass, the girl we picked up on the road, her eyes barely open.

"You've gotta be joking," Bob says. "Your face is still swollen out to infinity and we're heading for a swamp. If you get hurt before you're officially on the payroll, it'll be my ass they'll hang high."

"I think I saw some antihistamine in the first aid kit," I say.

She smiles cynically. "'Welcome to my parlour,' said the spider to the fly."

"Huh?"

"That swamp must be a pretty nasty piece of real estate for you to be inviting me onto your land, which I'm guessing you won't be so eager to do when you're in a sandbox."

I bristle. "Can't say. This is my first day at this job."

"Only two weeks greener than me, and yet an eon." Cass turns to Bob. "If you can spare some Benadryl, I might be ready for the swamp by mid-morning."

"Once your face has come down, and if you're not too groggy, you can help out around the kitchen," Bob says. "I'll pay you twenty for the breakfast dishes so you can earn your keep, but until I've cleared it with Head Office, you're just a guest."

A horn blares punchily. "Six-thirty, people," Bob bellows. "You know the drill."

I leave my breakfast half-eaten, grab my lunch and head for the exit.

"Blue one-ton, Noah," Lyndon says as I pass.

"What?"

"You're riding with me."

"Where we going?" Daniel snaps. "Why the hell did Therese tell us to leave our planting gear behind?"

"Empire Loop," Lyndon says, breaking off from the convoy of crummies to turn down a muddy cat road. "We need you to build us a bridge over a swamp. Bob says there's no other way we can get a trike through to stock the blocks on the other side."

"He'd better be planning on paying us for every second of down-time. I don't like plodding around in a swamp for squat dollar while your crew's creaming us out."

"My crew? I may be Bob's friend but friendship doesn't run as deep as a good poke, and it's Therese he's pokin.'"

Aleron leans forward over the seatback. "So what will we get for it?"

"I've cordoned off some cream for when you get done. You'll be paid the crew average — plus a bonus if the bridge is done by nightfall."

"After we have done the scuzz piles, right?" Aleron yawns, sarcastic punctuation. "Then the rest is cream. The Promised Land. Just over the next hill, on the horizon. But every time we get close to it, the Hendrix van is already parked there and Clem and his piranhas are capping off their cream-out with a four-course lunch and an hour-long siesta."

"They look like they should be riding camels the way they bandana those white cloths over their heads," Daniel says.

"Where you're headed, I guarantee you'll be adopting a similar dress code before the day is out," Lyndon says.

"Except it won't be a beach. Oh no, it would only be too fair to give all of us an equal shot at making some good cash."

"Look, I'm just the ferryman, okay? I'll take you from A to Z. You got a problem beyond that, then take it to Bob."

We stop at the edge of a pond that stretches for at least thirty metres over the road.

"I'm gonna hafta lock the hubs," Lyndon says, opening his door.

"It must've been coming down cats 'n dogs here last night," I say.

"God you must be blind or something." Daniel points out the four-foot-high beaver dam flanking the entire stretch of washout, probably the one Therese pointed out on the map.

"Why here?"

"Logging roads disrupt natural drainage, so they have to run culverts underneath — corrugated aluminum culverts, which amplify the sound of the water running through them. The sound of running water drives beavers insane. The water must be stopped at all costs. It's the instinct hardwired into the centre of their being."

Lyndon hops back into the driver's seat. "What's ours? Sex and war. We've been bred to fuck and kill each other."

"Speak for yourself," Daniel says.

"I just did," Lyndon says, throwing the truck into gear. "And the rest of stinking humanity, if the rest was half as honest about it."

"Okay, I'll admit to the first half, but I'm pretty selective about who I'd fuck or kill."

I tense up. "Looks pretty deep in the middle there. Think we'll make it?"

"What's this thing you have about water? First, you didn't want to be baptized. Now you're afraid of a little puddle. Can't swim?"

"I'd rather walk than have to swim out of a rapidly sinking truck." I reach for the door handle, but the gap in the vinyl moulding is empty.

"Bob bought the Conan at a police auction," Lyndon says, smiling into the rear-view. "Named for being the Schwarzenegger of crummies — the only one that can cut the gumbo and swamp-outs — aside from Bob's."

Lyndon slows the truck to a creep before dropping it gently over the edge of the washout, then accelerates to a steady crawl. Somewhere near the middle, water sloshing at the fenders, he stops. "Could be a sudden drop-off by the culvert, Noah. Maybe you'd prefer to get out and walk the rest of the way."

"Fuck off and drive, MacKerel," Daniel says.

The Conan, an old blue Dodge Ram, grinds forward on all fours. The tires spin only briefly before the truck mounts dry land on the other side, the sound of water sputtering from its exhaust.

"Horseshoe Swamp," Lyndon says, parking the Conan where the high Shield rock suddenly drops away to a vast sphagnum bog.

The white crew cab is already parked at the bottom of the steep grade. Bob is sitting way atop one of several log piles neatly stacked along the side of the road. Aleron and Daniel open the front door and hop out.

"You'd better watch where you step, Noah," Lyndon says. "The Chippewa say the sphagnum in an old *muskig* can be eight stories deep."

"You've probably got a story for every inch," I say.

"The bog sure does, and every one of them's a passed life."

I slide off the bench seat and push past him. Clouds of blackflies descend on my head — clouds so thick I'm breathing them.

"I'll see if I can rustle up some camels for quitting time," Lyndon quips. Then he turns the Conan around and speeds off.

Following Daniel's advice, I douse my spare T-shirt with Bug Off, slip my face through the neckhole, and tie the sleeves around the back of my head. Daniel slides into a green mesh bug shirt, and Bob splashes Deet all over his face and baseball cap. Aleron doesn't dope up or bundle up at all. Maybe he's one of those lucky planters whose blood isn't sweet enough for the flies, or maybe he just wants to avoid the humiliation of having to adopt the highballers' *kafiyah* without the status that seems to come with it.

Bob pushes himself off the pile and starts tossing logs off the embankment into the swamp.

Daniel frowns. "Won't the logging company be coming back for these?"

"They're culls," Bob says, still tossing.

"All of them? I'll admit I can see a few rotten cores, but most of these logs look like perfectly good wood."

"Some are legit culls, but on the harder access roads, some of the so-so stuff gets left behind when the piles become too depleted to fully load a hauling truck without having to stop all over hell's half-acre."

"I don't see what difference that makes."

Bob stops to wipe the sweat from his brow. "Some companies pay by the load, even the ones that don't expect their drivers to haul ass as if they do. Under those circumstances, I think you'd choose the one-stop shopping option any day of the week."

Pressing one nostril, Daniel blows the dusty snot from his other to the road. "Cull or not, they shouldn't be cutting what they're not gonna take."

"Cull or not, they've been left to rot," Bob says. "So we may as well make use of them. Ever seen a corduroy road?"

"You've gotta be joking. We can't just lay these over the swamp like you would over a muddy patch or a washout," Daniel mutters. "It's too deep. They'll float all over the place."

"Hey, just leave the engineering to me, okay? There are two types of corduroy. On muddy road you can lay the logs lengthwise, end to end. On water, you lay 'em like planks on a boardwalk. Two deep oughta buoy the trike and a loaded trailer over the deeper holes."

"Well, I hope you brought about a thousand yards of rope and an extra man because that's what it'll take to put it in and lash it all up by nightfall."

"Lash it up?" Bob laughs. "See that island of trees? That's the next solid ground — a good quarter mile from here. Anyways, we don't need to lash up a floating bridge, so long as we work from one sphagnum bed to the next. I've done it before — trust me."

We roll the rest of the eight-foot lengths from the pile over the embankment, then slide down to the edge of the bog. Bob picks up a log, and choosing the area of the swamp most matted with slash, lays it overtop. Aleron follows, then Daniel, then me.

Every time I bend down to place another log, blackflies swarm my face, bounce against my cheeks and eyelids (which Bob swears they do to "screef" through the bug dope) then fly off, repulsed by the halo of toxic scent emanating from my headdress. It keeps them from biting me, but it doesn't stop me from breathing them. "Hell," I gag, plunging my pinkie after the furious buzzing of a fly that has crawled deep into my bladderwort ear and bogged down in wax. "Stuff enough of these friggin' flies into a man's head and — I don't care how tough he is — he'll sell out his country within an hour."

Scowling into the glare of noon and through, Daniel passes me another log. "Sad part is the men who sold this country out sold it far more cheaply."

ONE. The sun has risen to its zenith. The swamp steams and bubbles; the leopard frogs kick their way out from beneath the corduroy as its undulates and shifts back and forth underfoot. The bridge is too narrow and unstable for four men to be squeezing past one another, so we form a chain gang to relay logs from the embankment to the end. By the time I've added another to the bridge, two more are coming up the line. But in spite of our system, we're only a quarter of the way across. The islands of sphagnum that snake through the swamp are becoming more and more sporadic, and the bridge is rolling and bobbing so violently with the accumulated undulations of so many footsteps that I'm constantly struggling to keep my balance.

Carrying the last two logs of the morning, Aleron stumbles past me to add them onto the end himself. Sitting on them, he removes his boots and dangles his feet in the cool swamp. "That woman who came in with you from town —"

"Cass. We picked her up on the road. She said she was a refugee of some other company."

"Señor Bark's camp?"

"Dunno. Didn't even catch her name till Bob got her to sign on the dotted line when she proved she'd earned her Brownie badge in big-top-raising ... I don't even remember him asking for it or her offering it before then. She's a bit of a mystery."

"Right now her face looks a bit ugly, but trust me, right under all the bites and swelling is a face that can sink a thousand ships."

"Launch — it's launch a thousand ships."

"Into what, wanker? A royal regatta? When you say launch, I see the Queen breaking a thousand bottles on a thousand hulls. But a face that can sink every one of those hulls is a face worth fighting for."

"I don't think she could be that dangerous."

"Not under ordinary circumstances," Daniel says, joining us. "But Bob didn't even come close to meeting his employment equity target. And all the women are taken. Kirsten's mine, Therese is with Bob, Mitra's Moira's girlfriend, Josie's taken with herself and the cook's quite taken with any young stud who's willing to take her. Jane Doe's dangerous, alright — she's the last available."

"She has nice eyes," I say, remembering how I'd silently cursed my satyr to keep at bay as her hips slid farther and farther up my lap driving up that first hill from where we'd found her. No use; I'd become a life support system for an erection.

Casting his eyes over the swamp, Daniel smacks his parched lips. "That moss looks almost good enough to eat."

I stand and stretch. "We'd better break for lunch. Before he convinces us all to go browsing."

We roll and bob our way back to the landing and climb the embankment to the road.

Flies blacken the crummy's windshield, spilling over the dash, streaming through the air vents. "We can't eat in here," I say. "We'll be carried off in millions of pieces."

"Shut the door," Daniel says, opening the hood on his bug shirt.

"You're crazy."

"They're claustrophobic. Once they're shut in, they'll be more intent on escaping than on sucking blood for their eggs."

"I dunno guys ..." Bob says, sliding into the driver's seat. "We gotta get this bridge in today and it's going slow." He takes his walkie-talkie from the dash. "Hey Jack ..."

Static. "Ya Bob ..." Static.

"Better tell Rose to set some dinner aside for us."

Static. "Anything else?"

I pick up the blue crew jug and shake it.

"Oh — we're running low on H_2O. Better dope up again, guys, and fill your canteens."

Static. "Everyone's nearly out here. I'll have to head back to camp for that."

"Save it till later then. Out."

Bob wolfs back the rest of his sandwich. "Better dope up again, guys, fill your canteens with whatever water we've got. We're staying out there till we've made landfall."

Looking back from the island, the bridge appears familiar, exotic, like a boardwalk across a rice paddy somewhere in Thailand, but nowhere near as straight, and probably much less stable. The sun has begun its long descent, and though the air is still clammy, it has cooled off enough for the blackflies to emerge from their shady places of siesta. I open my thermos.

"Any left?" Aleron asks, his hand reaching out instinctively before I even have a chance to answer.

I shake my head.

"Daniel?"

"Sorry Aleron. I finished mine over an hour ago." Daniel checks his watch. "Damn. Five twenty, and no sign of Jack. We'll die out here."

Aleron picks at the blisters that cover the pads in his palms. "We are done. We should go back to camp now, before the meat is all gone."

"Bob wants to beat a trail through these woods and out to the block on the other side before we pack it in."

"He's nuts," I say. "We won't be outa here before seven."

Bob rides into view on his ATC, the way a jockey rides a horse over a jump — knees braced around the saddle so he won't crack his nuts. He bounces down the embankment and out onto the bridge, gradually picking up speed as he gets used to the shifting logs. Halfway out, he's beginning to bog down, so he guns it. The logs slosh about and shift, sinking under the ATC's weight, resurfacing behind it, but they're staying in place, interlocked, even though he's driving so fast, the wheels spin on the wetter logs, spin the drier logs, and shred the softer ones, kicking up bits of sawdust in their wake.

As he nears the island, he gears down, just slow enough not to be thrown in case the front wheel jams in the shifting logs, just fast enough not to sink. Touching land, he dismounts. Daniel takes the free handlebar and they muscle the trike up the spongy embankment to the foot of the forest.

"D'ya get water?" Daniel asks.

"Couldn't. Jack said the Ministry of Health swung by camp just before he got there. The bacteria count in our water supply is high. Something's wrong with the filtration unit, so I sent him to Silver Dollar to pick up some iodine and extra bleach. I only hope he gets there before the store closes or I'll be up all night boiling water."

Aleron pales. "No water?"

"We'll find some here."

"In the middle of a swamp?" Aleron says. "We will surely get beaver fever."

"Come on, Aleron," Daniel says. "What's a little beaver fever? I'm sure most of the boys got a pretty severe case of it by now — even our latest case. Right, Noah?"

"Hey, I just got here."

"Buffalo chips," Bob says. "Green-eyed beauty of the opposite persuasion riding on your lap up ten clicks of bumpy logging road and you didn't once wish she was riding something else too? Or didn't you notice those eyes?"

"I saw more of her back than anything else." Her damp, dirty shirt, translucent with fresh rain, clinging to her bug-bitten skin and spotting badly over her right shoulder blade. Hiking out of her last camp, burdened with all her gear, she must've felt like she was being carried off a piece and a drop at a time. Right then, the collection of insect skulls glued to the top of Bob's rear-view seemed to make a whole lot more sense, but not the tent pole loosening the zipper on my pants.

"You haven't really answered the question," Daniel says. "Or don't beavers give you the fever?"

"Funny, wanker, funny." Aleron says. "If you ever get the real thing, you will be so busy shitting and spewing your supper, you will have no time to grease your pole, let alone joke about it. Jesus, all we want is some water — you would think we were asking for champagne on a famine relief project."

His mirth suddenly exhausted by an unappreciative audience, Bob glowers. "Look, I'm not paying you people overtime to hear you bitch. I may not have a degree in so-called forestry management, or water and soil conservation, but I know the bush as well as my own prick. I've worked in her crotch all my life and I hope to die here. So when I say I'll find fresh water, I'll find water. Here ..." He removes his knapsack and throws it at Aleron. "Suck on some fruit till then." And he hikes off into the woods.

In the knapsack is a grocery store vegetable bag containing three apples, two grapefruits, and an orange. We eat the citrus fruit first, stripping it with our teeth, spitting peels into the bog, sucking the juice from the flesh as if we're a brood of voracious fruit bats.

Minutes later, Bob returns to the trike, unhooks the bungees that hold his tools to the rack, picks up his chainsaw. "There's a moose trail leading to the other side, but it needs widening if we're gonna get the trike through. I'll be felling." He hands Aleron an axe. "You take out the smaller brush. Daniel and Noah can fill the boggy patches with slash. If we hurry, we can be outa here in half an hour."

Bob runs with his chainsaw, runs from tree to tree, yelling "Heads!" two dozen times or more, and in under fifteen minutes, he clears a path that must be three hundred feet long.

As Aleron and Daniel finish filling the last of the boggy spots, I follow him off the path into the forest's heart. Creeping along without snapping a twig, ear to the air, he seems to be stalking something. He stops suddenly, cups his hand to his ear, cocks his head to one side, as if listening for the earth's pulse.

"Noah — over here." He knows I'm following, probably knew it all along, accepts curious natures as long as they're there to witness his expertise. I slosh up behind him through the wet sphagnum. He crouches down by the roots of a fat old spruce.

"Hear it?"

"No."

"Bend down. ... Hear it now?"

A faint, muffled gurgle rises to my ears. He peels back a clump of lush green moss from a crotch in the tree's roots, exposing a clear, bubbling pool. Kneeling, he sniffs it, he licks it, he laps at it, he sticks his entire face in it and gulps and gulps and gulps. It's as if he can divine fresh water by its sound.

"Ahhhh," he sighs, smacking his lips. "This is the best water you'll find anywhere east of the Rockies." He splashes some over the top of his head. "Well, what're you waiting for? It's spring water, pure and good as a Cartesian well."

I pause, wondering if Bob is punning or mixing up his words, or blind in his faith in the water's purity. I cautiously cup a small palmful to my lips, water so sweet but so cold it numbs from mouth to stomach. Then I clutch the tree's roots and, bobbing for my own Adam's apple, plunge my face in; smashing deep into my distorted reflection, into a pool so icy it freezes my thoughts, just leaves me here hearing nothing but the pulse of the land against my own.

But then Bob calls the others.

The view from the top of the hill is like a giant diorama: twenty or more veiled and bandanaed hominid forms strung out along a quarter mile of floating corduroy, slowly snaking their way through the swamp beneath a hazy tangerine sunrise and the prehistoric cries and pterodactyl flight of a pair of great blue herons.

"Let's get a move on," Daniel prods from behind. So we stroll down the hill, stutter and roll the steps of upright beasts attempting to resist gravity, and join the caravan; the bridge undulating like the rollers of an incoming tide but hanging together — just — as Bob said it would.

We reach the end of the bridge: the trail we'd cut through the island's woods is log-jammed with planters. Steve is shuffling about, restless as a cooped hen.

"What's the holdup?" Daniel asks.

"Lyndon's swamped the trike. Anyone got the time?"

I pull my travel alarm from my pocket. "Eight-fifteen."

"Shit. Considering we've been up since five-thirty, it's sure shaping up to be a dog of a day."

"Well there's no sense in standing around waiting for the flies to wake up," Daniel says.

We squeeze our way up the line, along the thin trail to the far side of the island. Lyndon's swamped the trike alright — he's buried it up to its saddle in the Precambrian muck of the winter road he'd gambled would get us to the site without having to lay more corduroy, and now he's cursing the whole vast bog, unable to find anything solid within reach of his winch cable.

"Shoulda rented a hovercraft," Steve says.

"Cut the wise shit," Lyndon says. "It's gonna take me 'n Bob the morning to salvage the bitch, and the better part of a sunny afternoon to dry out 'er motor."

"What the hell are we supposed to do in the meantime?"

"We've already flagged your areas. You may as well pick up some of these spilt trays and get marching. Better carry all that you can, 'cause you're not gonna see anymore for a good long while."

We bag up the spilled seedlings, dew-wet, swamp-soaked seedlings, pack extra trays on our side bags and our shoulders and our heads, and begin the trek across the half-mile of muskeg that stretches out before us. The ground's almost as wet as what we'd laid the bridge over — even along the winter road, which probably hasn't seen a soul since spring thaw. Rivulets and creeks criss-cross its vast expanse: everywhere, the gurgle of running water draining north to Hudson's Bay.

We stop at a narrow channel. Steve drops his trays to the moss. "So, who's gonna take the leap of faith?"

"You're the one leading," Daniel says.

"Uh-Unh. I've done my share of faith-leaping. My life's a goddamned curse."

I toe the creek's edge. "Doesn't look like much of a leap to me."

Daniel sticks his shovel into the moss. "Here, we'll hold your trays."

"You've gotta be joking. An ant could spit across this trickle of piss." I step back and leap for the thick moss bed on the other side. Plunge right through, the swamp swallowing me whole ... the rippling, skylit mirror closing overhead. Sinking under the weight of my over-packed planting bags, I close my eyes tight against the possibility of long-extinct creatures, slowly fermenting in the organic still of eight stories of sphagnum. As the seedlings float up toward the light, dropping cloudy clots of soil from their roots, my bags fill with the bog's history, pulling me away from my own. My fingers fumble for the plastic clasps to release me from their weight. A shovel breaks the smoothing mirror. I cling to the hilt, begin to rise ...

Clutching the back of my shoulder harness, Steve leans back and hauls me up. I flop into the moss, coughing water.

I unclasp my hip belt and roll free of my planting bags, gasping for air, shivering in the crisp morning like something newborn on the land.

"You alright?" Daniel asks, barely able to keep a cork on his laugh.

"You fuckers!" I shout. "You knew this would happen —"

"Cool down," Steve says. "It happens to the best of us."

"Just because it happens doesn't mean you go around deliberately seeking it out!"

"We didn't know it had a false bottom," Daniel says. "Really! But now you know why I don't buckle my shoulder harness out here. Better to lose the bags and a few trees than your life."

"You've got to be kidding. You set me up for a fall and now I owe you my life? Are you two out of your skulls?"

Daniel stops laughing.

"I've got an extra fleece in my pack," Steve says. "If you need a hand salvaging your trees —"

"No. I need to know who the fuck I am."

They look at each other and shrug. Then they pick up their seedling trays and walk up the creek to where it narrows enough to prod the far bank with a shovel before crossing.

Finally, I reach the site. My legs are cramped with fatigue and the weight of the nine hundred sopping wet paper pot seedlings I'm lugging. Just about every other planter in the camp's passed me on the way — even Therese, and she was the last one to come up the trail. I drop my spare trays of trees in the shade of the cedar snag where

Daniel and Steve have made their cache, hang my soaked day pack on a root of its half-upturned trunk and open up my digital travel alarm on a stump, hoping that a day of sunshine will dry out its circuits enough to bring it back to life.

"Noah!" Therese whistles, waving me over to a long, skinny pocket cut into the treeline. "Hurry! I don't have all day."

I dump half the seedlings from my planting bags into an empty tray and cross the winter road.

"This is hardly ideal ground to be training you in," she says. "It's greener than Eden, so you're bound to lose sight of your trees almost as soon as you've planted them." She takes my shovel and a handful of seedlings from my bags, and plants a row along the treeline toward the back of the cutaway. Now she hands it back to me. "Here. You try."

I take the staff, point its long, narrow blade forward and thrust it into the moss, burying it to the hilt.

"Too deep," she says. "It's not about muscle. Just swing the blade out in front of you and drop it into the ground as you step forward. Let the weight of the shovel open the hole. Have a seedling ready in your hand as you bend to plant."

Following alongside, she watches as I plant my first trees. "Slowly," she says. She bends to tug and twist each seedling to check for firmness and exposed roots. Shallow tree, loose tree, tight spacing, long spacing, leaner, duff shot, poor microsite selection — before I have the chance to correct one fault or even understand what it means, she finds another.

"Duff shot."

"What did I shoot?"

"It's when you plant all or part of the root into duff instead of mineral soil or living sphagnum."

"Duff?"

"The decomposing, peaty, humus layer on top of the ground." She bends down, and grabs a palmful of dirt from a flipped-over hunk of dried-up moss. "See?" she says, opening her fist. "It looks like soil, but it hasn't broken down enough to clump up when I squeeze it. Plant a tree in this and all the moisture will be wicked out of its roots before the checker from the logging company even gets here to throw plots. A bunch of duff shots and one or two other infractions and you won't make payment on this piece, which means Flying Dutchmen won't get paid either. Worse, the quality of every planter's work on this contract will be questioned, and the checker will do everything in his power to slow us down until he gets perfection from us, in which case you'll be replanting your entire area."

"I can't be expected to test every spot by hand."

"I'm not asking you to. Here, you shouldn't need to test anything as long as you stick to the green sphagnum. But when we get onto drier land, you'll sometimes need to screef away the duff before planting your seedling. You can screef with your boot, shovel or hand, depending on how dense the duff is and whether or not you're in root mat." With the corks on her right boot, she claws at the ground, kicking back twigs and chunks of duff like a dog kicking grass over her scat.

In the exposed patch of muck, I replant the seedling I had "duff shot", a term I imagine was coined by an exasperated arborcide detective upon discovering that fields of the logging company's future harvests were dead or dying because of the gross negligence of a lowly planter, who had carelessly "shot them into the duff," tree-slaughter charges pending.

Fumbling in my bag to pick out one tree at a time without man-handling them to death, I struggle to pick up speed, trying to keep an even stride to plant each one exactly six and a half feet from the last, but the swamp sucks me down, the moss grabbing at my feet hungrily. I throw down my shovel. "How the hell can anyone plant a thousand trees a day in this shit, let alone three thousand?"

"If you're talking about Aleron, even he took a few days to break in, and he's descended from a long line of bean planters you could probably trace right back to the beginnings of the Aztec Empire. So forget about numbers for now. Just concentrate on planting 'em right. What you get paid depends on the checker's assessment of your quality as much as on your production." She picks up my shovel, offering me the staff.

"Did you ever plant like Aleron?"

"In my prime, I could have deuced him on any given day."

"No way."

"You don't think so? I've been in the business since Dutch started the first private reforestation op in the country, back when we'd spend half our time inventing better tools and methods for the job, so I've had a long time to master the art. Too bad not much else has changed since then; for all their free-ranging hair and ideas, few of the men on my first crew thought I was good for anything but a cook's apron. The day I planted six thousand trees in Alberta gumbo — that turned their heads right 'round."

"Six grand — in a day?"

She nods. "Of course, my record's fallen since ... to another woman."

"Then show me."

"I can't. You'll need to find your own rhythm, and that can only come with practice and by economizing your motions."

"How'd you find yours?"

"I used to think of a wheel, a tree for every turn — I'd really set it spinning. After a time, I ceased to think about anything at all. But the first thing you'll need to learn is how to find your last row of trees in all this green. Here —" She hands me a roll of fluorescent pink surveyor's tape. "Ribbon a stick every forty feet or so and toss it six feet to your open side. That way you can plant back along a line of moveable flags without losing your way. I've got to meet the district forester to go over the contract specs, but I'll try to check up on you this afternoon." She strides back toward the matted piles of slash that line the winter road.

"Hey, Therese," I call. "I don't think I get it."

She casts a knowing glance my way. "Don't think; plant."

"What?"

"It isn't the swamp that's bogging you down," she says, leaving me to face the muskeg alone.

Four and a half hours plodding around in the humid heat and teeming flies. Four and a half hours losing sight of my trees, bogging down in swamp, and losing it. Finally bagged out, I return to my cache, grab the cookies from my pack, only remembering water as the bog belches beneath my feet. I drink hungrily from my canteen, and eat thirstily. There isn't a dry piece of turf for miles but I want sleep so badly that I'm ready to curl up in the moss — false bottom or not. So I spread my planting bags between the roots of the cedar snag I chose for shade and kneel to the ground.

Pee-pipi-peep! A killdeer cries. Pee-pi-pi-peeee-ep! I scan the ground, greener than Eden, for its broken-wing dance, but it's nowhere in sight. Something touches my shoulder: I spring to my feet.

Aleron's standing there, polishing an apple on his jersey.

"That was pretty convincing. Know any other birdcalls?"

"A few here, a few from El Salvador — especially the songs of birds that fly between. That is how I met the woman I will bring here one day."

"Bird calling?"

"One morning on my family's farm. I was beating back the jungle with my machete when I heard a song I had never heard before. I listened to the bird again then sang back, hoping to call it out to the field. Soon, the song was getting closer and I was getting closer to finding its singer. As I looked for it in the branches, a woman stepped out of the bush, whistling and scanning the field with her binoculars."

"And it was love at first sight ..."

"For me. She was furious. She had been tracking a very rare bird and my song had lured her away from it. If I wanted to make up for ruining her day, she told me, I would have to come to the edge of the jungle each morning and sing its song. If I ever heard a reply, I was to contact her at the university. Of course, I did not wait that long." The shadow of a cloud passes over his eyes. He smiles. "So, how is the planting?"

"Shitty. I've only planted a tray and it's almost two. You've probably bagged out two thousand by now."

"Almost three," he concedes.

"Three? Ten trays in this crap?"

"*Crap?* This is cream, wanker — *ice cream*. Good as sand, really. Maybe even better."

"I wish I knew what I'm doing wrong. I've been using moveable flags, just like Therese showed me, but everything's so green that I keep losing them."

"Have you no eyes? If you want to be a highballer, you must lose the training wheels. You must be able to see every planted row without looking. Remember your line, like you have a map in your head."

"A map in my head through what? This muskeg's so barren there's nothing to lock onto. It just swallows everything in green."

Aleron's eyes soften: he can read my frustration, if only its surface. "Let me plant with you for the rest of the day, and I will show you how."

"Sure, but I don't see what you'll get out of it. If anything, I'll probably slow you down."

"No. You will speed up. Besides, there are too many highballers on my crew already, and they have cut up the land like a jigsaw puzzle. They are *loco*, like wolves marking their territory, and like wolves, they have no regard for each other when they lift their legs to lay their scent."

I shrug. "The land's the land's. I don't own any."

We bag up and share water from my canteen. Aleron picks up one of those planting spears I've seen back at camp — a staff handle pointed with a Sheffield steel blade barely larger than a seedling plug.

"Is it faster than a shovel?" I ask.

"You will see."

I lead him to my last row and, standing aside, wait for him to take the line.

"You first," he says.

"But I'm not fast enough."

"You will be. You have to be. Bob wants production."

"Look, I joined this circus two weeks later than everyone else, and this is my first day of planting. You can't expect me to lead when you plant ten times my speed."

"I think you are lazy, wanker. Your head is on the moon, your body in the swamp. You forget that when the season is over and you go back to the city, you will be working for peanuts and your meals will cost a lot more than a dollar seventy-five a day. You must be hungry for tomorrow today."

Steaming, I turn to the line and plant down it as fast as I can. Even though he's given me a head start, I know he'll soon overtake me. I think of a wheel, a tree for every turn, but the wheel's too big, so I make it smaller; smaller every time I hear the engine in Aleron's breath on my flank.

For half the run, I've kept ahead of him, but only because he's been planting two rows for my one, and now he's pulling even. My wheel's getting smaller all the time, but my steps are getting shorter and he isn't thinking wheels or engines or moons — he isn't thinking at all. Suddenly a sharp, bruising pain stabs through my heel, then another.

"You are slowing down, wanker. I'm going to catch up, and when I do —" He lifts his spear to take another jab at my boots.

"You won't be doing that when we switch places on the next run!"

"If we switch, I will leave you in the dust. No. You can lead for the rest of the day."

So we continue our crazed dance across the sphagnum, the hours blurring by with the bag-outs, as if in the cycle of our motions we've lost every split second between action and perception, being and seeing, Aleron poking at the ground around my feet relentlessly — even though he can see I'm winded and pouring sweat. "Let's go, wanker. The blackflies are waking up from their siesta. Believe me, you should be less afraid of my spear than their bites." He stabs at my heel again.

I fill with anger — my second wind. Plant the last tree from my right bag. I don't want to waste any time rebagging from my left, so I unbuckle my shoulder harness, let it fall past my waist like the straps of some exotic bra, and spin the bags around on my hips.

The sun is focused like a laser on my forehead. Blackflies are swarming up from the swamp, crawling down my black mudsuckers, biting their way around my ankles and up my calves. The duct tape I'd used to seal my socks over my pantcuffs this morning when I was dressing for the swamp has melted in the heat. "You're not gonna take me down, you little fuckers!" I yell. My body kicks into high gear, the pressure on my back eases. The land is pulling me along, my shovel a divining rod gone berserk. I pull away from Aleron, grunting like an animal.

Aleron gasps to catch up. "Feel it, Noah?"

I can't spare the breath to speak, so I just nod.

He's beginning to nose ahead but I'm hell-bent on not falling back. We curve away from the treeline, back toward the second cache on the winter road. My body feels light as my hand sifts through the cool soil in the bottom of my feeder bag. Aleron has pulled a couple of strides ahead, but I've finished first. I jog past him to get my knapsack from the cache.

"Bagged out?" he says, planting his last.

"Bagged."

He strides up beside me, pushing a button on his watch. "Three hundred in thirty-five minutes. You planted your last bag in twelve."

"A hundred trees in twelve minutes. I don't believe it."

"I only hope they are good." He sucks back a couple of mouthfuls of water from his army surplus canteen and hands what remains to me. Hiking along the trail we'd cut through the island forest, I consider looking for more, for the clear, cold spring — pure and good as a Cartesian well — that Bob found percolating up through the sphagnum in the middle of this swamp. But it's greener than Eden and yesterday's footprints have sprung out of the moss. My body tingles with heat. I feel as if I could have kept going, at least another run, but as we step out onto the floating bridge, the backs of my legs begin to burn, and I fade.

I gulp from the blue jug that's sitting between the rear doors of Therese's van, letting the coughing stream overflow my parched lips and spill down my chest. For the first time in my life, I'm thinking and feeling nothing but water.

CHAPTER FOUR

WEEK 1, DAY 4, May 18 — At dinner, Bob "takes the numbers." He calls out our names, alphabetically and crew by crew, and we have to call out how many spruce we planted that day. The hardcores and highballers call first and usually loudest; the quieter voices either had bad days or are excessively modest.

First night, I silently simmered at the humiliation of being forced to announce to the whole camp my meagre number, which Aleron had more than tripled, Jaegs had quadrupled, and Walter quintupled.

"A thousand," I mumbled when Bob called my name.

"Hear that, Buzzard?" he said. "He's already cracked a grand." Instead of heaping scorn, he shovelled praise for what he called an exceptional first day.

Yesterday, I wasn't so lucky, even though I'd been planting faster. After giving me shit and brimstone for "slutting" my trees into the ground, Therese made me replant my entire morning's work, which was riddled with double-planted rows and satellite lines.

"Eight," I whispered when my name was called at dinner.

"Eight trays?"

"Eight hundred."

"Eight hundred! What happened? After yesterday, I thought you might hit two grand, like Aleron did on his second day."

I no longer wonder why Bob won't take our numbers privately; even before I had to call out mine, the reasons behind his ritual were abundantly clear. It spawns competition, especially among the hardcores and highballers, who are constantly seeking to out-plant each other, and it shames the greeners and dog-fuckers into setting higher goals. But maybe that's not so bad. If I didn't know that the highballers are averaging counts of 4,000 trees (at 8.5 cents per plug, that's $340 per day), I might've quit this gong show by now — not that I've got any better place to go.

MAY 19 — Waiting for the dinner horn, I was invited by Ted, Tim, Josie and Judd, all from Lyndon's crew, to a game of hackey-sack. Soon, we were joined by Aleron, Jacques and Kirsten from Clem's crew, and Steve and Daniel from my own.

A seasoned highballer with experience in five provinces, Jacques swears by the game's therapeutic effects, which he claims limbers up stiff joints and tight muscles after a "day in the trenches" and helps to fine-tune eye-body coordination. "This is why hackey is the most popular game with planters, no matter where you go." But it also seems to be an antidote to the competition between planters for good ground and high tree counts, which, unchecked, could create a corrosive atmosphere in camp, or maybe open rifts between the crews as wide as those between the proletariat, bourgeoisie and upper crust. Not only is hackey-sack non-competitive, success at it depends on the co-operation of every participant. Each player added increases the difficulty of the common objective: "completing a hack," which is a fait accompli only when the extra-large egg-sized bean bag has been kept airborne for long enough for each person in the circle to have kicked, kneed or headered it at least once.

Completing a hack with ten people of varying ability and expereience was next to impossible, but I did get to know a little more about some of the planters not on my crew. Bob may not have a degree in water and soil conservation, but Josie does, which may explain the defensive and somewhat jealous undertone to Bob's outburst when Aleron questioned his ability to find pure water in the middle of a swamp. Topping that, Josie is now in the midst of graduate studies in scatology. Analyzing an animal's feces, she can determine not only its diet but also its approximate size, range, stress levels, sex, and, where the defecator is female, whether or not she is pregnant.

"A scat can be a virtual microchip of invaluable data on shier beasts, such as lynx and wolverines," she said, missing the sack and blowing another opportunity to achieve a hack. "To date, the research I've been involved in has shown that some carnivores of the boreal and mixed wood forests, such as foxes and wolves, are far more omnivorous than was originally thought. In fact, based on pollens either deliberately or accidentally ingested, we can even break down their dietary preferences season by season."

Hearing this, Tim scratched his spiky hair and asked, "So, from a piece of shit you can tell whether a bear had a side salad with his planter or simply ate a vegan planter's belly like a hagus?"

"Theoretically, yes."

"No shit, Sherlock?"

Tim, who looks like a younger version of that strummer from *Deliverance* (the guitarist, not the banjo plucker), is in theatre school, and by next summer, hopes to be kicking around the stages at Stratford or Shaw before trying his luck south of the 49th. Even though he has about as much experience in hackey sack as I do, he's a real pro at striking a pose of cool to cover up his ineptitude, often quoting his favourite lines from *Hamlet* and *Apocalypse Now*, as in "sprynges to catch woodcocks" when one of Josie's bullets caught him in the bag and "Charlie don't surf" when he wiped out in the boat launch chasing an errant sack with a wicked bias. Truth be told, Charlie don't hack, neither.

An "aggie" with a degree from Guelph, his home town, Judd's hoping to be among the first to establish a co-op organic hemp farm, and we're not talking about a grow-op for binder twine. He's biding his time waiting for "non-commercial hemp" to be legalized, letting his land lie in clover long enough to be certified organic. As a seasonal cabinet installer and now, a planter, he has ample opportunity to test-market various strains of his product; one of which filled the Pottery Barn bag he brought to the game. Something tells me he'll be planting trees for a very long time.

As others made their way to the big top from their tents and the shower, the circle of players grew, until it included the foremen, Jack and, very briefly, Bob; nineteen players in all. Very suddenly, the banter and joking gave way to intense concentration on the task at foot. Buzzard extinguished his Backwoods cigar and tucked it behind his ear for later. Although a more adroit hackey-sacker, like Kirsten, can keep the sack in play on her own for minutes at a time, all showboating was abandoned in favour of setting up textbook passes that could be easily headered, kneed or footed by the lamest of klutzes. On our twelfth or thirteenth attempt, the unthinkable occurred: we were one participant shy of completing a hack, and I was that participant.

"Cross the circle, Noah!" Therese prodded as Aleron kept the sack in play. "Quick! Oh my God, this is going to be our camp record!"

I ran over to his side but coming down, the sack connected hard with the steel toe of his workboot, flew up over my head and out of the circle. Passing by on her way to hit the horn announcing dinner, Cass looked up just in time to catch the sack on her forehead, let it roll down the length of her body to the tips of her bare toes on her left foot and kicked it up high. She caught it on the back of her heel, other foot, without more than a glance over her shoulder. This was merely the warm-up to a routine that would win her a gold at the summer games, were "hackey-sack, solo performance category," an Olympic event, and earned her claps and cheers until Therese lost her patience, smelling a hack of twenty. Finally, Cass toed a perfect pop fly right to me. Leaping forward, I shot out my left leg in a Judo kick, lost the sack in the sun, and hit a patch of slippery grass. My ass planted hard on terra firma, the sack landed smack in the middle of my forehead, then rolled to the dirt.

"It's good!" Steve proclaimed, as if he were the video judge on a disputed goal that went upstairs.

"Dinner's getting cold!" Rosemary yelled, and with a wooden spoon gonged an aluminum pot lid the size of a shield. Our throng of hackers streamed into the big top.

I looked up at Cass with a mixture of humiliation and amazement.

"I was a technical gymnast and baton twirler in a past life," she said.

"Really?"

"No, but I lost my high school trig credit to this stupid game. You?"

"I sacrificed my credit in hackey-sack to Scrabble."

CHAPTER FIVE

WEEK 2, DAY 1, May 22 — You wake up and you're there. There, you work all day. It is said that by the end of a season, you'll probably have seen every one else naked at least twice. You eat three square and fall asleep. You're there in your dreams and your nightmares, planting the gaps between days, dragging yourself by your shovel through trenches full of your fallen comrades till the wake-up horn predawn, and get up exhausted. If you're really lucky, when you wake up and see for certain that you've never left, you find that you're sharing a tent with someone else there, and you haven't kicked each other black and blue from your night of planting.

That's what it's like up here, 24/7: we live in our workspace and work in our living space. You could write an anthropology thesis on the integration of work and home in the planting camp alone and still have more than enough material to carry you through a long and illustrious career in the field. From what Lyndon has told me, it's nothing like the modern-day lumber camp, where the loggers are housed in heated trailers and eat in mess halls equipped with satellite TV and pool tables, where the only place you might find a woman is the kitchen. We could use a few more women here, but Therese says that out west, where reforestation is better established, camps typically recruit large numbers of women because they're more likely to stick it out a whole season. In some camps, the assistant cook or campee will babysit planters' brats for a reasonable fee.

There are no children here, but everything is centred on providing the planters with all that we need to do our jobs optimally. Jack, our tree-runner, often works till nightfall to stock our blocks with enough seedlings to carry us through till noon the next day. To Bob, there's no greater sin than letting a planter run out of trees, and the crew bosses (politically correct for foremen) are expected to hop on their ATV's and fetch for their own, if Jack falls behind or is sent to Thunder Bay — a two and a half hour drive — for supplies. The crew bosses assign us our pieces of land and make sure we fill them, monitoring the quality of our work and teaching the greeners some of the tricks of the trade. But their main job is to keep us motivated, especially when we're stuck in a scuzz pile (shite land where the planting's slow) or extreme weather (none yet, but I've heard they'll keep us working through conditions that would send the posties packing). There is no surefire way to spur on a lethargic, lazy, hungover, distracted or discouraged planter. Lyndon prefers boot-camp tactics, playing the drill sergeant to his grunts, sometimes forcing them to work an extra hour to meet the minimum daily production quotas he sets for each of them.

From what Aleron has told me, Clem takes a relatively hands-off approach to crew-bossing. Since, on average, the highballers have a couple of seasons under their belts and are highly competitive, he doesn't have to worry about motivating them; if anything, he spends most of his time and energy gently applying the brakes whenever they begin to sacrifice quality for production.

Therese, my hippy-dippy crew boss, favours embracing Zen as a means of shutting out all other-than-earthy distractions and plant-ing fully in the moment. Legend has it that a legendary planter, whose name I can't remember but who hailed from BC, set the first national record when, only halfway through a seven-year vow of silence, he planted 7,000 trees in a day — way up the side of a mountain!

The key, Therese says, is to remember that planting isn't a horrible distraction from our everyday reality, but the only reality we can touch with any immediacy. There are moments and sometimes hours when I'm there, when all I am is the hand in my bag and my shovel in the ground and the tree tucked into the hole and the heel healing it shut. The rest of the time, planting is a pleasant distraction from an awful reality I'm all too ready to shut out. So, here is my new reality, in the land of blackflies and muskeg and the explosion of spring, and I'll do what I must to be the best planter I can be.

The supper horn! I'm hungrier than a horse, and drooling like one of Pavlov's dogs. Knowing I'll be coming home to a smorgasbord each night is the greatest motivator of all. As the good book says, much depends on dinner; all the cook would have to do to start a mutiny is serve tasteless gruel after we've been planting in rain and rocks all day.

CHAPTER SIX

LINED UP IN the rain for the shower. There's just one shower so it's unisex. Jack runs it for only an hour before dinner and half an hour after to save on propane. There's twenty-four other dirty planters aside from me waiting their turn (not counting the support staff), so each of us is restricted to exactly two and a half minutes to lather up, shampoo and rinse, and another half-minute to dry off and get into our civvies. Worst of all is the narrow vestibule between the dry-shack and the shower stall, not knowing who I'll encounter, towelling off while I'm stripping or, conversely, stripping while I'm towelling off. I should be used to it by now, but I just can't get over the sensation that I'm always having to watch my eyes — especially when the who is a her. The moral majority tells me that, to avoid temptation and see her only as holy, I must cut her off at the head; the politically correct crowd demands that I correct my vision of her, make it more holistic, by cutting her off at the head. Should my eyes wander, fall below her neck, should I fantasize — thwack! — administer the whips of self-flagellation.

"Next!" a woman's voice calls.

I pick up my shopping bag of toiletries and slip through the tarp doorway into the dry-shack. Rain drums on the roof. Rainsoaked and muddied clothes, hanging from sapling beams above the smoking airtight, are steaming: men's musky sweat watered down by women's sweat, strong but more clean and saline. I spread my rainjacket over a chair, bob and duck my way toward the shower and step through the partition to the change vestibule.

It's the new girl — woman, I don't know why I think girl. Maybe because I caught a glimpse of her small breasts as she was turning her back to me, or because Lyndon's been calling Cass, *the new girl,* ever since she was put on his crew.

Now that her face is no longer so painfully swollen, her eyes and nose more defined, I still only catch glimpses — as she bends to dry her feet. As she throws the veil of her gaze over her shoulder.

My mouth goes dry. I lose a button taking off my greying white dress shirt. I slip out of my sandals, peel off my sopping wet pants; silent, eyes fixed on the dirt. Finally, I step out of my underwear. The drumming rain stops, and suddenly the tarpaulin walls of the shower shack glow orange. I try to squeeze by her as quickly as I can, without looking. But a bright red mark, five-pointed as a star, flashes from the whiteness of her shoulder blade as she snakes a rolled towel down her back: the dried blood print of a hand too big to be human.

CHAPTER SEVEN

AFTER WORK, IT'S the ghost images of the bloody print on the new girl's back instead of ghost seedlings that haunt the bare patches of earth on the path to the shitters. I've tried all day to match that print to hands — the hands of a large man, a giant — but gradually the hands have become mythological: sasquatch, abominable snowman — something with a large palm and widely spread but stubby fingers (I hold up my hand: *or with fingers bent to claw*).

On the branch of the fork leading to the men's, a faint grunt rises from a moss-coated and treed cluster of boulders. The grunt seems disembodied, like the boulders, picked up there, dropped here, a glacial question: what white force are you — carrier, or hunter? — or were you also deposited here to be taken by a mossy skin? Underbrush rustles, twigs snap.

I freeze. "Anyone there?"

There is a short pause, then a loud throaty growl like a bark stopped between lips and teeth.

I turn back for the fork, increasing my pace to a brisk step, a jog, a full-tilt run as the creature shadows me — browsing, preying, barrelling through the bush — matching its speed to mine; always alongside me but never in sight. Its sounds pull ahead, circle until I can no longer tell which side of the path it's on. I stop to wipe the sweat from my eyes, fighting the shakes to catch my breath as silently as I can. But its panting and snorts are closing on my flank. I clamber up a tree; damning myself for not knocking the muck off my treads when, mid-shimmy, I lose traction and start to slide down.

It growls, then claws at my foot. I grab for the nearest limb but it's too far out of reach. Peeled away from the trunk, I fall, and land on my hands and knees in the springy moss.

"Bear!" I yell. "BE—"

A hand cups my mouth. "Shhhh!" It's Lyndon. Laughing like a hyena. He releases my jaw and wraps his arm under my chest, locking it between my neck and shoulder to keep me from squirming out from under him. "You failed the test," he says. "But now you'll know what to do when you've got a real bear on your ass."

I reach back with my free arm, feeling blindly for his leg, his shirt — anything I can grab hold of. But like a boa, a set of handcuffs, he constricts; forcing it out with my breath. "Alright. What? What do I do?"

"Get down on all fours."

The dinner horn blares. Lyndon releases me from his grubby clutches and heads up the path for the big top; his laugh fading as it trails back to me.

I get up and brush myself off, watching the imprint of my hand slowly lifting from the moss, from the new girl's back, the black-furred paw of a bear, retracting two-inch claws bloodied with a redder mystery.

I wait up till dark, till everyone's in their tents, before rummaging by flashlight through the garbage pile. The night we arrived, Cass's tent was in tatters, "Torn in yesterday's squall, slashed by the branches of a falling tree," she said as she assembled the dome outside Bob's trailer, hoping that Bob would be able to fix it.

"That's funny — we had no squall," Therese said. "Your last camp is only fifteen clicks from here."

"Microclimate," Bob said, hunching over the mess of shredded nylon and twisted poles. "Could be sunny as a solstice day on our lake, pissing only two lakes over and we'd never know it." After a minute of close examination, Bob declared, "It's toast," offered her one of the spares left by planters of seasons past who, in the grip of bush fever, abandoned camp and all reminders; or who, rolling in the fall colours of Canadian green at season's end, donated decaying tents along with boots to charity or the woods — any takers.

"Christ, Bob's gone soft in his middle age," Lyndon sneered. "Not all that long ago he'd have charged her for it."

He must've felt sorry for her, knowing that the company she'd been working for had a reputation for being fly-by-night; deducting thousand-dollar sums from their foremen's pay cheques for scratches and stone chips to its crummies' already rusted, dented and dinged up finishes — sometimes defaulting on contracts and not paying any of their workers at all. Two seasons ago, Bob told her, so many workers had sued for back pay, so many MNR districts had seized the company's security deposits, that the banks decided it was too much of a credit risk to be granting it spring start-up loans. The president declared bankruptcy, moved himself, equipment and remaining assets out west to start up again under a new name. "Last season, he had the gall to visit his camps in a brand new BMW ...." Cass blushed, but Therese said, "It's alright — you can't know these things ahead of time unless you have friends who've been in the business awhile. That's why Mr. Bark has only greeners on his crews."

Bob started disassembling the unsalvageable tent, then stopped, eyeing his hands before wiping them on the thighs of his pants. "What's this sticky stuff?"

"Oh —" Cass reddened again. "I'm sorry, I forgot to tell you. It's sap."

"Sap."

"From the pine. It dripped sap all over my site from the time I pitched camp to the time it came down in the wind."

"Hmmph. Got under the fly too, I see." He eyeballed her again, but those were his last words on the matter.

Flashlight between my knees, I unroll the dome tent; marvelling at how neatly she's bundled it up for a landfill burial. The light blue fly is beginning to mildew. Flies, wasps and bees, frozen in their moments of ecstasy, float in the pine's blood, waiting for sap to become amber. But the sticky red body of the tent holds other moments — coarse ivory hairs left by a pastry brush, downy fine black hairs too coarse to be her shed. Tears too evenly spaced to have been cut by a scraping branch, spatters and smears of blood dried a deeper, browner red than the nylon and too large to be the swatted and squashed afterthoughts of bitch mosquitoes. The clinching clue is what the sap doesn't hold: the smell. I stick my finger through its congealing skin, touch amber to my tongue, but the taste that buds is honey.

CHAPTER EIGHT

THE CHILL OF early May nights has been eased out of the air by the earth's release of the past days' sun. Convection heat pulses up through the moss, the tent floor, my skin; holding me to the ground as if the gravity here has been trebled, which doesn't seem so impossible in light of the speed with which the days fly by.

No wind — just fingers of music (Bartram's guitar picking, Therese's light *pit-pa-tomb-a pit-pa-tomb* on Congo drums) reaching me through the trees and the mosquitoes' growing drone.

Rare bird's song — Bohemian waxwing ("*sr-r-r-r-ee, sr-r-r-r-ee*"), black-throated green warbler ("*trees, trees, murm'ring trees*"), birds of night rarely seen; birds of first and last light (white-throated sparrows and bitterns) whose voices trail off with the sunset.

"*Buzza! Buzz-ha-rd!*" Rosemary gasps hoarsely across the short distance between our tents. Giggles, grunts, more gasps and the snapping of twigs arise from the unbeaten ground beneath their now mated sleeping bags, and deeper into the bush, the mad mating thump of the male ruffed grouse.

She's almost old enough to be his mother. But maybe that's what he wants, what she wants. A bit of youth in exchange for a bite of wisdom. What he lacks in years, she knows from experience; what he lacks in years, she wants back again. I never try to make the private lives of any beings my business, but even when I do my best to avoid them, they make theirs mine. That's probably why Bob laughed his ass off when I practically vowed celibacy the day I joined the camp. It's hard not to be horny when, by the sounds of it, the whole forest is fucking.

It wasn't like this in prison. I was lonely, but never with desire. Four days and my prick never rose once. Not even at that made-for-TV movie they showed — *Futureworld*, no, *Westworld* — some flick about an adults-only Disneyland where frontier town cathouses are stocked with cybernaut whores. If you were married, would it be adultery, or just taking a ride? Theme parks like rags "for men's entertainment": more fuck for a buck.

When the movie was over and we were locked back into our cell, Hans, public relations officer for the All-Hallow's Eve Arboretum Day of Action and my self-appointed bodyguard, whispered, "The corrections authorities want you to dream such dreams, while they spike your bedtime beverage with saltpetre or something to make sure you'll never act on them. It's sort of like a catheterized catharsis, you know?"

"Get lost," I said. "They stopped doing that ages ago."

"Catharsis?"

"No. Saltpetre."

"Oh really? Then how come the coffee, tea, and hot chocolate are all the same muddy green tint?"

I jumped from my bunk and retched my cocoa into the stainless steel sink, helplessly watching as it drained down into the adjoined stainless steel toilet bowl; Hans laughing, "It was a joke, it was a joke!"

The next morning, he called from the top bunk. "Anything?"

"Not even a piss-on. You?"

"The cowgirls were cute, but there's no one waiting for my release either."

Hans wanted that more than anything: to look out through our caged window each morning and see his name among the dedications of love spray-painted on the warehouse wall beyond the barbed-wire-topped and possibly electrified fences: *Cliff — Hang in There XOX Nancy*; 2 Weeks 2 go, Not 2 Weak 2 Wait — Crystal Aug '85, etc. I guess I wanted that too: the promise that there would be someone to nurse my bruised ego when I got out.

Gazing at that graffiti the morning before our release, at promises so thickly layered they ceased to mean anything at all, I blurted, "Protesting is all for squat."

"Hey, we got one day to go, brother. It'll come back to you."

"That's not what I'm talking about."

"Yes, it is."

Two days past the gate, I got my cock back, but desire — think of the difficulties zookeepers have getting certain endangered species of animals to breed in captivity. I had to get farther out, needed to open every pore, wanted wind in my ear.

What do I hear now that every pore is opened?

I hear spring peepers bloating throats for a watery roll.

I hear the male ruffed grouse — th-th-thu-thu-thu-thuthuthth thump — wings still drumming air.

I hear a hollow knocking, antler on wood, coming from the lake. A bull moose calls: he answers his own echo. His rut more like a moan lamenting his story: it's May, spring — way past his mating season — and he hasn't shed his horns yet. I lie here, silent as a clam with a pearl growing moonsize stuck in its open mouth. I think this must be the male version of "expecting."

CHAPTER NINE

WEEK 3, DAY 2, May 31 — Lost two hours this morning to unloading trees from the reefer (planterese for refrigerated tractor trailer). It was my crew's first turn, so I shouldn't complain. Except that the $20 per head Bob paid each of us for the privilege hardly compensates for the downtime, or for the bruised and aching forearms from catching hundreds of flying trays of trees as they're being rolled off the back of the reefer, pulled from their bins and chain-ganged from planter to planter down to the edge of a creek where Jack can keep them watered. Even so, I planted six trays today — four of them Jack pine, as we've moved into drier, hillier ground. With a bit more focus and effort, I think I could crack two grand tomorrow, especially if Therese pairs me up with Steve or Daniel when we start our new block at noon.

Aleron told me that most of the highballers and hardcores prefer to plant solo, to avoid time-consuming moves and having to replant because one of their partners was slacking on the quality. But having him at my heels my first two days kept me motivated at a level that I haven't been able to sustain for more than a couple of hours at a time.

When I'm winded and burnt, when my shovel hand is cramping painfully around my staff, I try to imagine racing him across the muskeg, run after run — 300 trees in 45 minutes, a whole tray in half an hour — planting each successive bag-up faster than the last, stopping less and less for breaks, till I no longer have to eat or drink or rest at all. If I'm ever to keep that pace, my body must remember those movements till their so ingrained they're instinct and my mind must learn to switch off at will. But in the long hours of the afternoon, my head teems with memories and thoughts to fill the vast, empty expanse.

WEEK 3 DAY 4, June 2 — The temperature plummeted last night. The frost barely left the ground today. By mid-morning, we were planting in sleet. I'd forgotten my raingear and I didn't pack enough sandwiches to keep warm. My glove froze so stiff that I lost my grip on my shovel and kept dropping it. I'd just about given up on planting altogether, let alone 2,000 trees, when Lyndon pulled up in the Conan.

"Why are you sitting there, freezing your ass off?"

"I was freezing my ass off long before I sat down." I told him.

"Then you're not planting fast enough."

"I forgot my raingear." I clenched my teeth to stop them from chattering. "My fingers are so frozen I can't feel my trees."

"Fuck raingear. Raingear's for pussies. It's cold and clammy and it'll bog you down."

"Pussies? I thought Flying Dutchmen was an equal opportunity employer."

"We are," he said. "Cass is planting in a T-shirt and shorts, and she's on track for eight trays."

"Can I hop in for a minute to warm up?"

"Pussy," he said, and drove on.

I suppose he knew I'd probably hold my nose and take the bait; by the quitting horn, I'd planted the additional five trays I needed to reach 2100. Just as he'd predicted, Cass had planted her 2400, which makes her the highballer of the lowballer crew and Lyndon's pet.

At dinner, I sat at her table, still shivering from the damp, hoping to spark something out of nothing, a phoenix from the ash.

"I can't believe that Bob's worried we'll have a bad fire season. You know, I read somewhere that suppressing fires is actually wrecking our forests. Jack pine stands have adapted to burn every sixty years or so; without fire, their cones won't open and seed the ground for the next generation."

"Your point?"

"I dunno. I guess I'm fascinated by the idea that something so big actually thrives on its own destruction."

"It doesn't work that way with people," she said. Then she got up to clear her plate and took her dessert outside.

She's never once gone out of her way to speak with me, and ever since that day in the shower, she's made a point of avoiding me, as if I'd seen in her half-healed scar the heel that could bring her down, which makes it the one curiosity I'm both dying and loathing to ask her about.

CHAPTER TEN

I WAKE UP shivering — my nose and ears numb, my steaming breath frosting the nylon walls of my tent — the tent darker than usual for 5:30, sagging low over top of me under the weight of snow. I grab a sweater from my pack, struggle into it in the slight comfort of my sleeping bag, put on my old Habs toque. Then I roll over, pull the bag over my head, bunch myself up into a fetal position and shiver out warmth, waiting for the wake-up horn.

My entire body aches, especially my shovel arm. I've got the claw worse than any other morning this week. I try to rub the cramps out, but it's no use.

5:45 and the horn still hasn't gone but I can't sleep, so I reach down into the bottom of my bag, pull out the pants, shirt and work socks I put there last night so they'd be warm for the morning. My leather workboots, wet from yesterday's swamp, have shrunk in the freeze; I put on my runners, a second sweater, my lumberjack jacket. I unzip the tent: snowlight floods in so bright it would be blinding if it weren't for the trees. Four inches or more have accumulated; a few flakes are still falling through the still branches. The wind coming off the lake has blown a drift against my back door, frozen a skin of water along the edges of the shore. I brush the powdery snow off my tent and head for the mess, exposed patches of moss crunching underfoot, twigs snapping brightly.

Rosemary's making breakfast as usual, but hardly anyone is up.

"How's the fire coming, Jack?" Bob says, drawing himself a coffee from the urn.

Jack fans the mouth of the oil drum. "Wood's a bit damp,"

Bob walks to the mouth of the big top, looks out, shakes his head. "Fuckin' weather."

I serve myself a bowl of porridge and join him. "We're not planting in this, are we?"

"For Chrissake, Noah, what the hell do you think? The ground's frozen solid and who knows how long it's gonna stay that way ... shit! If it was only a little less snow, and a bit warmer, I'd send the crew out to plant right through — even if it meant risking a little quality."

Rosemary comes down the steps and hands him his breakfast plate.

"Ya, thanks." He picks a sausage, stuffs it in his mouth, chews on it thoughtfully. Then he glances down at his plate and gags. "Hey Rose, are we still having that problem with mice getting into the flour?"

"I don't think so. Why?"

"These ain't blueberries in my pancakes ..."

"Don't be silly — they're chocolate sprinkles."

"Chocolate?" Cass appears from behind the oil drum, where she has been sitting so silently that I didn't notice her. She's wrapped in a fluorescent orange ski jacket, her bony cheeks red from the cold, even redder against her blue scarf. "Chocolate pancakes — now that's what I call a real bear's breakfast!" She heaps four or five on a plastic plate, picks up the five gallon tin of maple syrup and pours a cold-thickened blob overtop.

I finish my porridge, fetch a couple of pancakes myself, pull up a lawn chair between Jack and Cass, and stretch my legs toward the faint heat of the smoking oil drum.

Lyndon tramps in. "Should I hit the horn?"

"Wait a half-hour," Bob says. "I'm gonna go back to my trailer to see if I can pick up a weather report on my shortwave." By the entrance, he pulls Lyndon closer and lowers his voice. "Go wake Clem and Therese 'n bring 'em to me. I think we'll make this the day off, move the whole crew to town till everything thaws. The last thing I need right now is a sick camp."

I watch them leave the big top.

"Hear that?" I whoop. "A day off!"

"I wouldn't count on it," Rosemary says. "If the weatherman predicts the temperature will rise above freezing by noon, he'll be sending you out to work. Anyway, if we go to town now, there's no way we'll be getting Saturday off too."

Cass puts down her plate, picks up a compact palate of cake-paints. She flips through her sketchbook, stopping on a view of an island that's about a half-kilometre off to the right of the boat launch. Then she looks out the mesh screen — the white everywhere, the forest on the other side of the clearing: spruce looking black, not so verdant as yesterday, where the needles on the undersides of their branches show through. She puts down her paints and sighs. "The view has really changed," she mutters to herself. "I can barely keep up."

Leaning closer, I shift my eyes between her painting and the view through the no-see-um mesh. "Cass, I hope I'm not sticking my nose where you don't want it , but isn't that the point of a still life or landscape — the artist's attempt to freeze the scene in the moment it first caught her eye and to portray it in a way that her audience will recognize?"

"Or the artist's admission that she can't do more than that in this medium? The scene's always changing; it's never still — not even momentarily. I can't freeze a transition."

"A leaf captured as it's falling off a tree, strobe light photos of a bullet passing through an apple. You can't freeze a transition or you don't want to?"

"Alright. What I mean is that I can't do it honestly. All I can communicate — and what I'm really interested in getting — is the tension and contradiction in the attempt."

"So you think artifice is dishonest because it might trick people into thinking they're getting sugar instead of Splenda or Toot Sweet, or whatever pretty name they have for the latest artificial sweetener? I know I can't swim in your painting, or that tamarack won't turn yellow and shed its needles when the one out there will. But I can appreciate it because I sometimes remember things freeze-frame, and from it, I can imagine what will and might happen. It's good. You shouldn't be so hard on yourself just because it doesn't reflect what you're trying to do, which, by the way, could most easily be done with a mirror."

"Thanks," she says quietly. "I still don't think you understand what I'm trying to do, and if you tried to assure me that the effort's noble I'd probably tell you to blow it out your ass." She licks the tip of a fine horsehair brush and begins lifting out some of the island's green.

Jack gets up to refill his coffee mug.

"While you're up, could you get me a cup of water?"

"The spigots on the water barrels are frozen, Cass."

"Then fetch me some from the kettle, if there's enough."

He gets a jar from the shelf, fills it with gently steaming water and puts the kettle back to boil on the Coleman.

Cass works quickly, lifting and washing out more and more of the green of her island, but only there, leaving the suggestion of snow. When she's done, she coats the entire page with a watery blue (water tinted with just a hint of blue) and puts it out in the dry-shack.

"I'm hoping the frost will leave a pattern when I melt it off," she says as she returns. "It may be an improvement."

The air is thick with snow again, as it must have been all night. The air is thick with lightly falling snow: I can hear each flake accumulate.

CHAPTER ELEVEN

We've been waiting in the lobby of the Shoreline Motor Hotel for well over an hour — packed in standing room only — with a couple of other planting crews from Kashabowie and Black Sturgeon Lake and all of our hockey bags, duffel bags, mailbags and garbage bags of filthy laundry. Finally, Bob and Therese step through the door.

"Hey, back off, will ya?" Bob shouts, pushing his way through the crush of half-washed bodies. He slaps an attaché case (so foreign in his hands) down on a bench by the window and snaps it open. Then he begins the crew-by-crew roll call for cash advances, starting with the highballers — Bartram ... Jaegs ... Westerly. ... Therese passes out mail from the stairway up to the C&W bar.

Bartram squeezes his way over to me, small wad of bills clenched in his one hand, backpack in the other. "Walt thinks the place will book up quickly, maybe before you've been called for your advance. We're taking a double with Aleron and Steve, and looking to get a coupla more roommates to keep it cheap, if you're interested."

"Sure," I say, a bit surprised that any of the highballers would want to room with a greener. "Whose name should I check under at the registration desk?"

"Actually, it would be better if you ask one of us in person later. The clerk's a bit uptight about overcrowding the rooms, especially with the manager breathing down her neck about collecting a per head surcharge. You'll probably have to sneak in by the back door or fire escape."

"Abramson."

Finally my turn. I squeeze through the mob and drop my backpack at Bob's feet.

"How much do you want?"

"A hundred."

"The limit's sixty," he says, entering that amount on my payroll sheet.

"How the hell is anyone supposed to get by on that?"

"Bunk up with some friends. That oughta leave you with enough for a few square meals." He looks up, holding out the pen. "Provided you keep off the sauce."

"Do I look like a drunk?"

"No, but bringing a crew into this town is kinda like inviting a bear to a picnic. We're not in our element anymore. The motel managers know it, the cops know it."

"They seem pretty happy to have us here."

"For now. But come tourist season, one wrecked room or bar brawl and we won't be able to go to town anywhere in the region. So I'd like to pen the animal energies of this crew for long enough to get them back to camp. Besides, this weather might not lift for days, and I can't afford to lose an extra day's production to a bender."

"Or to sore knees," I say. "So how about an extra twenty so I can go to that sauna I keep hearing about."

"Alright. Eighty. But that's as good as I can do."

I sign for my advance, and shouldering my pack, turn for the registration desk. Therese stops me halfway, leaning over the stair rail to hand me an envelope. "First mail since you got here, huh?"

"Probably my father forwarding my credit card bill."

Sure enough, the address is in his hand, neat and businesslike and functional as the place names on a map. Yep. Probably forwarding the bill for my charge card, which, last I looked, was maxed out from all my trips to Camping Co-op, Army and Navy Surplus and Sally Ann in my oh-so-green efforts to gear up and be prepared for this fiasco. I tear into the envelope so carelessly that I nearly rip it in half. Another envelope falls to the floor, marked with the official seal of the Office of the President of York University, addressed to my name and the house I grew up in, and (I flip it over) steamed open and resealed as is Father's habit when he suspects something's brewing that he should know about but that's really none of his damned business. I thumb open envelope #2 and pull out the neatly folded institutional parchment, wondering if they'd forgotten the plastic wax seal or, in these days of austerity, simply dispensed with the formality:

Dear Mr. Abramson,

In the past academic year, you have on a number of occasions conducted yourself in a manner unbecoming of a student and unacceptable to the standards of York University. Specifically, on October 31, you involved yourself in an unauthorized demonstration in the campus arboretum that prevented work crews from commencing scheduled improvements there. This demonstration, and your use of an unauthorized sound amplification device, were in violation of the Temporary Use of Space policy, contravened applicable municipal noise bylaws and disturbed the peace.

Later, on December 21, you were seen organizing and participating in another protest at the same location — in flagrant violation of a court injunction banning further protests and forbidding you and other members of Preach Our Practice from coming within a two kilometre radius of the arboretum worksite for the next year. Again, you were seen to be using an unauthorized sound amplification device. Additionally, several teeth on the blade of one Caterpillar bulldozer were reported bent, allegedly as a result of actions designed to delay or thwart progress on the project or derail it altogether — actions for which criminal charges of mischief and vandalism are still pending.

During these demonstrations, you interfered with the proper functioning of university programs and activities, contributed to the threat of harm to the safety and well-being of the campus community and failed to abide by reasonable requests and legal orders given orally and in writing by officials of the university authorized to secure compliance with regulations, rules, practices and procedures and also by police; all contrary to Presidential Regulation 2.

The arrogance of your actions and refusal to moderate your behaviour calls for harsh and swift corrective measures. Pursuant to my sole authority over student conduct, vested in me as President and Vice-Chancellor under Article 6 of the President Act, I hereby order you rusticated for a period of three calendar years, commencing May 1. During this period, and until you re-register, you will have no purpose on campus and are therefore asked not to attend the premises of York University. If you are seen on the premises, you will be issued a notice of trespass.

Yours sincerely,
Leslie R. Crustin, PhD.
President & Vice-Chancellor

Read again: "scheduled improvements to the campus arboretum" — pave paradise ... well, we all know the rest of that song. "unauthorized sound amplification device" — meaning a bullhorn, or a hearing aid to the listening impaired. "in violation of the Temporary Use of Space policy" — Me? I was only ever there temporarily, however involuntarily I left. Question for El Presidente: You call knocking down half the arboretum to make way for a parking lot a "temporary use of space"? "contravened applicable municipal noise bylaws" — like the diesel engines and chainsaws? "in flagrant violation of a court injunction ... prohibiting you from coming within a three kilometre radius of the arboretum worksite for the next year" — Okay, I didn't elect to drop all my courses the day I signed up for this tree planting gong show as much as I was no longer able to attend, since that three kilometre radius encompassed just about every classroom on the campus. "several teeth on the blade of one Caterpillar bulldozer were reported bent, allegedly as a result of actions designed to thwart progress ..." — or, more likely, as a result of the normal wear and tear of flattening a forest and dozing boulders and stumps the size of VW Bugs. Let me assure you — despite its brand name, a Caterpillar's no butterfly. "rusticated" — That one's so rusty I bet it didn't even make it into the Official Scrabble Dictionary. But from what I remember of my English 101 class, rustication was an old form of academic discipline meted out on naughty schoolboys of the Ivy Leagues for causing a disturbance (e.g., dallying with the daughters of important benefactors), for which they were sent up-country to cogitate on their misdeeds. I had no such pleasure earning mine. The university won't even refund my tuition for last term so that my father will stop kvetching about me "putting on that granola protester schtick to impress the chicks" on his dime. Rusticated: rhymes with fornicated, as in fucked.

The walls of the hotel room are like the walls of my jail cell and the walls of the classrooms I grew up in: thick, heavy cinder blocks an off-yellow colour that still make me wonder if the painters have pissed in the whitewash. Starving Artists' Convention paintings over the beds and the desk: conveyor belt landscapes, roller brush oceans, butter knife gulls.

When I booked in, there were already half a dozen others slated for this double room, and the numbers kept on growing. Buzzard was the last. The door swung open, banging loudly against the stopper, and he walked right in, shivering, the sleet still melting off his leather biker's jacket and pants. "Hotel's all booked up," he said. "I'm gonna have to room with you guys." He sat down on one of the two double beds as if staking a claim, removed his gloves, cupped his curled fingers to his mouth to blow the blue out of them. Daniel had told me that it was standard etiquette to let a homeless planter crash on your shag. But Buzzard didn't even ask, and I got the distinct impression that if anyone had any objections, no one was about to say so to his face.

Walter came out of the bathroom, towelling the remnants of shaving soap from the hinges of his jaw. "I'm goin' on a booze run with Jack. Anyone wanna split a two-four?"

"I'm flat broke." Buzzard said.

"Throw my laundry in with yours and I'll cover you till next day off."

"Next thing you know we'll be rubbing dubbing into the highballers' boots," Buzzard muttered. "Alright. Where's your shit?"

Walter grinned, nicotine-stained teeth as golden as his fleecy hair. "The Canada Post sack."

Everyone left for the laundromat to fight for machines, which I put off for later today or tomorrow; dreaming of an untimed hot bath. But two crews' worth of black-muck bathtub rings was more than the boiler could keep up with. So I had a cold shower, and I shaved. Then I used up every sheet of Shoreline Motor Hotel stationery drafting and redrafting a letter to Father but ran out before I could write one that I could commit to a postcard — which card I haven't decided yet, though there are several choice ones at the registration desk:

An aerial photo of the Shoreline Motor Hotel itself: whitewashed walls, maritime blue trim and balcony railings, permanently anchored one street inland from the shoreline and just down the tracks from the world's biggest grain elevators;

A caricature of a mosquito: "Ontario's Provincial Bird." An angler standing in the bow of a canoe, dwarfed by a superimposed mega-trout; head and tail curving up to the clouds from a belly about to burst through the gunwales, hook lost somewhere in its blossoming gills.

But most are of the Sleeping Giant: a sunrise over the island's 260 metre high chest; its summer colours that, from this distance, look like the patchwork of mosses and lichens that eventually overtake all boreal forest rocks but is the forest itself. Another view: an Indian in Chief's headdress painted to fit its contours, painted maiden kneeling at his feet:

> *MAJESTIC POSTCARD: A TRAVEL TIME PRODUCT*™
> *For revealing the secret of the great Silver Mine to*
> *White Man, Nana Bijou, deep water spirit, was turned*
> *to stone in a storm that forever flooded the richest silver mine*
> *ever discovered. Her legend lost, the Indian princess awaiting*
> *the great spirit's awakening remains a mystery.*

She has waited eons to rouse him from rock. She has stayed tuned to his silence — the breeze of his breath, the life that will remain rooted to his decay till the last stone rolls down, the only sounds of his sleep.

Father took a maiden to keep him awake. Lifting a glass twenty years later he still toasts her as his "child-bride" in wedding speeches — twenty years of somniloquies, the last repeating spark of the firefly (ephemerid); intervals of light and light decaying like an atom into longer stretches of dark. There is no crater open down to the lava pool; only a bricked-up chimney, only the flooded shafts of the mines I've dug in search. And since he vents when no one is looking, I don't know the time of death, only the degrees: slowing wingbeats, fading flashes, eyes cataracting, lava hitting water.

I buy this postcard and the one with the fish, not knowing which story I'll send him, and head back to my room.

He sat in stony silence throughout my first trespass hearing. Even after the sentence was handed down and we were safely out of the courthouse, he refused to say as much as a word to me. Over the long rush-hour drive back to the 'burbs, he wouldn't, or couldn't, make eye contact — not even once. He just sat there in the driver's seat of the family wagon, staring straight ahead, breaking his silence only when we'd pulled into the double garage, his refuge away from work and home. "You can thank your lucky stars that Justice acknowledged your youthful idealism and chose to be lenient with you," he said finally. "But Noah, the clock is ticking down. Soon, no one will have any patience for your antics and they'll cost you a lot more than a trespass fine, your tuition and mediocre grades put together. You're twenty now. It's high time you grew up." I was chomping at the bit to argue with him but there was no escaping the fact that, for as long as I could remember, growing up had meant growing farther and farther away from the things that rooted me to the earth, the grass between my toes. As much as I'd still like to, there's no sense in going head-to-head with him now; the chickens he'd warned me of have come home to roost — on his dime.

I step out onto the balcony to get some air, wondering if I'll ever be able to take the long train ride home or face Father's silence: a sentence worse than jail. Cass is standing in the parking lot, taking the brunt of the wind-whipped sleet, staring out over the Bay, the waves crashing over the breakwater and, miles farther off, against the feet of the cloud-shrouded Sleeping Giant. The steel steps of the fire escape are slick with ice. I slip and slide between our crummies and the prospectors' and arc-welders' trucks; sneaker-skating across a frozen puddle to her side.

"Nice island," I say. "Biggest one I've ever seen."

"Peninsula," she says. "But the weather makes it easier to pretend."

"Listen, there's seven of us going in on a room —"

"Got my own."

"Hey, Noah," Steve calls from the balcony. "We booked the conference sauna at Kangas for four. You coming?"

"I'm in. Cass?"

"Thanks," she says, eyes still held by the Giant. "But I really need to get away from the crowd for a bit."

I turn into the crosswind, pushing against the question that is threatening to ask itself, but before I'm halfway back to the fire escape, I know that it can no longer be contained. I return, this time stepping between Cass and her island.

"I forgot to ask ... how's your back healing?"

She cocks her head, pinning me with that same warning eye she'd used when she had to sit on my lap the day we found her on the road. "What are you talking about?"

"The wound on your back. I saw it the other day in the shower."

"You like staring at naked women?"

"I wasn't staring. It just caught my eye."

"Look, I feel clumsy enough about the way I came into this camp. The last thing I need is for everyone to know about another one of my accidents."

"Horseshit. You just don't want anyone to figure out that it wasn't an accident — that some pranking asshole in your last camp slapped honey all over your tent and you were attacked by a bear in your sleep."

She stands there trembling, her fists clenched at her sides as if to rein herself in. Then she breaks free, strides across the white line demarcating our parking spaces and swings.

Blinded, I stagger back and slip on the ice, feet flying out from under me, shoulder blades banging against the hollow metal of a truck door.

"There." She hunches over me where I lie, stunned as a clubbed fish, my head propped up against a tire. "In a few hours' time, you can have fun explaining that shiner, and you won't even have to worry about how you'll hide it in the fucking sauna — or in your motel room, for that matter."

In the split second before she runs for the shore, I think I can see her eyes soften. But perhaps I'm pretending a peninsula.

Once I've recovered my senses, I stomp back up the fire escape, enter my room, shoulder my hockey bag full of laundry and head back out before the screen door's even had a chance to blow shut. I scoop a fistful of ice pellets from the bottom step to press against my swelling left eye, and following the motel clerk's directions, head north along Cumberland, fighting the buffeting wind every step of the way.

Two or three blocks later, I enter the tropical warmth of a laundromat, the hot, moist air frosting thickly on the storefront window, muting the name painted there: the Cumber d ash 'N y. I cover my cumbered, ashen eye, squint my good one as if attempting to read an eye chart that's both blurred and inverted. As big as it is, there isn't a free machine anywhere in the Cumberland Wash 'N Dry — nearly all of them being used by planters, only a handful from our camp.

"Noah," Kirsten calls, waving me over to where she and Daniel are sitting along the back end of the island of washers. "Our clothes are in the final rinse cycle, if you're willing to stick around a minute. Hey, what happened to your eye?"

"Blackflies."

"Been there more times than I'd care to count," she says, not giving it a second thought.

I drop my laundry to the floor and unzip my jacket. "Is it always this busy here?"

"Never like this. But the weather update on the television said eighteen to twenty centimetres has fallen right across the north, from Dryden to North Bay."

"Geraldton's under twenty-six and the Kap's been hit with thirty-one," Daniel adds. "Flying Dutchmen's got camps both places, and I'd bet my advance that if they didn't move out of the bush last night, they won't be getting out today."

The washers hum into their final spin cycles. Kirsten and Daniel transfer their laundry into the shopping carts provided; I cram all my earthy belongings, work wear and civies alike, into a single double-loader to stretch my paltry advance. Behind me, Jack is cramming his wet clothes into some contraption that looks like a giant centrifuge. He spreads a towel overtop, slams down the lid, pops in a quarter, but can't get the machine to start.

"Damn piece of crap!" He pounds on the lid and hoofs it in the side. "All it extracts is quarters from my pocket!"

The proprietor, a sixtyish man with silver hair combed to one side and thick black-framed glasses, steps out from behind the dry cleaning counter. "Now what's wrong?"

"Your extractor. It ate my last three quarters. The least you could do is put up a sign if it's broke."

"It's not, but it will be the way you're treating it." The proprietor opens the lid, gently shuts it, and holds it down for several seconds after inserting another quarter. The floor begins to rumble as if the earth is crumbling away beneath it. "There," he says, refunding Jack's eaten change.

Jack bows his head. "I'm sorry," he says. "I just got word that the landlady who owns the spread I rent back in the Okanagan died last week and has willed it to the Communist Party of Canada, so I guess I'm a bit uptight right now."

"You're forgiven. Just do me a favour: Next time something's broke, just ask."

The extractor picks up speed, rattling a washboard-framed charcoal sketch of a woman's cloth-scrubbing hands from its hook to the floor. Jack stoops to pick it up but the old man stops him.

"Now that it's come down it may as well stay there for the day," he says. "That's why I bolted the washers to railway tracks. See?" he says, pointing to the steel rails running under all the machines. "Otherwise they'd be jumping around too." He starts back for his dry cleaning counter, then turns once more to Jack. "I know it's hard not to but don't assume the worst. Who knows? Maybe the new owners will let you stay on your piece or offer to sell it to you at a fair price. If not, maybe it's time to move on."

Jack nods, still sulking, probably wishing he'd never come to town, that the storm had somehow swung a wide arc around camp, that the bad news it brought him had come to him with a few more day's grace and not been borne on a biting wind. It would've come to him eventually anyway, as mine would've, I suppose; news travels fast, bad news by express mail or courier. But it would've come to each of us on his turf, without the added humiliation of an extractor eating his quarters or a girl blackening my eye or any of the collateral damage storms bring with chance encounters.

I blink. It's only now I've noticed that I've been seeing solely out of my right eye, my left eye is completely swollen shut. Kirsten and Daniel are folding the last of their laundry and packing it into their extra-large duffel bag.

"We're swinging by the liquor store to pick up some wine," Daniel says.

"Here's ten for a litre of any minimally acceptable dry red. I'll keep an eye on your stuff." I wink. "But only one."

Kirsten smiles. "We'll be taking a cab to the Shoreline after that to drop off our clothes, then over to the sauna if you wanna come along for the ride."

"Thanks, but I don't know if I'm up to it right now."

"You should come, Noah," Daniel says. "Walter goes religiously. For five bucks per head plus a loonie towel charge we'll get ninety minutes, but business is usually so slow on weekdays by this time of the year that the staff let us stay the whole afternoon. They even provide ice for your wine or beer."

"You'll come out feeling like a new man. And the desserts at the coffee bar ..."

"Tell you what," I say. "I'll go if Jack goes. What do you say, Jack? You in?"

Jack pulls his head from his drier and drops a pile of work socks and gotch on the counter. "I dunno," he says, sucking on his Lanny MacDonald moustache. "I really should be trying to get a hold of my new landlords. Besides, as old as they are to yours, my bones don't need the steaming they did back when I was a planter."

"Nonsense," Kirsten says. "We want to make sure you keep delivering all those trees on time."

"Alright." He sighs. "Here's thirty for a twenty-sixer of rye — any minimally palatable bottle. You can use the change to top up Noah's grape juice to a magnum. By the looks of it he's had a rough day."

The mural in the reception area at Kangas Sauna quickly melts all thoughts of the driving sleet outside. Men and women of various ages are crowded naked in two rows along benches. In the foreground, a middle-aged man is dipping a birch *vihta* in a pail of water, wiping the sweat from his upper lip, wrinkling his nose and clenching up his eyes as he breathes in the hot air. Seated along the same bench, a young woman with a *vihta* of her own is trailing its wet leaves across her back, eyelids fallen closed, corners of her lips curved up more subtly than the Mona Lisa's. Holding a large wooden ladle, another man scoops water over the lava rock. Steam rises almost unseeable around the figures, who are so slouched in relaxation that the breeze of an opening door would knock them over.

Kirsten taps the bell again. An elderly woman, hair permed in large flat curls, descends the stairs, carrying a stack of clean white towels, and steps in behind the register.

"Some planters from our company booked the conference sauna for the afternoon," Kirsten says.

"Flying Dutchmen?"

Kirsten nods.

"The conference sauna was already reserved by a group of loggers. So I've split your crew up over a number of smaller suites."

"We're looking for Aleron, Mitra, Moira and Steve," Daniel says.

"Ah yes," she says, checking her ledger. "They're in Number Eight."

We each pay our six dollars.

"Up the stairs to your left and right down the catwalk," she says, handing us two towels each.

The door to Number Eight is half-open. Mitra is lying nude on a cot, looking radiant in the grey light that falls from the skylight directly above — the watery shadows of ice melting on the pane beads over the contours of her skin. Seeing her like that, I'm suddenly relieved that our crew didn't get the conference sauna, where I'd be naked before everyone all at once and they'd be exposed to me. Mass skinny-dipping I can handle, no problem, especially in cold water. But no room could be big enough for thirty-odd asses, crammed onto a couple of cedar benches, steaming cheek-to-sweaty-cheek, mine squeezed in there somewhere in the middle — especially not with these skimpy towels.

Mitra turns her head. "You finally made it," she says. "There's some cold beer in that bucket by the coffee table and a bottle opener attached to the door. Feel free to grab yourselves a drink. Jesus, Noah. You get into a scrap or something?"

"Fly bites."

"Just like Cass a few weeks back when you two first joined the camp. Funny though. I could've sworn they've been easing up a lot with the drier weather."

"I thought so too. That's why I was caught completely offguard when I ran into a bad patch at the back of my piece day before yesterday. No bug dope, no head net. *Nada*."

"I guess they're still thick in spots in the wetter ground. But Lyndon says this freeze ought to kill the rest of them off."

Jack cracks open a bottle of Black Label; Daniel and Kirsten begin stripping down.

"Is there a washroom?" I ask.

"Opposite the showers."

I step through the sliding door in the glass partition and shut myself into the small pine bathroom, hoping that, by the time I've undressed, my hard-on will be gone so my shower won't have to be a cold one. One look at my grizzly face and swollen plum of an eye seems to take care of any worries in that department. Above the shoulders, I look like absolute hell. But looking down, I see I'm leaner than before, like I've lost some of my remaining boy fat, and for the first time in my life, I've actually got shoulders to speak of and a slight six pack.

I hang my clothes neatly over the towel rack and step out for a quick shower.

Even if there'd never been a sauna or Jacuzzi here, the six bucks would've been worth an untimed shower with unlimited hot water and enough pressure to blast the dirt from under my nails. I rub the fog from the glass partition and squint into the dimly lit sauna room. Empty! I shut the tap, grab a towel and go in. It's still hot from its latest use, but bearable enough for me to take a seat right by the heater. I slop a ladle of water over the rocks, sit back into the corner and carefully arrange the towel over my loins. My lips and scalp and nipples tingle as the steam billows up to the top bench and, rebounding from walls and ceiling, fills me with sweet cedar scent. The needle on the thermometer climbs steadily in the onslaught, the sweat streams from my forehead, stinging my eyes. I feel myself slowly regaining sensation and sensitivity in joints and limbs I didn't even notice had fallen asleep — my wrists, my knees, my funny bones, my fingertips jarred and jammed and frozen into numbness while planting and now awoken by this heat. Thinking of Cass, I wish the same could be done for hearts.

Jack pads into the sauna and throws two more scoopfuls of water — one undulating arc after the other — over the lava. Two bursts of steam billow up, the rocks hissing and squealing in the shock of shrinkage. Draping his towel around his neck, he sits back against the wall adjacent to mine.

"A hundred and eighty degrees," he says, squinting. "God it's really cooking in here. Maybe not too good for your eye. A shiner like that calls for ice. How'd you say you got it?"

"Blackflies."

"Flies? Now, ya see, I think that's just a cock 'n bullshit story. I delivered trees to the back of your piece from start to finish the day before yesterday, I didn't get one bite and I wasn't wearing the slightest trace of fly dope."

"Anyone could keep ahead of the flies on an ATV."

"Not when he's stopping to unload. Nope. There were no flies, Noah, and even if there was, I've never seen a fly big enough to pack a punch that could turn a fella's eye all black 'n blue like that — swollen shut, sure, but not mottling colours. So stop shittin' me, okay? If you're in some kinda trouble, here in town or back in the bush, you need to learn to trust somebody in this camp. I'm here to let you know you can trust me like you'd trust your own uncle."

"You're right. It wasn't the flies," I sigh, scrambling to come up with a more plausible cause that will also explain my evasiveness but won't subject me to the ridicule of the truth. "Oh, this is so hard."

"Go ahead."

"It was really stupid of me, but when I was planting my last few trees yesterday, I struck a really springy root with my shovel and the staff bounced up and caught me right in the eye. I could even feel my eyeball being pushed right back in its socket, and I swear that if I didn't have such a thick brow bone, it would've popped right out. It hurt like hell and was tender to the touch but didn't start bruising up like this till today."

"That's it?"

I nod. "Listen, I know it's not that big a deal but I really don't want it getting around the camp that I could be such a bonehead."

Uncle Jack shuffles closer to my corner and grasps my shoulder. "Don't worry about it, Noah. I won't tell a soul. But do youself a favour."

"What's that?"

"Cut down the staff on your shovel and fit it with a D-handle. Five or six bucks is a small price to pay for keeping your eyes and you'll probably plant twice as many trees."

"Aleron uses a staff, and so does Landells."

"Aleron's a bit of an anomaly, I think, and Landells — well, he's just a big freak."

I grip Jack's other hand in mine and shake it vigourously. "Thanks, Jack. You're a real friend. Well," I say standing. "I've had about as much steam as I can take. I think I'll go for a dip in the whirlpool."

"Bottom floor," he says, a tinge of disappointment in his voice. "Nearly the whole gang's there, or was, from what I heard."

I bolt through the door, partly to keep too much heat from escaping, partly to keep it from following me, and bypass the showers. Touching the handle of the sliding glass door, I see Moira standing over Mitra, gently rubbing her hips right about where mine have been sore from the weight of my planting bags. I've heard Moira say that she's been studying massage, and watching the way she works her fingertips around the joints between Mitra's thighs and hip bone, divining knots and strains and tension, she seems to know her stuff. Daniel is stretched out face down on a cot next to theirs, Kirsten kneading his shoulders. There is love in all their eyes. Like a bird-watcher stumbling across a mating pair of bald eagles, I don't want to disturb them or be the ground that forces them to part.

Jack exits the sauna and steps under one of the showers. "Whirlpool too hot for you?"

"Dunno. I haven't gone." I take the shower next to him to wash off the dirt I've sweated from my pores. "I've been thinking more about what you said to me, Jack. To be honest, I didn't get this eye from the end of my shovel staff."

"Well, to be honest, after giving what you told me some thought, I didn't think so."

"A girl in the camp nailed me in the eye and I didn't want anyone finding out about it, as much for her sake as for mine."

"Now, that's a more believable story, except that last bit sounds a little too altruistic to be true. So, who is she and what did you do to piss her off?"

"I accidentally found out something about her that she didn't want anyone to know and questioned her about it."

"You mean Cass?"

"Jack, you know I can't say."

"It was Cass. In my fourteen years in the camps I don't think I've ever met anyone who keeps to herself as much as she does. Besides, any fool can see how doe-eyed you get around her. Why else would you confront her with some juicy secret she didn't want revealed to anyone if you weren't hoping to draw her out of her shell?"

"That wasn't the only reason. It was also because I think she's been in some serious trouble."

"Gotcha!" Jack says, smiling so broadly that the corners of his mouth disappear under the twisted ends of his moustache.

"Alright, you got me." I sigh. "I wish I knew what to do."

Jack turns off his shower and begins to towel off. "I don't know if I can be much help. Women aren't exactly my department. But maybe you could start by telling her you're sorry for stepping on her toes and assuring her that none of what you found out will get 'round camp. Beyond that, you'll probably have to play it by ear."

Picking up his shampoo and soap, he heads for the massage lounge.

"Jack?"

"Yes?" he says, turning.

"About your problems back home."

He hangs his head rather sheepishly. "I don't suppose anyone could've missed my rantings and ravings, though it took a fucking extractor to extract them from me."

"Your new landlords are communists, Jack, not land barons or capitalists. They're not your run-of-the-mill Soviet-era communist, Stalinist or Maoist; they're the Communist Party *of Canada*. Your landlady willed them her property. They shouldn't need any reminding, but don't be afraid to tell them like it is if they do."

CHAPTER TWELVE

WE PULL INTO camp at dusk. The snow is gone except for crusty patches that have survived the sun in the shelter of the trees. Numb and hungover, I shoulder my duffel bag and crunch through the forest moss, finding with my feet the overgrown path that leads to my waterfront campsite: Buzzard's "bombproof" mountain tent, Mitra's Prospector, Lyndon's lean-to — each fragile in its own way in spite of its name or design, none a match against a falling tree and certainly not a bear. I reach the bluff, blink both good eye and blackened eye repeatedly but to no avail: my tent is gone. My planting bags are still hanging upside down on the staff of my shovel, the groundsheet's still spread where the tent had sat, the ropes that once held its tarp taut still tied to trees. But the tent's gone.

I replay that moment after Cass decked me, her eyes glowing red as the eyes of a nocturnal animal caught in headlights. Dazed, highway-hypnotized — which was more drawn to the other? She warded me off when I made the mistake of crossing into her space, but she should've known that taking my tent would be utter provocation.

The moon, full and haloed in the sky and the water, follows me as I storm across the moose path that runs along the bluffs and overhangs of the shore. "Cass? Cass!" in search of her dome.

"Cass."

A muffled yawn rises from the dark on my right, then the sounds of a match being struck repeatedly. Her dome appears, flickering neon pink. "What is it?"

"The question is, where is it?"

"Where is what?"

I switch on my maglite. "Don't play these goddamn games ..."

She unzips her doorflap and pokes her head out, squinting. "Oh, it's you. Would you mind getting that flashlight out of my face? It's rude."

I turn the beam to the ground: her face, underlit, is transformed: green eyes unveiled from the bone of her brow, picking up the yellows and browns in the freshly thawed moss, cheeks glinting smooth.

"You're looking for your tent."

"I wonder how you ever guessed."

"Look, I know what you're thinking. I'm sorry about Friday in the parking lot. I wasn't myself."

"Cut the shit, alright? Just tell me what the fuck you did with it."

"Hey, it wasn't me, okay? It was an act of God."

I focus the maglite beam to its sharpest setting, cast it in her eyes: inquisition of the sun.

"This is the last time I'm asking. Where is it?"

She points up through the spiky silhouette of the tree tops, lips quivering as she tries to force the upturning corners of her mouth back down. "The sky took it."

"You're lying."

"Ask Clem and Landells if you don't believe me. There was a windstorm Saturday and your tent got sucked into the stratosphere."

"And if I click my heels together three times I'll wake up cozy in my bag, thinking the whole weekend was just a bad dream."

For the first time since her arrival, she cracks a smile. "But it did! It blew way up over the trees. Clem and I drove after it in the Conan, thinking it would come down in one of the cutaways but —"

Laughter begins to leak through the spaces between her words. "But by the time we reached the main road, it was just a tiny dot in the clouds."

"You're laughing, you liar."

Finally the spasm seizes her fully. "Join the ranks of the homeless," she laughs. "A conservative god is in power!"

I diffuse the beam: she's telling the truth. "Well, I guess all I can hope now is that some goonhead air commander will embarrass himself internationally when he scrambles his finest squadron to intercept it as it's making an unauthorized landing on the White House lawn."

"I guess it wasn't insured."

"Even if it could've been, I don't believe in insurance. Half your premium goes to reinsurance."

"Reinsurance?"

"The companies that insure the insurers."

"Where does it end?"

"Where it all begins," I say, pointing my maglite into outer space. "God."

"Welcome to the Act of God club! Only, my tent wasn't ..."

"I know."

"No. You don't. There was only one other woman in my last camp, and some of the boys thought it would be fun to put a little wager on our asses, on who in their pack was going to bag one first, and which of us would be bagged first — over a hand of poker no less."

"So you gave 'em shit."

She nods. "That's probably when they put their pointy little heads together and came up with the bright idea of honeying my tent. There were baits for the spring hunt all around our camp, and the super's mutt had treed a bear twice the previous shift, so those assholes knew it was no joke. Worst part is they had an all-night piss-up in a crummy, waiting for the bear to show, and when it did, they just hooted and cheered it on. So I woke up with a bear on my back. Its claw sort of broke through the top of the fly, then it collapsed with all its weight right down on top of me. It must've thought the tent was solid when it reached for the honey."

"They waited that long before they decided it was time to chase it off?"

"Are you kidding? I chased it off. I reached for my shovel and backhanded it in the ribs. Poor thing fled into the treeline, moaning, those fuckers still laughing like hyenas."

"Jesus, Cass. If that bear had killed you, they'd be up on murder charges. You should've reported them to the police."

"A fuck of a lot of good that would've done when I was stranded with them in the middle of nowhere with no way of calling for outside help. My safety was in no one's hands but my own. As fast as I could, I crammed all my earthly belongings into my duffel and pack and tossed them into the back of my super's pick-up. Some of the fellas started jeering and hassling me then. "Where the fuck you think you're going in Chad's truck, bitch?" "Hey, maybe you prefer screwing the wildlife. The bear's a bull but maybe you'd like a sow better." Something in me snapped so loudly all I could hear was my pulse pounding in my ears. There was no way in hell I was going to leave them to follow me. So I went over to them, shovel in hand, and bashed in the windshield in their crummy, and when the cowards wound up their windows, I bashed those in too. There was so much flying glass I may have even blinded someone — I don't know because I tore the fuck outta there so fast that I didn't even take the time to turn on the highbeams and ended up ditching the truck in a beaver pond when I swerved to avoid a bull moose. I hated them for making me do that. I hate them for making me turn into an animal to defend my right to humanity."

Our eyes connect, only in the light of the moon now. I take her trembling hand, unable to fathom how she's managed to bear the burden of her secret for this long. Maybe it wasn't as simple as not knowing who to trust anymore; maybe she knew that her story would leave her as spent from telling as it had from living it.

"You don't need to sleep with your shovel here. There are more women — there's Therese, and she'd never put up with such absolute schmucks."

"Would you?"

I blink my blackened eye. "No sooner than I'd step between a sow and her cubs, or a woman and her island."

"Peninsula." Cass smiles. "It's getting late. Where will you sleep?"

"I dunno. Borrow one of Bob's spares, I guess."

"I think this was the last tent he had."

"Then maybe I'll curl up in a crummy for the night. It's a good thing I decided to wash my sleeping bag this week, or it might be in Oz now too."

"Too bad you gotta soil it up so soon. There isn't a clean square inch in any of those beaters."

"They're full of dirt, but it's a clean dirt, you know?"

Cass nods, then zips herself back in.

I turn for the moose path along the shore, the moons of the paraselene so perfectly kaleidoscoped in the air's icy lenses that for a moment, I almost forgot there's really only one of them. Gazing at the real moon, at the centre of that cross, I wonder if the moose that forced Cass off the road that night was one and the same as the bull that crossed the road and froze in front of the one-ton the very next day, when Bob was driving me up to camp. If it hadn't been for the eight to ten minutes it took Bob to clean and dress the cut to my head, thrown into the windshield going from sixty to zero on a dime, she might not have reached the road before we'd passed, and our paths would never have crossed. Fate at the flanks of a moose and ultimately, the fangs of blackflies.

Cass unzips her tent again. "Noah? There's room here, but just for tonight. Our bags stay separately sealed, and you'd better not blab about it, unless you want to look like a raccoon."

"I didn't tell anyone about the bear, did I?"

"Shhhh."

I return to my campsite. From my duffel bag, I pull out my sleeping bag and a change of clothes for the morning, then wrap the remaining laundry in the groundsheet and jam it under a log.

Cass has lit a candle to warm up her tent. "Five degrees in ten minutes," she says. "Maybe five in five with you here."

We stay up chatting, separately sealed in our bags, till the candle dies.

I awaken in the dark of midnight, our coccoons opened past our knees, our legs knitted together like the roots of trees, her cheek pressed into my shoulder, the seals broken in our sleep.

CHAPTER THIRTEEN

WE JUST FINISHED the last hour of the fourth day of an eight-day shift Bob's scheduled to make up for the three days lost to the snow and hopefully, to finish this contract. It's only my fourth week (if I count eight days as a week) and I don't know what day it is. I don't know the date, rarely know the time other than by the sun and the wake-up, quitting and supper horns (I stopped winding my watch some days ago and no longer need my travel alarm, which has only worked on and off since that morning I was swallowed by the bog). I haven't seen my reflection since the last day off, so I try to imagine my beard through my fingers, and avoid looking into the lake during the nightly jam down by the boat launch. (Last night, I was almost caught, but in the instant before our eyes locked, a fish leapt — shattering him, saving me. I turned my eyes to Cass's island before the ripples smoothed themselves out).

Aside from a strong craving for ice cream, to be cooled inside out after eleven hot days in the trenches, I haven't felt any need or desire to return to city or town. I could spend every day off right here with Cass, hiking overgrown roads, bushwacking up the chimneys of old mesas, canoeing off the map in search of a spot where in the light that stretches from sun to earth we might connect. Her offer to shelter me *just for tonight* was extended indefinitely because it's warmer that way, but the night after our unconscious embrace she draped a mosquito net between our bags.

"I don't mean to discourage you," she said. "But guys always want to skip the song and dance. You should watch the spider that spun that web on my laundry line. You might learn a thing or two."

"Like what?"

"She ate four suitors who'd come to tap a dance on her loom before the one who knew what strings to pluck came courting. He had to tie four of her legs to buy time for his getaway after the act. He should have tied all eight. But he probably died happy."

"Well that's encouraging."

"He knew the stakes. If I like your dance — who knows? Maybe I'll cut this net down."

I tapped my fingers against the bug net, spidering morse code for S-O-S as I inched my hand up toward her face, but she rolled up the magazine she was reading and swatted it off.

Ever since, I've been dreaming up dances that might get her to drop her guard. But the afternoon has cast a long shadow across these dreams.

I was spot-planting up a rock cap, divining dirt with each jab of my shovel, when a high-pitched whistling no louder than a whisper but unlike any wind or bird or breeze I've ever heard broke my trance. Innuk started barking. I turned around, scanned the treeline. Daniel, Steve and Mitra stood at the base of the outcrop, necks craned, heads bent back, shielding their eyes against the midday sun. Looking up, I spun around, but a deafening crack — the volume of a dozen thunderheads exploding all at once — ripped across the sky before I spotted them: a squadron of CF-18 fighter jets peeling past the sound barrier — already over the opposite treeline.

Aleron, planting along the ribbon separating his crew's piece from ours, dropped his bags and hit the dirt, covering his head with both hands. I threw off my own gear and ran down the hill to the bush he'd thrown himself under.

"Aleron?"

He wouldn't budge. He just lay there, curled up like an armadillo, face tucked into his knees. Arms curved over the top and back of his head, trembling beneath a fluttering length of blue flagging tape, breathing in short gasps and bursts.

"It's okay. They're gone now. They're probably just training."

He slowly uncurled himself and got up. He brushed himself off. His eyes remained frozen and distant, like the eyes of that moose Bob nearly hit the day I arrived, as if in anticipation of the impact he had swallowed his soul into the deepest pit of his stomach or spat it into space. Then, with a shake of his head, he snapped back.

"That's what we said back in Salvador — just practising. Then one day ..." He belted his planting bags back around his waist. "Yuh. They all just practise, but not for just nothing." Then he picked up his shovel and started planting back toward his cache.

I've never craved a newspaper as much as I have today. But even though I know Bob would let me listen to his shortwave if I asked, I won't. I won't even stop in town on the way to the next contract, if I can help it. Or maybe I'll stop only at the Cumberland Wash 'N Dry, avoid the tube if it's on if I can, if I can't switch it off.

Week 4, Day 7 — I've been watching Aleron closely these past few nights, kneeling alone by the boat launch, waiting for the timber wolf pups to set the whole pack off with their yapping. A wolf pup's cry sounds more human than canine — like a child's. A chorus of wolves and their whelps yelping, and Innuk will prick up his ears, stick his snout in the air and answer, more and more wolf in his straining voice than even his husky heritage can account for. That's when

Aleron rises from his meditative crouch and creeps up the hill toward the big top. That's when I follow, trying not to be heard, trying to figure out where his drive comes from, that locomotion which keeps him pumping three thousand trees into the ground each day.

After three nights of following him, one thing seems fairly evident: he's on a binge. All he'll eat for breakfast is a cold bowl of flakes. He'll pack only one apple and two oranges — and maybe a grapefruit — for his lunch. At dinner, he'll hardly eat a bite, or say a word unless spoken to, pass on dessert, and go back to his tent as soon as he's cleaned his dishes. But when he's sure everyone's gone to bed, he'll raid the food cache. As soon as he reaches the big top, he'll turn, click on his flashlight, and follow the flagged trail off into the thick forest. Then he'll start running, light-footed as if he'd been born here; sure of every rise and dip as the moss carpet rolls over fat red-rot stumps and old blow-down to the foot of the cache.

He doesn't even take any food back to his seat by the oil drum; he just unties the tarp, draws the machete he'd once used to keep the jungle from overtaking his family's farm, and slits open the taped boxes from the food wholesaler — not even stopping to read what's in each. Then he gorges himself. Strawberries, peaches, turnips, Spanish onions, carrots, other vegetables I wouldn't even dream of eating raw — it seems he has to sample every thing, each thing as it is in its raw state, in shaking hands, as if the world will end tomorrow, as if this is his last meal. And the cook thinks we have a bear.

CHAPTER FOURTEEN

I'VE BEEN WAITING up for the last traces of light to bleed from the sky. Aleron's also waiting — only he's down by the boat launch, waiting out the time he'd usually be spending raiding the food cache, and I'm up the hill, on my perch overlooking the lake, half waiting for him to come up, half waiting out the eternity Cass will make me wait before inviting me to slide into the heart of her hips. Not even a kiss blown through the mosquito net. So I've been leaving her tent almost as soon as she's fallen asleep, and waiting for the evening to cool to absolute silence, right down to the last spring peeper.

I stride down the hill.

The night is dark and glinty as a carboniferous pool of tar, and shot through with the cold fire of the Milky Way; its light reaching out to us from a time long before we were around to take it down from the sky. There Aleron's crouching, at the water's edge, grasping for beginnings in the lake's lazy lap. The stars are the problem. They can burn away so much. Everything after that moves sluggish and tired in comparison.

I tap him on the shoulder.

He glances up and nods as if he's been expecting me. "Let's go for a row."

"A paddle," I say, thinking he means Bob's canoe.

He points to a muted shape protruding from the shoreline brush — the stern of an old rowboat.

"I haven't seen that here before. You sure it floats?"

"Last Friday, when you were in town, an old prospector landed here. No gold, he said, but he had caught many gold eye."

"I don't feel right about taking it out without asking."

"He would have chained it to a tree if he did not want us using it. Come on," he says. "This is our last night here. Who knows? Our next camp could be a gravel pit with a dry creek for water. "

We take the old boat by the gunnels and feed it hand over hand into the lake.

Aleron holds the worn bow. "Get in. I will row."

The planks and ribs creak of dry rot beneath my crouched, unbalanced step. I sit against the flat of the stern and Aleron pushes off, taking up the oars to swing clear of the rocky shore. He steers us toward Cass's island and quietly rows us out. He doesn't say a word, and everything around us seems to respect his silence — even the lake.

Halfway out to the island, beyond earshot of shore, he lifts the oars and lights a cigarette.

"Didn't know you smoked."

He coughs and takes another haul. "Usually not. But I am not feeling my usual self lately."

"I noticed."

"The day those jets flew over the block —"

"They're still flying, aren't they?"

"In my mind, they have never stopped, but I did not expect to see them all the way up here."

"They were Canadian Air Force — probably half their entire fleet. Odds are they were on a training exercise or redeployed from Petawawa to Cold Lake, Alberta."

But Aleron looks unconvinced. I suppose he's thinking that, even when jet fighters armed with sidewinders (or whatever slithery name the offence contractors have trademarked to naturalize their missiles) aren't making their purpose obvious, they are on standby to do so at a moment's notice.

Out of the black, a dark shape skims over the water, flits up over the gunnel and lands on the bottom of the boat. Aleron bends down, butts out his smoke and gently cups his hands around it.

I lean forward and reach into my jacket pocket. "Let's see what you've got."

"No light," Aleron says. He opens his palms: slowly, the huddled black shape stirs, stretching its leathery wings and hissing itself into a flap over the squirming object held fast in its spiky little teeth.

"Jesus!" I jump to my feet, nearly capsizing us. But instead of fluttering up into my face, the bat folds up its wings and settles into the calloused flesh of Aleron's palm, contentedly munching on the half-hatched dragonfly nymph it's fished from the water.

Aleron sure has a way with animals. I have seen stray killdeer chicks hop right into that same open hand and stay there long enough for him to return them to their nests, and the rabbits, fox and grouse, that have fled at the sound of my shovel, turn and follow at his heels. Now he sits before me, stroking the ears of a wild bat.

I take my seat again. "You must smell of trust."

"No. An animal can tell your intentions by how hard you hold onto it." He rolls the bat onto its back and gently unfolds one of its wings. "The bones are much like the finger bones in our hands. See?"

I nod.

"We tore the skins that once stretched between our fingers soon after we moved onto the land. We only remember that all life started in the same sea when we try to master it, then forget it like a dream after waking. And still we credit our hands for our mastery."

The boat bumps up against the rocks of Cass's island; chattering and clicking its clicks of echo-location, the bat takes wing, flapping off into the dark veils of shoreline spruce. Aleron takes up the oars again and rows us back toward the centre of the lake.

"We had many bats back in El Salvador," he muses. "Only they were much bigger, and fed on the blood of our cattle."

"Vampire bats?"

He nods. "I still feel sorry for them."

"Sorry?" I shudder. "If any flying bloodsucking rodent ever comes after me or mine, I swear to God it'll be making an appointment with the heel of my boot."

"That is why the animals will not come to you, Noah. You refuse to take the time to see the world through their eyes. In El Salvador, the bats have had a sad history, like ours — like mine, really."

On his family's farm in Chalatenango province, it was not uncommon to see blood trickling down the necks of the cows when he went out to milk them in the morning. Because their pastures were on the edge of a jungle, it was as natural for the bats to feed on the blood of their herds as it was for his family to live off their cow's milk and the corn and the beans they grew.

The civil war changed everything. The government suspected that some of the farmers were supplying the rebels with food. They sent the air force to drop gasoline rockets on jungles and crops. They sent the army to set fire to houses and fields. Some fled to nearby caves. Others hid among the rows of corn.

(Aleron stops. A stiff breeze has blown up and pushed us within a stone's throw of the rock-strewn shallows; he takes up the oars, and rows us back to the middle of the lake.)

Armies are meant to defend their people. The army that entered Chalatenango shot anyone who coughed or ran from the smoke of their fires, and took others away. As they were leaving, they dumped the bodies of those they had tortured into the wells, and shot all the cows. Since then, the bats have had nothing to drink. So now when they come in the night, they must drink from the children. They lick the neck first, secreting a venom onto their tongues that numbs the skin, and makes the blood run faster. The children have been sick because they lack milk, so many bleed to death. Now the bats go hungry and are hated.

Aleron casts his gaze over the broad sweep of the lake and falls silent. For some minutes, we drift, turning counter-clockwise, closer and closer to shore. My father should be in this boat, face-to-face with the implacable enemy that the pinstripers and Pentagoners have conjured up from the sons and daughters of farmers: their nightmare of a red dawn. But perhaps being up here has made me forget just how hard time has frozen him — a pointed finger punctuating a stock lecture on how Hitler had caught us with our pants down.

We slip within a stroke of the boat launch; Aleron takes up the oars again, and begins to row us out.

"Maybe we should head in," I say. "Finish this around a campfire."

But he continues to row us out from the beach, as far from any land as this lake will allow, as if there's something hidden in the shoreline brush, listening, waiting for him to make the mistake of talking. He drops the oars — this time without lifting them again — and looks me straight in the eye. "I lost my father and brother in those fields. If I had a gun, I would have killed every one of those widowing bastards. But I had nothing but my life, so I ran." His voice cracks with shame. "I have been away three years now and I'm still running, trying to save the money to bring my mother and my woman over."

I want to say something that doesn't sound like a drugstore condolence card, but can't even say "Words escape me."

The keel of the boat grinds up against a sandy beach — the western shore of Cass's island. Aleron stands, stretches, and takes to the land.

"Where you heading, Aleron?"

"To piss, to shit. Maybe to vomit." He smiles sardonically, then turns for the trees.

"Wait—" I stumble out onto the beach. "What if everyone in the camp pitched in half a day's planting? Would that bring 'em home any faster?"

"I was not asking for your charity, wanker," he replies from somewhere in the woods. "Only for your ear. Besides, this is a delicate matter. If I wanted everyone and their mothers to know, I would have spilled my guts at the mess table."

Turning on my maglite, I hike up the beach, following the sounds of his bushcrash. Seedling afterimage: ghost Jack pine planted six by six in the sand. I close my eyes and rattle my head, but can't shake them from my sight.

"Noah!" Aleron's voice filters up through the treetops. "Over here!"

My feet find a narrow path, strewn with moose droppings, and cut through the heart of the island toward its northern shore.

Standing small in the forest, he's looking up through a break in the crowns — a phosphorescent green curtain rising and falling, undulating across the sky in oceanic swells. I turn off my light.

"Ghosts," Aleron says.

I smile, invigorated and giddy from the faint background crackle and hiss of electromagnetic emissions. "Aurora borealis."

"What?"

"Aurora borealis — the northern lights. Never seen them before?"

He shakes his head.

"Some people used to think it was sunlight reflecting off the ice at the North Pole. That was before anyone knew that light is made up of particles that travel in waves. The particles ..." I pause, trying to recall all the details I had to memorize for the astronomy mid-term I wrote just before I was forced to drop out. "The particles are charged like tiny magnets, like iron filings — you know, those piles of iron shavings our elementary school teachers gave us to play with? We'd pour them out onto a cardboard sheet and hold a magnet underneath and they'd arrange themselves into a pattern, revealing the magnetic field ..."

"Ah, yes," he nods.

"When there's a solar flare, a large amount of these light particles are thrown out into space in the form of magnetic radiation. They blow to Earth as the solar wind, and are drawn to the magnetic fields around the North and South Poles —"

"Like a compass?"

"Like a compass," I nod, amazed that I haven't lost him, and even more that I haven't lost myself. "When these bits of invisible light strike the magnetosphere, they glow, like when you strike a match, or when fireflies rub their tails between their hind legs."

Aleron nods, mouth twisted and brows furrowed in confusion. I know he didn't get all of it, that some of the more scientific terms are words for which he might need a comprehensive English-Spanish dictionary as much as I needed this vision to understand them. I took that astronomy course — the only science course I've ever loved — just last winter, and some of the details are sketchy, except the Latin. *Aurora borealis* — Northern Lights. *Aurora Australis* — Southern. Lights above the boreal forest. Lights above the down-under. Easy multiple choice. I failed the theory question, but if I'd had this picture we have before us now, I would have aced it. I wonder if there is someone down under, in the outback, making religion out of the lights: a mirror reflection of our own. The Innuit and Cree must have done, and the Ojibway here.

Silent, we walk down to the water. The lake is still as a photograph, so still I can't tell where the spruce on the opposite shore ends and their reflections begin. Out where I can see no shore, sky and water are one. Lights Above, Lights Below — 'up north' doesn't cut it anymore: if the Aussies have the outback, we have the up-beneath. I try to explain all this to Aleron. He just breathes it all in with the cool air and smiles.

"Let's go," he says. He strips down, leaves his clothes on a cedar snag overhanging the shore, and hops onto the pebbly beach.

"You're crazy. It's only been a few weeks since the ice broke off the lake."

"Come on, wanker! The chance may never come again. Besides, the cold cannot catch you as long as you keep moving."

His official excuse for such machismo masochism. But I know the real reason: he wants to swim in the Lights, to have their blessing. He even tries to catch some in the water he cups in his hands.

I throw off my clothes, climb down the overhang, step up on a rock and dive in. Surfacing from the confusion of dividing and multiplying bubbles, I swim over to him, his short, lithe figure dancing in the shallows.

"Race you back to the boat," he says.

"I'm not much of a swimmer."

"Neither am I, so we will run."

"Through the water? What about our clothes?"

"We can row back for them. Come on! You have to keep moving if you want to keep warm."

We race down the shoreline, slowing and slowing until the deepening water pulls at our knees, our feet miring in nightmares, our heads swimming a dream. Balls deep, he pulls ahead, lifting his knees high to thrust himself forward. Unable to keep up, I fall back, and naked as the day I was born, take to land, running hard and fast against the cold. It's as if we're streaking through Cass's watercolour, as if we've just seen snow for the first time.

CHAPTER FIFTEEN

DAY OFF, JUNE 14 — Spent today moving to someplace way up a road that's supposed to join up somewhere with the mighty Graham, a logging road that has been extended and added onto for so long that it now stretches for several hundred kilometres north of the Trans-Canada. Neither Cass nor I know exactly where we are, since our unsigned road's barely passable, and winds and rolls like a serpent through the patchwork of forest, cuts and "regen" blocks, and beyond into a wilds that nearly pinches it off completely. Tomorrow morning we'll pitch a skeleton camp (no shower or dry shack) as we're slated to be here for only two weeks before we head on to the final show for the Ontario season somewhere up beyond the northernmost end of the Armstrong highway. Hopefully, we'll get the big top up and shitters dug early enough for some R and R.

The campsite is even more of a paradise than the first. Rapids spill down through the forest and beneath a bridge just high enough to ride a canoe under if you duck. The river widens into a narrow lake a skipped stone beyond where we're pitched. I haven't been down it yet but Aleron and Daniel paddled the camp canoe out as far as they could before dusk forced them to turn around. A river of lakes, Aleron called it. Endless, endless. From what he saw, untouched.

Based on his description, I'd place us somewhere on the Kopka River, a bit northeast of the lake that is its source, which would mean we're straddling the timeline. My Official Ontario Road Map doesn't show any roads leading there, but it's from 1982 and from what I've seen, hardly any of the tertiary roads, extensions, loops and shortcuts that branch off the main routes are ever drawn in. Then again, maybe our river isn't on the map. I guess I sort of hope that. The paper (and perhaps other authorities) wants to know its name and location more than I do. I'm just as happy with Aleron's name for it, the River of Lakes — happier knowing it by maps that haven't been drawn by my father.

I think I've found a heaven you don't need to die to get into.

We ease Bob's red Grumman canoe into the water by the log bridge. I load my knapsack, Cass's blanket, and two cans of Jolt Cola under the yoke and drape a life jacket over each thwart. Cass takes the stern and I push off, running a few steps through the shallows before hopping into the bow. We pick up our paddles and swing the canoe away from the white of the rapids, negotiating around drowned rocks that, under an overcast sky, we wouldn't have been able to see.

Several canoe lengths beyond the bridge, the rapids diffuse into flat, still waters: the river widens into a long, narrow lake, wild rice breaking its glassy surface almost from bank to bank, shore to shore. Yet beneath the calm, I can feel the strong thrust of the river's undercurrent pushing against my paddle.

"Noah — blueberries!"

I look where she's looking: there, along the shore, where pine-dotted ledges squeeze the lake into a river once again, a thin carpet of berries bobs beneath the thick underbrush overhanging the water.

"I thought blueberries grew closer to the ground, like strawberries.

The ones coming up in the cutaway are only half as high as my shovel blade, and few of them are ripe yet."

"Maybe the clear-cut's too exposed for them to grow any better. Anyway, half of what we've been planting is old cut block left fallow for too long, then doused with Vision or whatever pretty name they have for defoliant these days."

"What are you talking about?"

"Oh yeah, I forgot. You're on Therese's crew. You've probably never seen a chem-block in your life. All I'm saying is that these berries are safe to eat."

We glide toward the left bank. Cass lays her paddle across the gunnel, reaches into the shadows of the shrub and plucks a few ripe berries.

"Here ... taste," she says.

"You sure?"

"Then smell them first, for god's sake. I'm not trying to poison you."

I cup some leaves from the bushes to my nose: they smell like blueberry, so I eat.

"Good?" she asks, smacking her already purple lips.

I reach under my seat and open my knapsack to get the treat I'd bought in Thunder Bay. With my new fishing knife, I cut the fruit into quarters. "I have a surprise for you."

"Something sweet?"

"Yes."

"Chocolate?"

"No."

"Maple fudge from that gas bar on the edge of town?"

I turn and hold out a slice of the fruit, bleeding off the end of the knife.

Cass' smile fades. "Pomegranates?"

"Translation: seedy apples. Passion and temptation fortified in a fruit, if you believe Greek mythology."

"I believe they're too fidgety."

"But so is love."

"I thought you were talking about passion, and passion's like this
—" She lifts her paddle and combs it back and forth through the
bushes: hundreds of blueberries — ripe and plump — rain into the
canoe. "That's the way the First Nations used to harvest wild rice,"
she says, her smile turning bluer with every handful.

"You know, Aleron was right about you. He said that underneath
all those bites is a real beauty."

"Hadn't you noticed that yourself? Or have you been standing in
for him all this time?"

"No. I think I sensed it that day we picked you off the road and
you rode into camp on my lap."

"I think you sensed it that day in the shower."

"Is that where you felt it?"

"I'm not saying I felt anything. All I'll say is that you look a lot less
sexy with that bloody blade in your hand and that red juice dribbling
down your chin."

I rinse my knife in the river and slip it back into its sheath.

"I think you're starting to burn," Cass says. "Pass me the sunscreen."

I pass the bottle back to her on the end of my paddle. Keeping a
low center of balance, I turn around, step over my seat and kneel gingerly in the bottom. She squeezes a blob of Solar Eclipse Liquid
Shade onto the fingertips of her less calloused tree hand and reaches
across the yoke to smooth it over my cheeks and brow, finishing with
my earlobes. She shakes the dregs of the sunscreen into my palm,
and shutting her eyes, cranes her neck as I lean forward to paint her
face. Protected for the time being, we take our seats and pick up
our paddles.

Strokes unceasingly strong, face calm as the moon's, Cass paddles
us out from the bank and downstream, the log bridge slipping out of
sight as we enter the narrows; the only sign of the big top a wispy
trickle of smoke rising above the treeline.

The river opens up into another lake, much longer and wider than the last. Along the shores, layered ledges, tiered and pastry-like, stagger up from the water, thrust up through one another to a height of eight stories, their reflections staggering down; rock on rock, broken only by small clusters of Jack pine and their mirror images.

"Let's park the canoe and picnic atop that cliff," I say.

Cass steers the canoe into a small inlet carved into the shoreline by some glacier that passed through ages ago. I leap onto the finger of shield rock, pull the bow up the smooth, submerged ledge and lash it to a pine trunk. Cass fills the brown paper bag from my pomegranate with blueberries, then stuffs it in my knapsack.

"I'll go first," Cass says.

"Maybe I should. I used to climb cliffs like this when I was a kid."

"What if I slip? Nobody'll be there to stop me."

"Alright. You go first. Just watch out for loose rock."

The first tier is easy: a gentle grade with plenty of footholds and crevices, and narrow sills where we can stop to catch our breath. But the next tiers will be harder to achieve, seeing the lichen-covered rock from a new perspective now — a view, information, my father's maps couldn't provide; despite all positives of a distant perspective (nothing on Earth looks all that bad from outer space), the subtle contours, smaller lakes, animals, and people — anything you might become attached to — are always left off. Maps: you can draw lines through them, shade whole continents the colour of evil, pinpoint the silos — yours, theirs — sketch in the calculated paths of projectiles, and you'll never have to hear anyone scream. Or you can shade one-fiftieth of your country green and say, this is what we're not touching, and still log it, selectively.

A stream of pebbles and dirt trickles onto my head. I look up: Cass is hanging from a sapling that's slowly peeling away from the rock.

"There's a toehold to your right," I call.

Her feet grope blindly along the sheer rockface. But the sapling's roots tear loose from their crevice and she skitters partway down the cliff before her feet find a narrow ledge to stop her.

"Grab onto the rock with your left hand and lean into the wall."

"As if there's anything better up here to hold onto."

I scramble up the brittle, loosely knit dolerite to her side and hold out my hand.

"Oh no," she says. "No way. The price is too high."

"Just take it!"

"You'll probably brag to Aleron and it'll be all over camp by noon tomorrow. There's no way I'm going to end up owing you my life."

"We'll call it payback for putting me up in your tent the last two weeks."

"I can't. I was doing myself the favour."

"Really?"

"I wasn't sleeping after the bear attack. Having you around made everything feel a bit safer."

"You could've borrowed the camp mutt for that."

Another length of root peels away from the rockface, dropping Cass farther back from the ledge. "So, should I wait to paint the rocks or take my chances on breaking my neck throwing myself into the lake?"

I lean down and reach out to her. "Grab my arm!"

"No."

Hanging onto the ledge, I drop my free hand onto her wrist and pull her hand from the sapling. "If you don't help me to help you up, we're both going down. Satisfied?"

Finally, she closes her hand around my wrist; I pull her in close to the wall and she starts toeing her way back up.

We scale the cliff side by side. Reaching the plateau of the last tier, we pull ourselves up into a brilliant sun and verdant breeze; lichens baking, orchids swaying on stony perches. The view curves on forever — the rolling forest cut only by the river of lakes and the odd string bog and not a cutaway in sight.

"You'd've chosen death or paralysis over this?"

"Water?" she mumbles, passing her canteen.

I take it; she spits a jet into my face, and laughing, turns to run.

I drop my knapsack on the shaded side of a rock I'll easily recognize later and spring after her, out of the sun into the dank smell of vegetation steeping in its own sweats.

Cass weaves in and out of the trees, jumping roots that snake out beneath the moss, laughing uncontrollably past the charred stumps of an ancient fire, deeper into the thickening woods. She drops from my sight over the top of a boulder-strewn slope. Her laughter stops.

I run up the hill, bracing myself for another one of her tricks. But she's just standing there, her back to me, in the crater-like depression below, her head bent back as far as it can go. Looking up, I see them too: a cluster of white pines at least fourteen stories tall. They've survived fire after fire. They'd been missed by the men with the Swede saws, or maybe left for the circle of light that filters around and through their bushy crowns and turns the shrubless carpet of needles at their feet a coppery gold.

I join Cass in the cool of the bowl — maybe a long-dried-up pond, maybe an ancient crater.

"My God."

"esses," says Cass.

"Aren't we through with actresses? Male or female, they're all actors."

"We can axe actress, waitress, but not seamstress or goddess."

"Why not?"

"Seamster may rhyme with Teamster but I've never heard of one — no man would take such a low-paying, labour-intensive job. When I think of God, he always comes out male. Goddess is female and can be just as powerful, and more in the right ways."

"What's it matter? These trees don't have a sex."

"They're feminine to me."

"That's your association."

"No, it's your appropriation. You've taken the animal kingdom, lionized yourselves. Women have to take what we can get, what you've left — crumbs, the backwoods. That's our starting ground, only it's not crumbs; the backwoods is undervalued."

"Except for its lumber products. Look Cass, these trees are sexless. They're not pineapples; they're androgynous."

"Physically, yes."

We walk to the base of the nearest pine, its roots so enormous they look like they've erupted through the forest floor, pulling up a massive mound of earth and a blanket of moss around themselves. We scamper up the damp hillock and try to link arms around the trunk, but we'd need two more of us, or more.

"I've never seen trees this big anywhere in Ontario," Cass says.

"In Ontario? I've never seen a tree this big in my life."

Cass combs her fingers through the long, deep ridges in the pine's thick bark, as if she can read something — its age, the flow of its sap, who else had touched it, when. "Let's eat here," she says. "Hey, where's the goods?"

"I left them back by the cliff. I thought you'd want to eat where we'd have a view of the lake."

"Well go and get them before some animal does."

I swing around the fattest trunk, jog up the side of the crater, and retrace our route back to the cliff. The rock where I'd dropped my knapsack had the face of an old man, bearded with moss, on its north side. But now, all around, the rocks make too many faces, chiding me for my forgetfulness. In the slash, in the dissolving morning mists, a seasoned planter could leave his warm-up jacket hanging from the snaky growth of an uprooted poplar, several hectares away from his main cache, or on an odd-looking rock, and still find it an hour later on the next run, or even six or seven runs later, among all the other odd rocks and uprooted poplars. But the forest hides many things, makes orientation difficult for me, an animal of the field. So I look for other signs: depressions in the moss or hunks of moss turned over, broken branches, bent saplings — where had we been?

I hear a caw-cawing, violent wing beats: ravens, probably feasting on our grub like they used to eat my lunch when I was a greener and didn't know that I should be packing it in a steel box or heavy canvas bag. I run in the direction of their sounds. There they are, by the rock, jabbing holes in my knapsack with their beaks, plucking out berries like grubs from a rotten trunk, fighting for position: possession.

"Scat!" I hiss. "Take the high road outta here!" They scatter, raucous caws and wingbeats; my knapsack bleeding pomegranate from the holes they punched.

By the time I get back to the crater, Cass has fallen asleep, nestled among the cones in the needle-sprinkled moss, between the tentacle roots of the most giant pine. I bend down in the spongy moss, scoop a handful of berries from my knapsack, hold my stained hand over her face. "Cass ..."

Her eyes open slowly, blink lazily as her vision comes into focus, and widen. She sits up, her other-worldly expression dissipating. "I was dreaming about swimming alongside one of those shark-size sturgeon that Bob said the explorers found in the MacKenzie River. For a second I thought your hand was the tail end of a lunker about to drown me in a motherlode of her caviar."

"Blueberries I got, but if you're looking for fancy fish eggs you'll have to find yourself another catch."

I cram a handful of the tiny, plump fruits into my mouth. She tilts her head back, cranes her neck and opens her gullet like a fledgling sparrow: I bend over and kiss her, slyly tucking an unchewed berry under her tongue. Laughing, she reaches for the brown bag and stuffs her own cheeks, and in a minute, we're rolling in the moss, trying to force-feed each other. Pine needles woven into her clothes and hair, she backs me against the tree trunk. I try to scramble over the roots, but she pins me there like an insect, with her arms, my own laughter, her kiss.

"So, why haven't you told me what you're running from?"

"I'm not."

"Oh? You worry about eating a few harmless berries, and you can't bring yourself to tell me you're a fugitive?"

"You're mistaking me for somebody else."

"Really? So you're not the Toronto tree-hugger charged with busting a CAT in the chops."

I stiffen. "You've been reading my mail ..."

"You read my back," she says, pressing her lips against my ear.

"It was nothing like that, you know. I was just trying to save this one tree — nothing even all that special — just a maple, an old decrepit maple with a crotch big enough for me to stretch out in and read."

"It must've been a pretty big tree to hold a galoot like you, and special if you were willing to face vandalism charges for it."

"Listen, I'm no vandal. I'm not even a fugitive or an activist. All I did was bind myself to a tree to stop them from taking it out. Honestly, the lock and chain cost me more than my trespass fine and the Admin's pissed off that they wrecked five pairs of bolt cutters trying to cut through them, so they trumped up the charges. Legal Aid told me they won't even make it to court."

"I'm sorry to be the one to tell you this, Noah, but being banished to the hinterland for three years for tying yourself to a tree and barking chants through a megaphone makes you an activist, whether you like it or not."

"No — the real activists came afterwards, in droves and out of the woodwork, after the student press got a hold of it. I'm not an exile either. I came here because —"

"Shhhshh!" She whispers, nuzzling up against my cheek. "Can't we just pretend?"

She slides her hands up my T-shirt, glides her fingers over my abdomen, ribs, chest and pulls the shirt over my head, off my arms. My hands find the small of her back and I take her shirt off. The drone of blackflies and mosquitoes is converging on us, but we don't care that we'll be fed on — we are feeding each other, ourselves. We strip off our shoes and jeans, each other's work socks and underwear. Rolling into the bed of needles (airy moss and soft needles) and still softer, each other's arms. Sweat and perfume indistinct in the smell of pine: the uncultivated world's neither-nor — a carrion flower, vegetation smelling of flesh, flesh grown fragrant from vegetable — not like the world of our arguments. But how could I say it to her? Love in the woods is a perfect geometry, a symbiosis ...

She smells like the sea: that's where we all came from originally, that's where God came — big fish, sperm whales, hammerhead, man-o'-war, manta ray, manatee, Neptune, monster squid, Scylla (wrap-me-round), Sirens (lash me to the mast), Charybdis suck 'er down; funnelling to the depths, stirring the heavens, dethroning gods and draining oceans (she draws me in) but to where? (to the picture) what the? is there a the? ... questions: why he scrambled coughing, amphibious, up a beach — from.

She turns around, moves her mouth up to mine: our tongues, twin, twine, play with each other for a while. I stop, pluck a pubic hair from between my lips. Hers, or mine, tucked there by her? I have a picture I did not take: she enveloped me in darkness, in lightness, a sea.

CHAPTER SIXTEEN

"Joan of Arc had a house in the suburbs,
went door to door for the NDP.
Her husband Dave was an image consultant,
helped the Tories sweep to victory.
Brought the PM and his nuclear family
all the way from Comeau Bay.
Funny how he had them to dinner
as Joan was hitchin' it for Thunder Bay."

Reaching back to the seed of the song, sprung from the rhythm of my spade slicing sand, I croon from the shadows in our darkened big top, the red glow of the oil-drum stove we're sitting around faintly illuminating Cass's beatific smile and glinting off the varnished rosewood belly of Aleron's guitar. We've had a few brew, and a couple of joints, and we're making up the rest as we go along, Aleron stringing as I'm singing her praises:

"Joan caught a bus to the Seventeen Highway
oh Canada, oh Trans-Canada!

in the Sault hitched a ride from a trucker,
took her all the way to Upsala.
Ordered a Number Four in Betty's Truckstop,
the fellers watched her as she wolfed it down.
Betty came out, wiped her hands on her apron,
said, 'Honey, welcome to our one-cab town.'"

Our song rings with a truth that can only come from spontanaeity — so true that I wish we were taping it. But we don't have any recording devices, and life is such a work in progress, none of us knows where the song will end:

"Now, Maxwell turned his head to hear his car mentioned,
said 'I'm the taxi — where you wanna go?'
Joanie said, 'To a tree planting contract
sixty clicks above the Graham Road' ..."

In the song, I've changed her name to Joan to protect her identity. She really was nearly hitched to one of the Prime Minister's image consultants — a young turncoat-come-Tory who taught the PM to don bifocals to look grandfatherly when talking down to the Opposition, and to take them off with the gloves. Now she's kicking herself because she knows her ex learned that from the sage/savage switch she trips with her own eyes. Only, I've condensed the story a little. She rode into her first camp in a cab but into her second on my lap. Even though I didn't know the first thing about her, I could smell the freedom that was trailing in the wind, which had caught the hair of a woman who'd taken a new name from a dream. And for the first time in a while, my life didn't feel like such a jail:

"She sang, 'One two three, it's the eye of the hurricane,
the calm between the storm,
Come all my brothers

tell your sisters and your lovers
how you'll keep their babies warm.
One two three, it's the eye of the hurricane,
the calm between the storm,
Come on, my lover,
tell your sisters and your brothers
how you'll keep your baby warm.'"

WEEK 5, DAY 4 — Plâge. Cream. The Promised Land. Just over the next hill, at the next block, a day away on another cutaway. I'm finally clueing into the reasons for Daniel's cynicism, except when it comes to Bob's promises of good land, I don't think it's his penchant for exaggeration speaking as much as his way of hanging carrots to motivate us through the shite. When we bog down there, he sends out the foremen to crack the whips. It's classic operant conditioning: when the dinner bell stops getting the dogs to drool and mush, it's time to flog their furry asses. Once they've completed the assigned task successfully — say, hauled your sled from the Alaska panhandle to the Florida panhandle — throw them their bones and shower them with praise. Save the chuck steak for another day.

Today was such a day. Therese had promised us all week that today, all the crews would be going to a cream block so big that it will last us through the end of the contract, and that our crew would be there first to stake out our ground. After three days of progressively stonier ground, we'd certainly earned it. But when we got to the turnoff for Paydirt Lane, which Jack has been stocking all week in anticipation of "record production," Therese blasted right past it, ignoring Steve's queries and Daniel's cries of protest and foul play, past the blocks Lyndon's crew had been in, right to where the catroad came to an end at a landing, where Clem's and Lyndon's crummies were already parked, their planters milling about the tree cache, none of them very eager to bag up. An ominous sign.

Therese turned off the engine. "There's been a slight change of plan."

"A slight change?" Daniel bitched. "We're supposed to be starting the cream block today."

Therese sighed. "And we will, later. But first we have to work with Clem and Lyndon to finish this brackie block. It's too big and snarly for one crew to be in alone while the others are off in the pay dirt."

"What about the smeg we've been in for the past three days?" Steve griped. "I didn't see Clem or Lyndon volunteer his crew to help us get through that quicker."

"They've been in similar ground," Therese said. "Anyways, this isn't their piece. Bob gave the foremen the choice of either drawing straws for it or cattle-planting it. None of us wanted to risk our crews being stuck there alone for the next two days, so we agreed to a cattle-plant."

"Let's just get this done," Moira said, opening the door.

The most memorable lecture of my all-too-brief career as a university student was in the ever-popular Inhumanities 101 course, Greek and Biblical Traditions, and delivered with great flare and brimstone by a visiting professor and scholar of classical Greece and Rome (and ex-pat of the USSR), Dr. Pavel Lichenov, on the topic of hell. For the ancient Greeks, there could be no worse hell than an afterlife of endless, fruitless, purposeless toil. Witness Sisyphus rolling that stone ceaselessly up that hill without any real objective other than following orders to get it to the top — only to see his dreams of task completion and a smoke-break repeatedly dashed on the rocks when he loses his grip or hits a snag just before reaching the summit, or worse, pushes too hard on his final heave-ho, overshoots his mark, sending it right over the peak and crashing down the precipitous slope or chasm on the other side — Poor Old Michael Finnegan, Begin Again. To the ancient Greek, then, hell was paved with good intentions that had a uniformly bad outcome: no fulfillment.

To a planter, hell is paved with cobblestones — acres and hectares of cobblestones that have been scarified with some contraption that scoops backhoe blade-sized holes every three feet in a five-on-the-dice pattern, taking the little dirt and moss that once was there, leaving nothing but holes full of cobblestones in which he is expected to plant trees.

Overwhelming sense of fruitlessness to his efforts? Check. Nothing could feel more fruitless than combing over twelve hectares of stone-filled holes with forty pounds of seedlings strapped to your hips and two dozen other planters desperately jabbing their shovels and spears into the same hole, all hoping to hit dirt, sparks flying off the tips of their Sheffield steel Excaliburs as they hit Shield and the ground-down remains of erratics instead, and, after three hours, not planting a single tree; thus, not pocketing a single dime.

Ceaselessness of this fruitless toil? Check. Bob eventually put a stop to this nonsense once it was determined for his report that "the ground had been sufficiently covered," not by any actual trees planted but by the foremen's rather haphazardly placed flagging tapes; by which time the thirty person line-plant that in some way, shape or form is supposed to resemble an orderly herd of cattle, had quickly collapsed into chaos. But we all left the area with the sense that it has yet to be reforested, and in our worst nightmares, we will be planting it again and again for all eternity.

Purposelessness to complying with an order to complete an impossible task? Check. This one needs no explaining, but for further illustration, see cool war-vet Paul Newman versus the anal prison warden in Cool Hand Luke. I would've made a heck of a lot more money today than I did planting by taking a baseball bat to Thunder Bay parking meters set at 1950's Port Arthur hourly rates, and I would've been more richly deserving of my sentence. Oh, I forgot — I've been rusticated for martyring myself to a stupid tree simply because I liked to read in it, only stupidly, stupidly, I didn't even wait for sentencing; no, like a true martyr of the lemming variety, I romanticized this torture and actually volunteered for it. I'm sure President Leslie Crustin, PhD., would be delighted to learn that the punishment fits my crime.

Not that it's all bad, or none of us would be here. In true Skinnerian fashion, Bob tossed us our bone. He had to, seeing that even Walter Westerly, his top planter, his Achilles, was apoplectic about having to participate in a cattle-plant, which he called a "cluster-fuck," and he threw so many sparks from his shovel with his ballistic curse-riddled thrusts into Shield that he nearly set a dried-up moss bed on fire. Bob promised us the afternoon off, so we packed up our gear and piled into the crummies, Cass and Aleron riding on either side of me in the Suburban, and took off on the forty minute drive back to camp.

This is where the plot sickens. Peppering his Skinner with Machiavelli, Bob changed the game plan again to make that bone taste all the sweeter and his dogs that much more grateful. Halfway home, his voice came crackling over Therese's walkie-talkie.

"Wanna pick that up, Daniel?" Therese asked.

Daniel turned down the volume on Steve's tape of Colin James. "Ya Bob."

"I've got great news. We just picked up some extra work. Thirty thousand trees, but they're old bare root stock that has to be planted today."

Every one groaned in unison.

"I was thinking, if we go to the reefer, unload 'em now, we could have 'em in the ground by sunset."

"No way," Steve said. "I can't wrap my head around the idea of unloading another friggin' reefer right now, not after the dog of a day we've just had."

"You're passing up a chance to salvage it," said Therese. "At least you could cover your camp costs and beer money for the next day off."

"I have to agree with Steve," Daniel said. "The day's a wash. Bob can't get us psyched to kick off work early then tell us on the ride back to camp we'll be planting till dusk or till every last pine's in the ground, whichever comes first."

"He can do whatever the hell he pleases," Therese said. "Now give me the walkie-talkie. Where are we meeting the reefer, Bob?"

"Back at camp."

Our second collective groan was deafening.

A white reefer trailer marked with the government of Ontario's trillium logo and the slogan "Forests for the Future" had been unhitched in the landing across the road from the big top. Like clockwork, we poured out of the crummies and lined up at the back of the trailer. Jack and Bob backed their trucks into place so that some of the boxes of trees could be relayed straight into their tree racks. Aleron and I unlatched the big double doors and swung them open. Jaegs, Buzzard, Mitra and Kirsten hauled out the roller ramp from the undercarriage and hooked it into place. I was just about to climb up into the back of the reefer so I could start unstacking the bareroot boxes onto the coasters when Bob grabbed my arm.

"Let me, Noah. You've worked hard enough today."

He and Jack took my place and Aleron's, so we took up positions as receivers along the ramp.

A minute or more must have passed before we could hear the first box slowly rattling along the rollers. There was something distinctly untree-like about the sound the box made as it rattled and clinked its way out of the darkness of the reefer and toward daylight, yet something intimately familiar to all of us. But before any of us had guessed it, the first case of beer flew down the ramp, so fast that it slipped right through our hands.

"Stop it, damn it, stop it!" Buzzard cried.

Cass caught it just as it was about to plunge off the end, and handed it off to Jaegs.

We raised our voices in an eardrum-beating cheer. Seven more two-fours followed, each proceeding down the line, in the bucket brigade style we always use to unload trees, to their new destination: the big top. For the butt-heads, there were cartons of smokes of every conceivable brand and for the teetotallers, candy bars. There were also trees, about fifty thousand in fact, but they were neither old bareroot nor destined to go into the ground today. So Cass and I took time to go blueberry picking again, though in easier to reach and less buggy climes, and even managed to squeeze in a nap.

To cap it all off, Rosemary had prepared a great feast, in part to use up as much of the leftovers from previous dinners to make more space in the fridge and freezer. The buffet table was decked with cold cucumber soup and garlic bread, Greek and Caesar salad, and a cold rice and raisin curry. As for the hot dishes, there were more than I had the stomach for: Aleron and Landells helped Rosemary with tray after tray of lasagna, and moussaka, and burittos, and perogies, and stir-fried veggies, seafood fettucine and Thai peanut chicken. Dessert consisted of Mitra's family-recipe baklava, cherry cheesecake, Aleron's Special Tequila-Spiked Fruit Salad, Rosemary's Nanaimo bars and fudge.

For two hours, we gorged ourselves, drinking our beer and toasting the cook and her assistants. Once we'd settled down with our coffees and teas, Bob took his place at the top of the kitchen steps. Buzzing on sugar and alcohol and caffeine, we banged on the tables with mugs and bottles and cutlery.

Beaming, he raised his hand; the din faded. "I know today was a tough one to take, and I'm sorry for putting you through it, especially since it wasn't a money-maker. But the ground you'll be moving into now is among the sweetest cream I've seen in my life, and — no exaggerating — it'll last us till the end of this contract. In fact, it's so sweet that we expect the trees will be flying into the ground so fast it's gonna be hard for us to keep up, so you'll have a sleep-in and ten o' clock start tomorrow to give Jack and I an extra jump start on stocking the blocks."

The cheer that went up funnelled up the conical roof of the big top and into the dusk, my voice included in the chorus. Bread and circuses. But a meatier bone than expected. Save the chuck meat for another day.

WEEK 5, DAY 6 — Beach, plâge, crême, cream. Whatever you want to call it, pay dirt has a unique ring to it. The sound of a shovel hitting pay dirt is like the sound of an old cash register drawer unlocking and sliding open, and between yesterday and today, my blade has opened that drawer seven thousand three hundred and fifty times. That's an average of three thousand six hundred and seventy-five trees per day and about six hundred dollars after camp costs, cha-ching, cha-ching.

Three thousand a day for one week, Bob told me at breakfast, and I might make Clem's crew when he and Therese sit down to reshuffle the planters, and it's easier to highball when your crew gets the lion's share of the cream.

3000/day come hell or highwater and I'll be a highballer.
4000/day or more and I'll be a hardcore.

Spelling out numbers like those does such feats a bit more justice than jotting them down numerically, and there isn't a planter in this camp who isn't feeling high and mighty for breaking wide open a personal best. Even the slowest nose-pickers on Lyndon's crew are hitting 2400, and Cass, his fastest, isn't far behind me. But for seemingly impossible numbers, the hardcores have it, hands down. Walter's been averaging six thousand, and Landells, with his cut-down two foot staff-handled shovel, a close 5800. Tonight, we gave Kirsten a standing ovation for being camp highballer with a count of 6500.

An anthropologist of workplaces might expect us to be spent and cranky from our work, and would likely be baffled to see us up playing cards and guitars till one in the morning when we have to rise before the sun. But pay dirt is easier in every way, on the joints and back as much as the psyche. Some of the old rivalries between the crews are also beginning to melt away. Even Lyndon, who normally derides Clem for looking like "the Man from GLAD", has been caught up in the giddiness; after they finished tabulating camp production earlier this evening, he cracked open his best single malt, poured Clem a dram, then offered up libations to anyone who happened by his table. "To the sunniest of solstices," he said, raising his glass to the fiery red orb sinking into view through the mouth of the big top. "To early dawns and late dusks and everything that comes in between."

The sex has been as sweet as the cream. Quickies in Cass's tent before the breakfast and dinner horns. Lingering in the river, just beyond the bend, before and after bathing and rebathing. Risqués on a bed of folded tarps under the Prairie Schooner. Now that all crews are planting together in a sandflat that stretches almost to the horizon, and I've been working a piece right across the road from Cass's, we've made the odd foray in the forêt. We've humped twice atop a high wall of logs stacked along the road during last winter's harvest and once, to cool off, in the back of a reefer, almost screwing ourselves royally when the trucker returned to haul the empty trailer back to the nursery in Dog River. Luckily, he heard us banging against the rear doors and, when he stopped the rig to let us out, accepted Cass's explanation that I'd suffered a heat stroke and needed to be moved to the nearest cool, shady spot, where she could administer first aid. Lucky for us we're in such an enormous clear-cut.

I've been just as lucky with my fishing rod. Though I've been more of a dabbler than an angler up till now, the sheer abundance of fish in these waters has got me hooked. Yesterday after work, in my half-hour of fishing from the big rock below the bridge, I caught seven. The pike were easy: you can see them sunbathing, just below the surface of the still, shallow waters on the south bank of the rapids. Casting farther out into the middle, right into the boiling white waters,

I hooked two rainbows. The three walleye I landed were schooling where the river widens into a pool and the rapids calm to a dark, gurgling green.

I owe my great luck to Aleron, whose one fishing tip two nights ago has proven to be as fruitful as the lessons he gave me in planting. He was sitting in his lawn chair atop the bridge, watching as I dipped my rod from the rock below. Downstream, a big-bellied moon was floating up in the gap between the banks. Behind us, the sun was just setting into the treeline. The moon reddened.

"If you wanna catch alotta fish, you should fish tomorrow," he said. "Fishing's always best the day after the new moon."

I know it can't last, and I wonder when the weather will turn, but every day in this nameless place has been like the day after a new moon: in one way or another, teeming with light.

CHAPTER SEVENTEEN

"NOAH, YOU AWAKE?" Cass whispers hoarsely.

"Wide awake for ten minutes now. It sounds too big to be a raccoon or a fox, but it could be a wolf, couldn't it?"

"Noises can be deceiving but that's the stench that clawed into my back."

We lie back shaking, waiting for it to go, its pungent gamey smell growing stronger, its snuffles and snorts louder.

"Oh shit," Cass mutters. "Shit, shit, shit," the shadow of its head falling across the curved nylon wall of the dome, the shadow of its right forepaw expanding as it reaches for the eaves above our front flap.

I open my mouth, but nothing will come out. I can just see the headline: "T-Bay Planters Mauled, Half-Eaten," among the others that have appeared in the local papers over the season — about B.C. planters killed in an overloaded crummy that plunged over the end of a washed-out bridge, about planters struck by lightning. My leg jerks up involuntarily. The creature grunts and barrels off through the bush.

Cass sits up. "That's it. I'm outta here."

"Wait —" I unzip the ventilation flap on the front entrance and cast my flashlight beam through the no-see-um screen. "Clear," I say, but now I can hear something foraging the forest floor around the other side of the tent. I reach past Cass to check the rear screen.

"Aa—ahhhh!" She jerks toward me. "He's poking his nose into my foot."

I hang onto my breath, focus the beam on the screen, yank down the rear flap. Eyes luminesce out of a broad, richly furred face, then vanish. The snapping and crunching of its slow retreat through the underbrush fade until they can no longer be heard above the white noise of the rapids. We bail out through the front flap and run up the path along the river.

"There's something strange about that bear," I say. "It's red — rust red. I thought black bears were the only kind we had in this part of Ontario."

"Black, red — who in hell cares?" Cass snipes. "I'd just like to know where the dogs are when you need them."

"Becky had a run-in with a porcupine just after you turned in. Poor mutt's nose looked just like a pin cushion. Jack and I tried holding her still so Tim could work the quills out, but the barbs were lodged too deeply. So Jack took her and the trike to town for repairs."

"What about Innuk?"

"Last I saw of him he was sleeping by the mess."

"Maybe the bear got 'im."

"We would've heard it."

"I heard him barking, but I was half-asleep."

The mess is exactly that — a mess. The coolers have been over-turned, their lids torn off, and remnants of cheese, eggs, and butter are scattered all over the place. Up in the Prairie Schooner, the door's been ripped off one of the fridges; its stark light falling on the white rivulets that are leaking down from punctured milk bags, trickling through the dusty linoleum floor, and dripping down the steps.

I knock on the screen door of Bob's and Therese's trailer. No answer, so I rap on the window. "Bob?"

Cass presses her ear to the screen. "They're stirring ..."

"Better go see what's up," Therese groans in a muffled, drowsy voice.

Bob shuffles blindly to the door, fumbling to tie the sash on his robe. "Mind switching that fuckin' light off? ... Jesus, what time is it?" His whole face is one pissed-off squint.

Cass checks her watch. "Ten to two."

"What are you waking me up for at this goddamn hour of the morning?"

"There's a bear in camp."

"Where?"

"Down by our tent. We don't even keep our soap or toothpaste there."

"Is it still there now?"

"Well, no — it ran off after Noah shone a light in its eyes. But —"

"Sounds like it spooks way too easily to be much of a worry. But if it'll help you to sleep any better, you can always claim one of the crummies."

"If the kitchen's any indication, there'll be No Vacancy in any of the crummies."

"What?"

"Kitchen's trashed," I say. "It turned the mess inside out."

Bob grabs his ball cap off a hook, and reaches behind the door for his .306. Stepping out, he hands me one of those car battery flashlights. "This one's more powerful."

Cass quickens her step to stay within the protective halo of the beam. "Lyndon told me a warning shot usually scares them off for good."

"If he's still green, he'll listen. But if he's been baited ..."

"Here, in the middle of nowhere?"

"The middle of nowhere is where the bears are, and the spring hunt's still on. There'll be bait stations all up 'n down these roads, and some on the edges of old cutaways."

"Shoot the hunters then. We have to live and work here."

"The MNR doesn't issue tags for that, and it'll be impossible to get one for a black bear this late in the game."

"The bear I saw isn't black," I say. "It's red."

"Then maybe you saw a fox."

"No way."

"Shhh!" Cass hisses.

A bulky shape lumbers out of the darkened big top, carrying a long, rectangular object in its teeth, and cuts across the landing toward the bridge.

Bob stops and sights the animal through his scope. "Quick — shine the light. ... Mother." He lowers his rifle. "You're right. It's a cinnamon bear."

"A *cinnamon bear*?" Cass repeats.

"A freak of nature something like those albino black bears we've got on the west coast."

"So it's like a spirit bear, only it's a *red* black bear," I say.

He nods. "They're very rare. Few sows ever have them, but the ones that do might drop a cinnamon bear in every litter."

"Well," Cass snorts. "Stinks the same to me."

"That's musk," Bob says. "It's a boy." He raises the scope to his eyes again, tracking the bear as it scrambles up the shoulder to the road. "An adolescent, maybe three years old. With one of our ten-pound blocks of cheddar in its teeth ... and a pronounced limp." He squints. "From losing the outer two toes of its left forepaw. Probably got caught in a trap and gnawed them off to get free."

The bear crosses the bridge and into the dark of the forest. Bob loads a shell into his gun.

"You'll have to kill him, won't you?" Cass says.

"Can't. Don't have a bear tag. The MNR could shut us down and seize the entire camp if I do."

"Can't doesn't mean won't."

"I'm not going to let him walk off with the store, if that's what you mean. Ten to one he's stashing his spoils at a cache maybe fifty metres off the road before coming back for more. And when he does, I'll fire a warning shot."

"What if he doesn't listen?" I say. "I don't want to see him killed, but what about us?"

"It would have to be a pretty clear-cut case of self-defense — he chases a planter or attacks a dog or tears up someone's tent. But if he keeps this up, I'll have to get the MNR to dispatch a conservation officer to set up a baited bear cage. Once he's caught, they'll drive him fifty miles into the middle of nowhere before releasing him. That should give us more than enough time to finish up here in case he's one of those bears with a strong homing instinct." He seats himself in a lawn chair in the mouth of the big top, lays his rifle across his lap, and lights a cigarette.

My nose wrinkles up. "God does he reek."

Cass nods. "Of course, as bad as he smells, there's the distinct possibility that, after all he's been put through, we stink a lot worse to him ..."

"Noah, I can't sleep here," Cass says, grabbing the elastic waistband of my shorts as I'm crawling back into the tent. "Let's find a crummy."

I pass our sleeping bags out to her and we carry them back to the road.

"Which one?"

"The rental van Lyndon's driving has the plush seats." She reaches for the handle on the sliding panel door. "It's locked."

We try all the other doors but they're locked too.

I sweep my beam through the windows, over the seats: huddled shapes stir and turn and writhe like caterpillars disturbed in the midst of metamorphosis, heads shrinking away from the light, retracting under blankets. "Damn. No wonder we're the only ones up. Everyone else must've abandoned their tents hours ago."

We peer into Therese's Suburban and the Hendrix, but both are packed to the rafters. All that's left is the Conan, and Jack's been using it to truck trees. We open it up and start to brush off the soil that has leeched from dozens of runs of seedling trays onto the rear seat.

"That bear may be rare but I'll be a lot happier when it's gone," I say.

"Doesn't seem fair that he should have to be relocated or shot after he chewed half his foot off to free himself from a leg trap — especially not if it's bear baits that attracted him to the people food that lured him here in the first place."

"It might not be fair but the damage is done. I'm sure you would've felt much safer if you'd had a gun to face the bear that crashed your tent in your last camp. Smacking it with a shovel was risky."

"If I'd had a gun I'd have been tempted to train it on a few of those men long before they'd had the chance to honey my tent. That bear and the cinnamon here are only symptoms."

"True. But there's no way you'll ever convince people from around here to give up the spring hunt as long as the local economy depends on it. Even if you could, this bear's gone bad."

"No. He was made bad."

"Gone bad, made bad. Same difference."

"Noah, the distinction matters."

"Not to someone who was mauled half to death."

"I nearly was, and ultimately, I know that bear wasn't to blame."

"You know it now, but at the time, you were ready to kill it if necessary. Otherwise, you wouldn't have smacked it with your shovel."

"And now, I'm ready to campaign for an end to bear-baiting."

"I wish you luck. Remember that court injunction my university obtained to keep me away from the arboretum and essentially off the campus entirely?"

"What about it?"

"The day I tried to find the registrar's office to drop my courses, I got lost in a subterranean rat's maze of hallways and ended up outside the door of a department I never knew even existed: *The Centre for Practical Ethics ...*"

"Ha."

"Ha? I laughed like a madman. I couldn't stop. It was so uncontrollable that I got scared and ran around the goddamn place for twenty minutes trying to find a way out. It was like trying to hold it in long enough to find a washroom after a night of heavy drinking; you know, once you let go — dambusters, and you're wet with it. Finally, I found a fire exit. I ran deep into the arboretum where I laughed till I was hyperventilating. The next day, campus security issued an Alert to be on the lookout for a man who'd been seen running through the sub-level of the Behavioural Science Building, acting strangely, and was subsequently heard roaming around in the woodlot. I think they had me pegged for a stalker."

Cass sighs with fatigue. "Your point?"

"Since when have ethics ever been practical? If they were, we'd be in Utopia right now, we wouldn't have centres for practical ethics because there wouldn't be any other kind and the bear wouldn't be endangered or a threat."

"Isn't Utopia worth the effort?"

I sweep my shirt sleeve across the bench seat one last time. "I dunno. The effort, maybe, but not the price. People, as a species, seem to need their dramas and scandals and flaws to grow, or at least to light the fire under their asses to get off their duffs and do something with their lives. Perfection would get boring. Ask yourself what life would be like without setbacks and disappointments and tragedy?"

"You know what I think? Enough tragedy is thrown down on our heads randomly by nature without certain members of your *species* spurring it on deliberately."

"Hey, my species is yours and vice-versa. I'm not advocating wilful destruction. If anything, I came here thinking that by planting trees, I'd be fixing it. I don't think that anymore. Paradise isn't something we can make or fix. Maybe we can find it, but when we do, it never stays that way for long. That's why it's probably better to be nomadic — pick up and move before the perfection of a place dies in your head or your heart, or we can do too much damage to it."

"Too bad that's so impratical."

"Why are you so angry with me?"

"I'm not. I just wish you wouldn't start these deep, philosophical conversations right when we're about to turn in. They give me indigestion."

We roll out our bags, get in, and lock the doors behind us. At first, we try to lie together in spoons, but the seat's not wide enough. Reclining with our backs to one another, we each swing our feet up against the windows, hers against the passenger side and mine against the driver's side, and rest our heads on each other's left shoulder.

"Your head makes a hard pillow," Cass mumbles, squirming to find a more comfortable position.

"Then let me be on top. You always sleep with your head under your pillow anyway."

"Your head makes a hard pillow."

WEEK 6, DAY 1 — Bob met with some Big Cheese in the MNR today to arrange the delivery of a mobile bear trap tomorrow or the day after. He came back from Thunder Bay around dusk, armed with bear repellents for the crew bosses — exploding flares called bear bangers to deter a bear at long range and cayenne pepper spray in case of an up-close and personal attack on the block.

"Maybe everyone should get one of each," I suggested. "I wouldn't mind paying a few bucks for the extra protection, and I'm sure just about everyone would feel the same. It can't be nine-thirty and already most of the camp's in bed. I'd be in la-la land too, if I could get any sleep."

"I know this bear-scare business is exhausting," he said. "But the forest is too much of a tinder box and all that slash baking on the blocks is even drier. One misfired flare could spark a blaze. A panicky planter who accidentally sprays cayenne into the wind may as well be handing himself to the bear on a platter, blind and seasoned to boot."

When I pointed out that the crew bosses can't be everywhere at once, he told me that, starting tomorrow, each crew will be cattle planting so the crew bosses can keep constant vigil over their flocks. "But," he ceded, "it might be a good idea to train at least one other person on each crew how to use them properly, just in case a foreman's not around or unavailable for some reason. You wanna come along for a test firing of one of these bangers? I'm gonna shoot it out over the water, just to be safe."

Standing atop the bridge, Bob aimed the pen-sized launcher down at the river and released the clip. The flare flew out over the rapids, whizzing about fifty feet before striking the water. But instead of sinking and fizzling out, it skipped like the best skipping stone you've ever seen across the surface of the pool and landed smack in the middle of an old beaver lodge. Though surrounded by water, the islet of mounded sticks burst into flame, the fire shooting up a good ten or twelve feet.

We grabbed a couple of piss-packs and hatchets off the back of his one-ton and made a beeline for his Grumman canoe, but by the time we reached the old lodge, the fire had consumed most of its fuel and was drowning in its own greed.

"It's even drier than I thought," Bob said. "Much drier. I'll have to make an announcement at breakfast tomorrow. No smoking anywhere on the block, not even at the caches or on the roads, unless it's in the shelter of a vehicle, from now until we've had a good rain."

CHAPTER EIGHTEEN

SHIFT 6, DAY 3. Utopia: A Planter's History — All week, the ground has continued to be one non-stop cream pound, and the mood throughout camp as celebratory as on the solstice, in spite of the slight damper the bear has put on it from time to time. As Bob and Therese had predicted, average production has been increasing by the day. Today, Walter noted, the camp planted more than double the number of trees claimed as the world record for trees planted in a single day in Guiness' good book, and the title-holders had more than three times the planters on hand.

This dramatic spike in our production and earnings has both increased the spirit of generosity (especially with spirits, tobacco and other smokables) and eased reservations about splurging on non-essentials, creature comforts and absolute frivolities. Perhaps the most notable effect has been on the stakes at the gambling tables: whereas before, most were reluctant to wager more than a quarter on a poker hand, now that we're in the cream, even the most timid or conservative players routinely ante up an entire tray or box of seedlings, depending on what stock they were planting that day. At eight and a half cents per tree, that's $25 or $43 per ante! Losing parties usually have the option of paying winners the wagered trays in cash (which may have to come from the loser's next advance); mutually agreed upon goods (especially spirits, tobacco and other smokables, but sometimes, the home-baked sweets or premium chocolate included in the care packages sent up by concerned moms); or services (taken for three trays by Buzzard, Moira opted to pay off her debt in the form of two 45-minute Shiatsu massage sessions, which would have been three, were it not for Buzzard's gargantuan stature). Otherwise, losers are expected to settle their debts by putting their seedlings where their mouths were: i.e., informing Bob during the next evening's production tally of their actual tree count for that day, and their adjusted tree count, after forfeiture of losses to the winner, whose tree count is also adjusted accordingly. Maintaining these two as distinctly separate figures is particularly important to Bob, who is adamant about knowing the precise numbers of seedlings planted by each planter and each crew in each area, lest any questions or concerns later arise about the accuracy or honesty of a planter's tree counts, or the density of seedlings in a particular plantation.

This evening, Lyndon invited me to play backgammon. I politely declined, and when he asked why, I made the monumental error of explaining that I'm not one for games that depend on rolls of the dice.

"It's just a game," he protested. "You don't have to put up one red cent."

"It's not that," I said. "I just prefer games of skill to games of chance."

Lyndon's eyes narrowed. "A chess player, eh?" he said with contempt. "Well, comrade Fischer, I'll have you know that backgammon has been around in one form or another for more than 5,000 years and is considered by some to be the most realistic game of military strategy ever devised."

"Strategy? Give me a break. Where's the skill in rolling all your men home on some lucky dice while your opponent is stuck on the bar, unable to get off because of several unlucky rolls?"

"The skill is in keeping your opponent on the bar by minimizing the number of spaces he has to roll onto the board as you're trying to roll around and hopefully off the board, or, if the shoe's on the other foot, keeping your head till your luck turns. Keeping yourself from giving up or not tossing your hat in the ring in the first place depends on your ability not to confuse fortune with fate."

"How is a roll of the dice keeping me out of the game — or, at least, from playing like I'm still in it — the least bit realistic?"

"It's realistic, city boy, because the ancients who invented it recognized that every now and then, life throws you for a loop with something you never expected would be dropped on your head, and whether you like it or not, you have no fucking say in the matter. Not with all the degrees and wisdom and skill and chess moves in the world. Father killed in a logging accident? Roll of the dice. Bumping into the identical twin you were separated from at birth? Roll of the dice. Unplanned pregnancy? Roll of the dice. Snowstorm in June? Roll of the goddamned dice. Hell, we didn't even see that mother coming. So, we had to wait a couple of days in T-Bay for everything to thaw so we could get back to work. Did we quit before we gave the weather a chance to turn? Fuckin' right we didn't. Because we knew that, sooner or later, the weather would turn and that if we quit, we'd lose everything. Same as the dice."

The silence was deafening.

I couldn't resist. "I thought you said it's only a game."

After Lyndon's impassioned defense of backgammon, this pithy observation drew a substantial draft of laughter, and Lyndon's ire to the rafters.

"You know something, Abramson? You're a real turd."

"No, MacKerel — really, I'm not too little a man to admit that you've done an admirable job of convincing me. Still wanna play?"

"Sure, but now it's gonna cost you something. Betting starts at one box, and don't tell me you're still planting trays 'cause I'm a stickler for detail when Bob's taking the numbers."

"A box, eh? No dice."

I was just about to brush my teeth when barking erupted from the far bank of the river. Innuk immediately arose from where he'd been sleeping by the oil-drum stove and tore out of the big top in the direction of the bridge. Soon, Becky's barks were being countered by snorts and growls.

"Hey Abramson," Lyndon called, catching me before I'd quite made my exit. "Maybe I can interest you in a wager on something more lifelike."

"Shoot."

"Which dog would you bet on to be the first to tree the bear, Innuk or Becky?"

The question barely merited a moment's consideration. Though a husky, Walter's Innuk was bred to be a lead runner for the dog sled and hardly weighs twenty pounds wet. Of very square build, with a mass that must verge on eighty-five or ninety pounds, Jack's black Lab, Becky, on the other hand, is imposing. Her favourite game is to dive after five-pound rocks thrown from the bridge, and retrieving them, swim them across the river and back to Jack. Once, in one of her and Jack's more ill-timed moments, she waded into the path of Jack's projectile and took a sizeable cobblestone in the ribcage without as much as a whimper or grunt, though when she returned with the exact grenade tightly clenched in her canines, her brown eyes did register some anger, despite Jack's profound apologies and efforts to make it up to her.

"A slam-dunk," I said. "Becky, hands down."

"Somehow I knew you'd say that. What d'ya say? A box of trees, and since I rarely plant these days, I'll sweeten the pot with a brand new bottle of Glen Fiddich. Of roughly equal value, give or take a few cents."

"What if both dogs tree the bear, or neither?"

"Then we each take back from the pot what we put in — nothing lost or gained. But if the bear is treed, the dog that is closest to barking up it or right underneath it is the winner."

"Deal."

By this time, Innuk had entered the fray, and both dogs could be heard padding along the opposite bank in rapid pursuit of their quarry. As we crossed the bridge, we could see that Jaegs, Aleron, Mitra and Moira, Kirsten and Daniel, along with planters who'd pitched their tents there to escape the bustle of camp central, were all up on the road, nervously eyeing the woods. Walter stood down on the riverbank with Jack, who was packing Bob's rifle.

"Seen 'im yet?" Lyndon inquired, eyeing the sizeable tracks in the sand.

Walter pointed to a gap in the juniper bushes. "They followed him through there and up that slope somewhere."

"Gonna plug 'im if they flush 'im out?"

"Naw," Jack said. "I'll fire a warning shot. That's usually good enough to scare off a bear for good. But if he lays as much as a toe on either of our dogs, or charges any one in this camp, I'll take him out."

For awhile, all that could be heard were the distant sounds of snapping branches and the occasional outburst of barking. Then, as dusk fell, the sound of excited pants and the thudding of running paws advanced on us. Suddenly, a bulky, dark shape burst out of the bush. Jack raised Bob's rifle to his eye; blinded in the glare of a dozen flashlights, the ruddy bear veered off to the right, along the treeline toward the road, with Innuk chasing his tail.

Lyndon laughed. "What I tell you?"

"He hasn't treed him yet," I grumbled.

Just then, Becky flew out of the woods and leapt onto the shoulder, cutting off the bear before he could reach the road. Planting her large paws firmly, Becky bared her bright canines and growled deeply.

"You were saying, MacKerel?"

Jack ran up to the road to get a clearer shot should the situation call for it, but no matter how he positioned himself, one or the other dog was always in the way.

The bear turned to ward off Innuk, crouched in the tall grass, yapping incessantly at his heels. As Innuk inched back, Becky advanced, snarling. Cornered against a rock, the red bear rose up on his hind legs, turned, and growling with a ferocity nearing a roar, lunged at Becky with his good paw. Jack fired a shot over the bear's head.

Yelping, Becky retreated over the bridge and cowered under the Prairie Schooner. His way to one side clear, the beast resumed his flight, Innuk snapping at his rump as he clambered up the nearest tall white pine, sending him almost to the very top, where Innuk, tiny Innuk, would keep him for the next three hours, till Walter finally called him off.

Lyndon turned to me, grinning his gap-toothed grin. "So Abramson, will that be trees or Chargex?"

"It shouldn't count," I muttered. "Becky was clearly spooked by Jack's shot. It whizzed right over the back of her head."

"No dice."

CHAPTER NINETEEN

CASS AND I are standing in the mouth of the big top, eating our slices of lemon poppy-seed cake, when the two conservation officers who'd hauled in the mobile bear cage pull up in their trademark spruce green MNR pickup, two tranquilizer guns on the gun rack on the back. Bob, Therese, Lyndon and Clem file past us to greet the c.o.'s.

"We always aim to get them in open ground," I overhear the older one saying. "But to be on the safe side, we'll need to draw up a site plan of the entire camp — just in case ..."

The greener one, whose acne suggests he can't be much more than a year past forestry school, follows Lyndon around, quickly sketching the layout of camp central before crossing into the forest, ostensibly to map (more meticulously, I hope) the locations of our tents.

"What the hell are they bothering with that for?" Cass says.

"It's so they won't accidentally plug any of us in case they have to chase the bear through the woods."

"A lot of good that'll do if they're shooting in the dark."

"We'll be safe. See?" I point to the halogen lights on the roof rack of their pickup.

"Wake up, Noah. Those lights won't go very far in these woods, and a tranq dart doesn't have a guidance system. If they accidentally shoot you, you'll be comatose before they even find our tent. But maybe that's okay. You'll be asleep anyway. You just won't wake up before the trees we've planted are ready for harvesting."

"I think we should stick to sleeping in the crummies till this is over."

"I'm sick and tired of the Conan. It's cramped and dirty, and now those Ministry goons are on night watch, and they've parked themselves within spitting distance. Christ, it's like being parked next to the vice squad at Lover's Leap — always dreading that tap on the fogged-up glass and the blinding light because the springs are gone, and you know damned well that if you can hear all that rocking and squeaking inside, it's gotta be twice as loud outside."

"I thought that element of risk was a turn-on for you. But if you'd prefer to be embare-assed by the bear, we can always go back to the tent."

She doesn't even crack a smile.

We end up in the Conan again, since nobody else much wants it, and nothing else is vacant. But we make no sounds of squeaking violins because, I try telling myself, she's bushed from planting on no sleep. What I really fear is that she's going soft on the bear — maybe in a way that only she can — and growing angry that I'm not willing to leave to chance something already unpredictable. She certainly hasn't appreciated hearing about my little wager with Lyndon, who, as her foreman, has taken great pleasure in recounting his version of events to her over and over ever since; leaving her with the indelible impression that I have a sadistic streak — a redneck side that might, from time to time, predispose me to betting on cock fights, U.S. versus U.K. pitbull fights, bull fights, and Russian roulette.

It's on nights like these that I fall asleep cursing my parents for naming me after an unsuspecting farmer with no seafaring experience divinely chosen to pack breeding pairs of all the world's land-roving species — but only the innocent birds and bees — aboard a boat he would build to contract in time for the purging flood. The good book says it was God's great reckoning. Velikovsky says God was a close brush with an errant planet, that sucked and swept the seas inland, rained hellfire and brimstone on Jerusalem and environs, and stood the Earth still for several days on its run-up to the finale: reversing sunrise and sunset. And so the Great Flood seeped its way into mythologies the world over — including Velikovsky's. I can't say which story is more true; I only know that being named after one of the biggest stars of the Bible next to Moses and Abraham seems to increase others' expectations of me, whether or not they're conscious of it.

I stir around midnight and get out for a piss break. The c.o.'s are sitting up waiting in the cab of their pickup, drinking coffee from a thermos, just as they were three hours earlier. But not long after I go back to bed, they start up the engine, turn on the high-beams and drive off.

Ten minutes later, through the Conan's dusty windshield, I watch the cinnamon bear limp out of the bush to shit where the trademark spruce green Ministry pickup had been parked.

WEEK 6, DAY 7 — Cracked four grand wide open today, planting the creamiest piece of real estate I've seen all season! All day long, I was racing the quitting horn, especially since I knew we'd be pulled off the plant an hour early to unload a reefer. When Therese came by to pick me up, and saw the stack of empty trays at my cache, she said I should stay to sow up the piece, as the nursery was delivering only a half-load, and everyone else from our crew had finished their land. By the time they returned for me, I'd planted two more trays for a total of 4500 Jack pine — a whole tray more than Aleron and only one short of Walter, Kirsten, and Jaegs, I later learned when Bob took our numbers.

"You'll be planting on Clem's crew starting next shift," Therese said, handing me a frosty bottle of Northern Light after the daily production tally.

"Thanks. But what's it matter whose crew I'm on now? We're all in the same dirt. Besides, you're in cahoots with the big boss should the ground take a downturn. I've been thinking I'm well-placed right where I am."

"Same sand, different sandbox. With the numbers you're planting now you need the room to grow. But you can still hang with us after work if it's not too below your station."

For the whole day, I was one with my purpose — maybe for the first day in my life. Now I'll be planting with planters who plant as though they are one with their planting every day — who know no other purpose, who "don't think; plant," who plant for tomorrow today and every day from first bag-up before the sun's burned off the mist till their foreman hits the horn at five or five-thirty or six, as the sun begins its long, sluggish descent toward the western horizon.

CHAPTER TWENTY

DAY OFF — ON the big rock below the bridge, I finish filleting the last of three rainbows and scrape off the wood slab I've been using as a cutting board. The sun's white light splits in the prisms of their skins as guts and skeletal remains are sucked under the boiling rapids and churned up where the white water calms to a dark, gurgling green. A raven lands in the shallows of a pool along the bank to scavenge an intestine, but just as suddenly abandons its claim, flying off to an unseeable perch somewhere on the edge of camp.

"*Oso! Oso!*" Aleron's shouts echo overhead. "Everyone out — quick!"

"Get the fuck out of here, you stupid animal," Cass shrieks. "Go! Or I swear I'll bean you with this pan."

I sprint up the embankment and across the landing, crouch down behind the Conan and peer over the hood.

The bear is sitting back on his haunches right in the mouth of the big top, his cinnamon red fur ruffling in the slight breeze. Trapped inside, Cass, Aleron, Mitra and Moira are yelling and shouting, banging pots and clanging pans. But the noise is barely enough to keep him at bay.

I run around to the other side of the big top and pull two of the foremen's shovels out from under the Prairie Schooner. Hunched forward, I march on the bear, clanging the blades together.

"Move it! Now!"

He glances at me as if I'm nothing more than a minor irritation, grunts, gets up, shuffles back a few feet to one side of the entrance, sits again. Nostrils swelling and jowls dripping with drool, he waves his snout in the air to see with his nose what he can't with his eyes. He fixes his gaze on my hands — my unwashed, scale-caked fish-slimed hands — and slouches forward.

I stop clanging and slowly back away, the bear getting up to follow.

"Noah!" Aleron calls. "Make noise!"

"I'm in fish guts up to my elbows, for Chrissake. He's looking at me like I'm the goddamn dinner bell and dinner in one." I stare into the face of the bear, looking for some sign of fear in his eyes, for then our feelings would be mutual. But there is none.

The hair on the nape of my neck bristles up. My entire body starts to shake. "I'll try to lure him 'round back to the bear cage. The conservation officers who towed it into camp baited it with a bag of fish-heads."

"Forget about the cage," Cass says. "That piece of circus junk has been parked out back for the past few nights and the only thing it's caught is Jack's Newfie lab — twice."

"Then honey the damned bag. That worked well enough on your last tent, didn't it?"

Cass scowls. "My tent was hit by a falling tree, remember?"

The bear advances with slow, lumbering deliberation.

"Look, I don't have time to debate this. There should be a bucket of honey somewhere in the kitchen."

"*Later,*" she says, disappearing into the Prairie Schooner.

"Come on, Red!" I bang my shovels with renewed vigour. "Follow your pied piper ..." *Clang!* "For he's the Sugar-Daddy who'll lead you to Sweet Salivation! Or I'm a bear's breakfast." *Calanngggh!*

Backing around the circus tent, I stumble ass over tea kettle on one of the guy ropes. The shovels fly up, rebounding from the ground, but I manage to hang onto them. Eyes glued to the steadily advancing bear, I spring to my feet. *Clanghh!*

"Hey," I call as we round the big top to the back. "Haven't you finished honeying that bait yet?"

"Patience, my friend," Aleron says, crouched in the cage and pouring the last dribbles of a five-litre pail over the bag. "The door is very easily triggered."

He throws the empty pail to Cass, crawls out, and lays a trail of sandwiches down the trailer ramp.

"Not like that," Cass says. "You should've put a couple in the cage — one right under the bag."

"There's no time for that!" I shriek, banging the shovels furiously and scowling for good measure, hoping that he'll see I mean business and think twice before taking another step toward me.

Aleron tosses the last sandwich into the cage, grabs Cass by the arm and pulls her into the poplar brush; I drop one shovel at the foot of the trailer ramp and plunge after them.

The bear pauses to look around. He lowers his broad head to sniff the staff of the shovel and limps toward the foot of the ramp.

"Yes!" Cass whispers.

He licks the first sandwich, flipping it twice with his long tongue before wolfing it back. Now he ambles up the ramp, quickly snapping back the other three. But as soon as he reaches the door, he stops, turns, and lumbers back down.

Cass sits back and sighs in frustration. "He's too smart for a completely wild bear. He must've been caught and relocated before."

"Really?" Aleron says. "Would you willingly enter a cage if you were not absolutely compelled to do so? Or step into the steel that will only remind you of the trap that took your toes?"

"But we've sweetened the pot."

"The pot must be sweeter than freedom itself. By now, his shit will be blue with berries."

The cinnamon circles around to the front of the trailer, rears up on his hind legs and climbs the cage. On top, he stuffs his snout as far as he can between the bars, and with his tongue, tries to grab the rope, but the pulley wheel from which his manna has been suspended is too far out of reach, and the spaces between the bars are too narrow, even for his severed paw. He sits back, sticks his nose straight up in the air and moans.

"Look at him!" I laugh. "He's drooling for it now. He has no choice but to go in."

Holding onto the bars, the bear swings his rump down the side of the cage, and lets himself drop to the ground. He makes his way up the ramp again, hesitates, then slowly enters. Inside, he inhales the last sandwich. The honey, melting and dripping to the floor, draws his head up closer and closer to the bag. Finally, he opens his jaws; his tongue extending, curving, and twisting like a tentacle to catch the amber drops. He snuffles with pleasure, his eyes glazing over, rolling up.

Now he stops, lowers his head, and snaps his teeth shut. His eyes trace the rope from the bag through the pulley to the door. He turns. I spring from the bush to trip the stick in the hinge: the bait drops and the spring-loaded gate slams shut, catching a few hairs from the bear's tail as he bolts down the ramp and back into the forest. Sweet freedom.

CHAPTER TWENTY-ONE

WEEK 7 DAY 1 — Bob's furious. There's a hunting lodge on a lake several kilometers down the main road from the turnoff and "your gracious hosts and guides" refuse to take ownership of the bait station that Cass found in the corner of the cut block where Lyndon's crew has been working. He cut the bait and took it down to the dump along with the garbage from camp, but suspects there must be others along the treeline of the massive clear-cut, all up and down the main road and branches. To add to his worries, the c.o.'s have been here for the past three nights now, and they still haven't snagged the bear, even though the bear has kept coming. Each night, they've stayed up later and later. The first night, they left around midnight. The night before last, they stayed till one. Last night, they were here until two-thirty. But the bear always shows up ten to fifteen minutes after they drive off. It's as if the bear can smell Ministry, the Ministry in natural resources.

Week 7, Day 2 — Even though we'll sow up the rest of the cut block in two or three days and with it, the contract, we're taking extra measures to secure the food supply. Rosemary chains and padlocks the refrigerators after she's done packing up the dinner leftovers. Bob stacks the coolers in a sling net then winches them up a tree using the cable on the front of his one-ton. But this has only made the bear more determined and aggressive. Last night, he tore into the rear vestibule on Buzzard's brand new $450 Yeti dome and made off with a six-pack of Jolt Cola — so stealthily that no one heard a sound. He didn't even bother taking his spoils to his deep woods cache on the far side of the river; Rosemary found all six empties scattered around the shitters when she got up to start breakfast.

You could tell, more or less, the order in which they had been consumed. The first two cans were chewed beyond recognition — brand name or otherwise. By the third, he'd learned to use his jaws like a can opener, neatly cutting around the top and peeling it back with his teeth. Number five, he'd discovered, probably quite by accident, the tab that is conventionally used for opening a pop, only it poured too slowly for his liking; hence, the neatly placed single-toothed puncture near the base of number six, which he appeared to have shot-gunned.

"Jolt Cola — All the sugar and twice the caffeine of the leading colas," Therese read from the least chewed can. "Tabernac! Now we have a hyperactive pubescent male problem bear juiced on the most addictive stimulants known to humankind."

"That pretty much sums up most of the boys in this camp," Cass said.

"A most desirable trait in the human of the species," Rosemary said. "As long as they ply it as well in the sack as the furrow."

"Sometimes I wish more of them would ply it to something more constructive ..." Cass said, shifting her gaze to me. "Like getting Bob to tell the owner of that goddamn hunt camp to keep his sacks and buckets of bait away from here."

"Angry young men grow into grumpy old men," Therese said as if speaking to her younger Fate. "After they've hit their share of brick walls. The best you can hope for is that they'll be more practical —

and smart enough to store their pop well away from the tent. Right, Rosemary?"

Rosemary reddened. But Therese decided to go easy on Buzzard, for in his haste to sling the foodstuffs before dark, Bob had missed the two-four of Muskoka Cola under the Prairie Schooner, which, for some unknown reason, the bear left untouched.

On the morning drive, the Highballers are a lesson in Zen, in the absolute conservation of energy. Kirsten sits in the lotus position on a mat in the back, eyes shut in meditation. Aleron and Josie exchange hand massages to relieve the claw. Jaegs sits up front — pitch-black sunglasses covering the whole upper half of his face, breeze blowing back his hair, sipping an herbal power tea concocted from ginseng and other stimulants timed to kick in as soon as he steps out of the van. Jacques sleeps. Bartram snores. The only exception is Walter. I don't think Walter ever sleeps; he pounds out the beats on the seat back the way he pounds the ground, singing at the top of his lungs, albino blond hair zapping bone-straight out of his skull with the feedback of Jimi's burning guitar. His mother had probably learned as soon as he'd teethed not to feed him chocolate, but then it's precisely for this reason that he now has no need for Zen, and such a ravenous appetite for land that Clem almost always puts him in his own large piece, such as all the ground on the right side of the road.

When we pull up to the block, the side doors swing open; our trademark "Purple Haze" echoing across the cutover as we spill out and scramble for the cache, racing to be the first to bag up. Clem remains at the wheel, pours himself a cup of coffee from his truck-proof aluminum thermos.

We swarm onto the block like a stampede of panicked animals — planting into and around one another, cutting satellite lines, creaming out all the sand by the road in minutes. Then we cut up the rest like a jigsaw puzzle, each of us claiming his or her own piece. That's usually when Clem hops out of the van and starts shouting at us about leaving holes. "Neither rhyme nor reason!" he yells. But we completely ignore him; after all, no checker has been able to find a single missed spot or fineable fault in the history of this crew.

Clem's fears are understandable. The highballers each have their own styles, so you'd think that when they plant together, it would be chaos. To me, it still is, but the veterans know each other's styles so well that they can anticipate and adjust to one another on the fly. Jaegs calls it "an articulate frenzy." Bartram calls it "jazz."

We finish the day atop a plateau in the side of a large hill, gazing down on the sand flats below, on the hectares and hectares of clear-cut we've planted these past two weeks, the end still two or three days up the slope and beyond the peak, where we'll meet my old crew and Lyndon's — all converging on the same height of land. I know we're not reforesting in any true sense of the word, that a plantation of two-by-fours and bum-wad does not a forest make. But already I can see wild flowers, small shrubs and shivering aspen poking up in the peaks between the furrows, filling in some of the gaps, and I can't help but feel that we've left our mark and made it against the large-scale destruction of an indiscriminate, mechanized harvest. To the naysaying, canvassing enviro-critics who'd call us complicit, I say at least we've planted our timber frames and ass-wipe, and yours and your children's and grandchildren's, and the paper for your pamphlets.

CHAPTER TWENTY-TWO

A CONVOY OF 4X4S roars up to the big top. Doors open, slam, bottles rattle as cases are passed from man to man, their voices raised with the two to three beer each has probably downed on the way.

Rosemary groans.

"It's your desserts, you know," Cass says, depositing her dishes in the wash bin. "They really like your cheesecake."

"Don't fool yourself, honey," I say. "They're here for sweets they can't get in their camp, and — no offense — I'm not talking about Rose's desserts."

"Is that what brought you here?"

"Partly, but those log heads are all practically old enough to be your father."

Half a dozen loggers barge into the mess. George, who first discovered Rosemary's culinary delights on a solo visit a week ago, slams his two-four down on the oil-drum stove and proceeds to offer up libations.

Walter, Buzzard, and Bartram are first to the pole; Aleron and I are not far behind.

"Remains of the day are on the back table, boys," Rosemary offers before they've had a chance to ask.

The six men crowd the table, heaping generous portions of apple crisp into cereal bowls and dowsing them with Carnation. Beer in one hand, bowl in the other, George slides along a bench, supposedly to make room for his crewmates, till he's practically thigh to thigh with Mitra; the others draw patio chairs into our circle, strategically interspersing themselves among the remaining women.

Twisted cheeks, broken and missing teeth, multiple-jointed noses — each of their faces looks like it's been hit by at least one falling tree: gnarled as burly old ash trunks. One catches me staring and points to a long, jagged gouge that starts at his forehead and cuts right down the bridge of his nose. "Oh, this," he says. "An old white pine. And that's just where one of its branches scraped me. The crown dropped right down on Frank over there 'n busted his neck. Put him outta commission for nine months. Had to wear one of those haloes. See the screw scars in his temples?... Lucky, though. Damned lucky."

"Well then, the shit musta run outta mine." George opens his shirt to his belly, revealing a healed-over puncture wound the diameter of a Frost fence post. "This is where I was damn near impaled by a spruce top that kicked up under the wheel of my skidder and punched through the door." He rebuttons his shirt and sparks up a tailor-made. "So," he blows his smoke. "We hear you've got a little problem."

"Oh?" Cass says. "Who told you that?"

"Our crew boss says you've got a problem bear."

"I guess you could say we've been having some problems settling on boundaries. But he was here first and we'll be done and gone in another couple of days, so —"

"Boundaries?" George laughs. "That's a quaint way of putting being in the thick of a territorial dispute with a bear. And to a problem bear, well, your encroachment in his neck of the woods looks a lot like a declaration of war."

"You know what we do with a problem bear, eh?" says the one with the scar carved down his nose. "I tell you, we had five come 'round our camp last winter. We dropped 'em all."

That word again — *dropped* — so casually into conversation. Bob told us of a sow who'd *dropped* a cinnamon bear every year, as if giving birth could ever be as easy as dropping bears with high-powered rifles, or dropping entire forests with all-in-one harvesters, delimbers and stackers. Drop of death; drop of life. The paradox must be in the blood. The connection must be in the falling action.

Scowling, Aleron sits his beer on the oil drum. "What do you kill them for? I have seen your camp. You live in bunkhouses and trailers. Your kitchen and mess are indoors."

"They get into the garbage, that's what for," says Frank, who still bears faint tan marks indicating where screws had held his halo in place. "They're pests, just like the 'coons and skunks."

"Skunks?"

"Shoot a skunk and it'll only stink once." He laughs.

Aleron downs his beer and slams his empty on the drum. "If you try to shoot the bear, I will stand in the path of your gun."

Frank rises and, grinning, sights Aleron through the scope of an imaginary rifle. "You know, buddy, you ought to be sure of who you're talking to before you go shootin' your mouth off. You never know who might be tempted to take you up on your offer." He squeezes his imaginary trigger.

"Frank." A pot-bellied man with a very red face and a salt and pepper crewcut is standing in the entrance, holding a real rifle. "Si' down."

The big top falls silent. Cass eyes me nervously. I pull my chair across the circle to her side.

"Are you deaf or something?"

Frank slowly eases back into his chair. "Hey, that looks like my gun."

"It is. Got a problem with that?"

"I don't remember you asking."

"Friends borrow, Frank — sometimes without asking. But I'm your crew boss."

"It's alright Joe. Be careful with it, eh? It's brand new." He turns to Aleron. "This shrubbie here's from Greenpeace or somethin'. He says he won't let us take care of the bear."

"You spike trees too, kid? Eh?" Scarnose says. "Or have those llamas on your hat been grazing on your brain? Get your fucking priorities straight. We cut 'em and you plant 'em. You don't have a job without us."

"I think you are mistaken," Aleron says. "Without us, you will be out of work in another twenty years."

"I'll be retired by then."

"So will your children," Cass says.

"Oooh, look —" Scarnose jeers. "It's Mother Nature in the flesh."

"You know," I cut in. "With smarts like yours, it's a wonder you haven't made foreman."

"You wanna take this outside, wise-ass?"

Cass pinches each cheek of the offensive organ. "Your ass is so wise it deserves the Nobel," she whispers.

The screw marks that has held the halo to Frank's forehead redden. "No use in wasting your breath on him, Chuck. Chicky here's obviously the one wearing the pants. Got something to say, little lady?"

I clear my throat. "The lady was just saying that whoever's manning the guns is doing a half-assed job. He missed the porcupine that quilled the camp sled dog, and twice failed to cite the Newfie lab for taking the bait in the cage, which robbed us of our best chance to capture the bear without having to shoot it first. And then there's that ruffed grouse — still beating about the bush for a mate, or beating off 'cause he can't find one — and a really shrill loon maybe about a click downstream. Noisy creatures. They keep us up all night."

"Outside, dumbfuck!"

Cass giggles. "So that's why you've been acting so dumb lately."

"Let me handle this, Frank," Joe says. The burly crew boss crosses the floor to the oil drum and leans Frank's gun against the centrepole. "Look, I take no pleasure in having to destroy a majestical animal, but I've been working in logging camps for close to twenty years, and I've seen enough problem bears to know that if you don't put your foot down, someone's gonna get hurt. From what your foreman's told me, you've got a problem bear. He's not at all afraid of people, and he's getting bolder by the day."

"Which foreman told you that?" Cass says.

"Lyndon."

"Really? Did Lyndon also tell you the bear's been treed by a dog that's less than one-tenth its weight?"

"He's afraid of dogs now, but each time a dog chases him or trees him and nothing happens, he learns to be less and less afraid. Sooner or later, he's bound to turn around and clout that mutt across the jaw. That's all it would take to break its neck."

"Listen," George chimes in. "You've got a problem bear, right? Nobody's doin' nothin' about it — not Bob, not the MNR. You're all losing a lot of sleep and your camp's being torn apart. Your safety is our concern."

"Then let the MNR stay here until they can catch and move him," Cass says.

"The MNR? I'll tell you two things about the MNR. They can catch 'im and move 'im to Timbukfuckin'tu and he's still likely to find his way back here. Number two — unlike the MNR, we'll wait up here all night, and the next night and the next — whatever it takes."

Cass stands. "I appreciate your concern, but it's not problem bears that worry me — it's problem people. You see, I have a battle scar of my own ..." With both hands, she grabs her shirt at the collar and yanks it open. Buttons fly off in all directions, popping halo man in the nose and Scarnose in the eye. She allows just a glimpse of her palm-sized breasts, then turns her back to them, her shirt sliding down her arms, bunching at her wrists. "A bear left that claw mark on my shoulder, but the men who baited it were the problem ..."

"I'm in love," I whisper to her back.

Aleron smiles, eyes tearing. "I think I'm in love too."

I return to our tent site, lower the knapsack containing our toiletries from the branch, quickly brush my teeth, and haul the sack back up. I sit on a fallen tree until dusk finally sets in enough to let my spirit rest, though I know I won't sleep until the last light melts from the edge of the sky around eleven.

"Come to bed," Cass calls from the tent.

I kneel and open the fly.

"Quick," she says. "I just finished killing all the mosquitoes."

I dive in and she zips up behind me.

"Are you sure you don't wanna sleep in the Conan again?"

"It's too cramped and dirty," she says. "Besides, I'm getting used to Cinnamon's visitations."

"If he comes, it'll be bullets flying, not tranq darts. Those log heads are smashed out of their skulls."

She sighs. "I know we shouldn't sleep here, but I'm so sore and tired, and there's no privacy. ... Come here and cuddle up ..."

I roll into her arms. Stroking her hips, I marvel at their soft flesh and sudden bone. "On moving day," I whisper, "We'll get up early and paddle downriver to picnic on that rock." I rub her shovel shoulder, and she groans and winces and smiles in cadence with the stages I work out the knots.

She rolls onto her chest. My fingers follow the river of her spine to the two knobby little bones just above her bum.

"Noah?"

"Yes?"

"Do you think it'll still be there?"

"The cliff? The cluster of pines? Of course."

"No — I mean, do you think it'll still be the same?"

"More or less. Hopefully better."

"Better? Didn't you say it's better to be nomadic — to move on before the magic of a place dies in your head or heart?"

"I said perfection, but I like magic even better. It makes you forget that a place you were at wasn't perfect."

She tenses and rolls onto her side to look me in the eye. "Are you saying you remember it differently from me?"

"Looking back, we could've done without the flies."

"Is that all that stuck in your mind about that day?"

For the first time, I'm aware that something I said days ago has been worrying her ever since.

Taking her hand, I kiss the lifeline in her palm. "If that's all I remembered, I wouldn't have suggested going back there. And if the magic is gone from there, we'll find it someplace else — together."

We're picnicking atop the cliff, sprawled out together on Cass's down sleeping bag, popping blueberries the size of wine grapes into each other's mouths as we watch the sun peek in and out of the swift-sailing glacial clouds. "Perfect day for a swim," I say. Cass smiles. "Maybe we should go for ice cream." A loud bang rings out from somewhere over the pine grove, followed by a flash, the clouds suddenly swirling shut like the aperture on a camera. Lightning. "Stay down," I say. Another strike, the bang louder and more synchronized with the flash. An enraged wail cuts through the woods, followed by men's whooping and hollering.

I bolt upright, the clifftop killed by consciousness.

Shrieking, Cass sits up and points. "They've shot him." Her voice is trembling and teary.

"I heard a shot, but —"

"He's wounded."

Sounds of aimless crashing, the fear of being hunted, converge on the tent. His breathing is hard and arrhythmic and strained; his moaning like a suppressed bark — a *woof* stopped between lips and teeth, then allowed to escape in a puff of breath. He sounds like he's trying not to be heard.

Flashlight beams weave in and out of the trunks, throwing the shadows of leaves and needles and branches across the tent fly. I can hear Innuk and Becky sniffing and panting frantically as he pads through the moss and sparse underbrush.

"Where's he at?" asks the voice of the man who'd worn a halo.

"Over here!" Scarnose calls hoarsely. "Look — blood."

"There he is! There!"

Two deafening cracks, bullets whizzing by our tent, splintering wood. The bear wails, lets go a weak growl and begins to run. But his flight's reduced to a stumble.

"Hit 'im?"

"Missed. But he's tiring."

Cass reaches for the zipper.

"No!" I grab her by the wrist and yank her hand away.

"Let go Noah."

"It's too dangerous."

"You don't think I know that already? My eyes are in his bloody head, and I can't get out. We've got to stop this."

A bright beam sweeps back and forth across the vent on the rear flap.

"Watch it! There's another one here, Joe," says the man who'd worn a halo.

"Jesus, there must be fifty goddamn shrubbies in these woods."

Another shot.

Bartram shrieks.

A loud thump. Everything stops.

"Got 'im!" the crew boss shouts.

"Nice shot," Scarnose says.

"Right behind the ear," halo man says.

Cass weeps. I swallow, but it's like swallowing blood, choking on clots. I just feel sick and empty.

"Ey! 'Ey, *tête a merde!*" Buzzard's yelling. "You shitheads shoot all over the forest like no one was here."

"Back off, buddy."

I reach for the zipper, and now Cass grabs my hand. "We'll go together. No circuses, okay?"

"I'm not here for the scenery anymore. These dumbfucks are wrecking it."

The night is moonless, but we can see them in the now static weave of flashlights — the man who'd worn a halo, holding his rifle in both hands, trying to walk away, Buzzard grabbing his shirt sleeve, trying to pull him back, halo man jerking free.

"Hey," Buzzard grips onto his shoulder and swings him around. "What are you going to do with the bear? The MNR could seize our camp if they see it, lying there like that. You should take it away on your truck ..."

"You're a planter. You bury it." He releases the barrel of his rifle and shoves Buzzard back a few steps. "Ain't that what you shrubbies do with your trees anyways? Dig a big hole 'n bury them — more than ten at a time, from what I've heard."

Buzzard lunges forward but halo man cross-checks him with the gun, then butt-ends him in the chest. Winded, possibly broken-ribbed, Buzzard crumples to the ground, gasping.

"Buzzard!" I crouch down to help him up, but he's rolling around, coughing, clutching the side of his ribcage.

"That your name kid — Buzzard? Well, Buzzard, next time you pull a stunt like that I'll break your fuckin' beak. Got it?" He jabs the butt of his rifle at Buzzard's face, stopping a centimetre from his nose. "Got it?"

Aleron steps out of the dark, the light glinting off the edge of his drawn machete as he touches its cold, broad, curved tip to the back of halo man's neck. "Back where I come from, this is what we use as a Swiss army knife. A single blade, so many purposes. I kept it sharp for beating back the jungle, and if necessary, my enemies. How it will be used in this neck of the woods is your decision."

"He's got a fuckin' bolo knife?" halo man says.

"No Frank," his crew boss says. "A machete."

"A machete. What the fuck do you think we're playing at here, eh? Indiana Jones?"

"Doctor Jones was facing his opponent — hardly a fair set-up for a duel between a man bearing a sword and one pointing a gun. But in case you doubt the strength of its bite, this machete has cut down trees much thicker than your neck."

"Aleron — don't," Cass pleads.

"You will unload your gun and give it to my friend. Noah, stand up please."

"It ain't loaded."

"Do it, Frank," his crew boss says.

Frank extends both arms, offering up the rifle.

"You're sure it's not loaded?" I say.

He nods. "Never handled a weapon before, eh?"

"Never a gun."

"I'll take that," Bob says, stepping into the stand-off. "If you want it back, you'll have to return tomorrow to remove that carcass."

Frank crosses his burly arms over his barrelled chest. "Your foreman invites us in here to do what should've been done the minute you spotted that bear and now that we've done the dirty work for you, you treat us like we're the scum of the earth? I've a good mind to report you to the union for this."

Resting his forearm against a tree, Bob leans forward, getting his face right in Frank's. "I'm the supervisor here, not my foremen. *Capiche*? If you want to tell the union about how you came here uninvited by me, and pissed to the gills, started shooting all over the place at two in the morning, be my guest. Now get the fuck out of my camp."

Joe and Scarnose hustle Frank — the man who'd worn a halo for nine months for cutting the wrong tree — out to the landing.

"Watch out for spotchecks," I call after them.

The truck doors slam, and they screech down the road, punching their horns till they're out of earshot.

The corpse is sprawled out on its side, its jaw hanging half-open, the pads of its three good feet sticking straight out, the remaining toes on the fourth curled inward as if it had been limping, its red coat mottling in the morning light that passes through the trees.

"Thank God its eyes are closed," Cass says.

I stroke its fur and feel its claws and find the bullet hole of the fatal shot behind the ear. "I hope we won't have to carry it all the way out to the road."

Cass begins to retrace its path from Bartram's blood-sprayed tent — the site of the final shot. "It came through the underbrush here ... It. ... Funny how corpses lose their sex."

We follow the drops of blood and bloody paw prints that stain the moss, and the blood-tipped leaves and needles he fled through: out to the road, around the big top, past the Prairie Schooner, to the bear cage. Up the ramp. ... Inside.

CHAPTER TWENTY-THREE

UNDER THE BARREN shelter of a dead pine tree limb, a fly-covered, blood-stained burlap bag twists in the breeze, unfurling a stench far worse than the bear's.

"See how high it hangs?" Aleron says. "A consolation prize for the trophy that can reach it. Look, the blind is right above it." He draws his machete and with one swipe — *thak!* — cuts the bait from the twine, Cass catching it in her outspread arms.

"God it's ripe," she says, wrinkling up her nose. "Here, Noah, you'd better take it before I start to smell more attractive to the bears than to you."

I try dragging the bloated bag along the crude path by its cinched-up top, but by the time I reach the road, it's threatening to burst and spill its rotting contents on the shoulder. Holding my breath, I wave off the flies, pick it up in my arms, stagger it onto the tailgate of the Conan, and shove it under the cap, right between the baits we stole from the first two stations. High noon. Flies and the stench of death overdone. Three sacks of sundry animal remains, seasoned with egg shells, bacon fat and vegetable peels, and however many more bags or buckets of bait we find by the telltale pickup tracks in the sandy

170

shoulders of the road between camp and the turnoff for the lake. All for deposit on the boat launch of the Bull's Eye Hunting Lodge.

Back at the bait station, Cass is climbing a ladder of bark slabs up the pine that houses the camouflaged blind, a hammer in her belt, a sheet of paper in her teeth. Aleron is sitting back against a fat white spruce, scribbling a note on a clipboard he took from the dash.

"What are you doing?"

He passes the sheet to me. "A thank-you note for our hosts."

Bang bang bang, Cass's hammer rings.

Shooting a baited bear is like abducting a kid from a mall.

Faint lines run like veins under the surface of the page. I flip the sheet over. "Shit, Aleron. It's bad enough that you're rubbing their noses in it, but on the back of a fucking forestry map?"

"His is pretty tame compared to mine," Cass says, dropping from the last rung to the ground. "*Shooting a baited bear is kinda like luring Lolitas with lollipops.*"

"Nice alliteration, but I think you're missing the point. You're leaving hate mail on maps of the cuts we've planted."

"So ..."

"So? Here," I snatch the pen from Aleron's hand and hold it out to her. "You may as well be leaving your autograph."

Aleron clears his throat. "You surprise me, wanker. Did you chain yourself to trees under a false name?"

"Alias Dudley Do-Right," Cass says.

"This isn't a joke," I stammer. "I'm already facing charges of vandalism and criminal mischief for that bullshit the university trumped up about me bashing in the teeth on a fucking bulldozer, not to mention contempt of fucking court for violating a court order. If we draw heat up here, they'll start running names through their database, and — poof! — I'll wake up to find my ass in the back of an OPP cruiser, sailing to Thunder Bay on a sea of other charges, including criminal mischief and defamation of character for comparing bear hunters to pedophiles!"

"Relax ..." Cass says. "We're leaving for Armstrong tomorrow."

"Where they'll find us if you insist on leaving those notes."

"You think you've got worries? Aleron hasn't even had his refugee hearing yet. He could be deported."

"And you'd let him take that risk?"

"Noah —"

"I am perfectly able to decide for myself," Aleron says. "I have freely chosen to do this, as is my right."

"Your choice can't be free, Aleron, if you're not fully informed or aware of the consequences. Of all of us, you have the most to lose. What about Cass?"

Her eyes tear up. "How could you even think that I wouldn't lose if they sent you to jail? Or if Aleron were sent back? I'd be so angry that you'd be front page news every day."

"Did you ever ask me if I want to be?"

"Noah, I was nearly killed by a bear that was trained to eat our food. The same stupid practices lured a genetically rare bruin into this camp, spoiled him, and ultimately killed him. If you go to jail for trying to stop bear baiting, especially around work camps, there'll be so much public outcry —"

"That they'll have to release me? Tell that to the judge. The MNR pulls in half a grand on every bear tag they sell to a Yank, and the lodges, hotels and taverns a hell of a lot more. My days of martyrdom are over. I'm not going to be put in a cage again — ever."

Aleron sheaths his machete. "What will you do to avoid capture for standing up for your beliefs — hide out in a church basement, join the foreign legion, plant trees for the rest of your life? Or will you just abandon them like orphans?"

"Look, I don't want to bail on either of you, but we have to tone down this action. Even if you don't give a damn about what happens to us, don't forget what we told Bob. We're borrowing the Conan to run the garbage to the dump now so that we can load it up with camp gear tonight and get up to Armstrong as early as possible tomorrow. How do you think he'll feel about his truck being impounded as evidence?"

"Bob will explain everything that led up to this," Aleron says. "He and Therese are old granolas with big hearts and they can talk their way out of anything. Besides, hunters from that lodge put baits near our camp and some by the ground we were planting. Do you really think they would call the police?"

"The hunters are a cash cow. Besides, as far as the law is concerned, one crime doesn't justify the commission of another, not even in retaliation."

"As far as I'm concerned," Cass says, "a message has to be sent, and we should have the guts to say who it's from."

"The hunters don't have to know who cut their baits — if they're all cut, word'll get around to the logging camp, and they'll know who; they just won't have any proof. But if we leave our fingerprints all over this, at best, the MNR will be called in to investigate and we'll all go down, and at worst, we'll be visited by a bunch of pissed up, pissed off hunters."

"Let them visit," Aleron says. With a rock and a salvaged nail, he hammers his declaration to the dead pine. "I have run to the edge of the world and I will not be pushed off it. I will no longer be a fugitive from myself."

CHAPTER TWENTY-FOUR

ARMSTRONG

DUNES. WE HAVE to wear dark glasses to keep the sand and its glare out of our eyes. We have to brush the sand off our plates before we heap them high with dinner.

Bob says that it's because of the microclimate. Two weather fronts constantly rub up against one another, producing a pressure ridge — a great divide in the sky walled in by clouds. Storm clouds unlike any I've seen before, all swimming around that big blue eye, which (according to bait shop lore) has stayed wide open for over a month. That eye, Bob says, is why it hasn't rained here all spring.

Cass thinks the eye is a tiny pocket of an ozone hole that's gone undiscovered: though the only one she's heard about is over Antarctica, she suspects there must be one over our Arctic too. Maybe the earth's rotation on its axis swirls the atmosphere around, causing all holes to collect at the poles, she says.

Aleron's dubbed this place "Armpit." He says he heard that when you slash and burn a huge chunk of rain forest, it stops raining there, over the bare spot. So why not here, over a northern clear-cut? Trees make their own rain, he says, as surely as they breathe.

Lyndon starts his chainsaw to fell a tree for the centrepole.

Cass drops the pots she's been unpacking from the cupboards. "The white pine? Has he lost his mind!"

"It isn't very large," I say, battening down the tarp on the Prairie Schooner. "Far from old growth."

"For Chrissake, Noah, it's the only tree standing on our site." She squeezes past me down the steps. "Hey!" she yells over the drone. "Don't you think it might be nice to have at least one green thing standing closer than a quarter mile from the mess?"

Lyndon idles the saw till it sputters and coughs to a stop. "What?"

"I was just thinking how great it would be to leave that tree where it is — you know, to perk up the scenery a bit ... maybe for a little shade." She sticks her hands in her pockets, and shifting from one foot to the other, toes the sand; first in no particular pattern, then, as she looks down, drawing sideways figure 8s. "Besides, that tree's got a lot of cones in it — future babies."

Lyndon smirks. "Hah. Well, if you wanna haul a log from around the other side of the lake, go ahead — be my guest." He holds out the saw in a gesture of white offering.

"Lyndon." Cass puts her hands on her hips.

"Time's up." He yanks the starter cord again and lurches toward the trunk.

"Lyndon!" She steps forward.

"Heads!" he bellows, levelling the biting teeth into the trunk; dry then pulpy sawdust flies out till all that remains is a thin lip of wood and bark. He cuts the motor and gives the tree a shove.

The pine leans away from him a bit, then hangs up in the air, the wind shifting and shifting, blowing in crazy ways. Finally, the tree teeters, but instead of falling straight down it falls into a slow spin; gyrating counter-clockwise (the sound of grass skirts in ecstatic dance) in a circle so tight it appears to vibrate from butt to top, the cone it's cutting through the air ever widening in circumference, the needles whooshing as the trunk sweeps out and spirals down — our eyes are transfixed, our feet unable to break the circle of its spell.

"Jump!" Bob yells.

I throw myself up against Cass: we crumple into a tumble of limbs down a dune, my face spinning up to catch a glimpse of the pine plummeting after Lyndon, its crown reaching for, catching his ass.

"I'm hit," he yowls. "I'm hit!"

Cass scrambles to her feet, gives me a hand up. Buzzard and Aleron, who've been lying flat on their bellies, fingers knitted over their heads, move to get up too. But Bob's already there, hunched over Lyndon, who's pinned under the pine's cone-heavy crown.

He has sand on his lips. His jeans are ripped right down his left leg from seat to mid-thigh, and he's bleeding from a long scratch that deepens to a gouge in his pale ass-cheek. He wipes his mouth with his wrist, looks up at Bob, and now at Cass. He keeps his eyes glued to her as he squirms out from under the tree's top and stands.

"Never, never rush a man when he's cutting a tree." He jabs his shaking index at her face. "Understand?"

"Lyndon ..." I drop my hand on his shoulder to restrain him, but he throws me off with an angry shrug.

"Understand?"

"I didn't —" Cass shakes too, but more like the tree had. "I stopped."

He turns to Bob, still pointing at Cass. "She's danger, man. A walking menace. She nearly had me killed."

Bob looks from one to the other, from his enraged eyes, to hers, blurring with suppressed tears. "The three of us will talk about it later," he says. "Right now we've got a camp to get up. Lyndon, go see Tim about that leg. What are the rest of you gawking at?"

"But Lyndon —" Cass' voice breaks. "How could you think —? It was random." She bursts into tears and runs off toward the lake.

I don't know if I should follow, or leave her to whatever island she might find. The one lush island at the centre of a lake surrounded by deforested pine barrens. The islands she retreats to in her water-colours when she's too damned proud to let anyone tend to her wounds, especially not a man, especially not her lover.

"You should go after her," Aleron says, looking at me as if he can hear every one of my thoughts.

"In a few minutes. She needs time."

"Do you want me to speak with her?"

"Maybe we both should. Lately she's been feeling a bit overwhelmed by all the lumberjocks." I smile. "You miss your girlfriend ..."

"I love to cook for her."

"And I bet she loves to be cooked for."

"Beans, spicy fish, a bottle of red wine from Chile ..."

"A warm bed."

He nods.

"You'll cook for her again, sooner than later I'm sure."

"I only hope the land on all of our blocks will be as good as it is here."

He fixes his eyes on the south, and I turn mine northwest, toward our small lake.

By the time I've crossed the hot dunes to the shore, she's paddled Bob's canoe halfway to the island.

"Cass!" I call. "Hey Cass!"

But she just keeps paddling.

I strip down but stop at my underwear when I notice the leeches choking the shallows where the lake is lapping at my feet.

CHAPTER TWENTY-FIVE

THROUGH THE SIDE mirror, the dust trail Bob leaves in our wake extends as far back as the most distant hill. Somewhere in the thick clouds that plume out behind us are the rest of the crummies in our fleet, their passengers sweltering, dying to crank down all the windows, choking on dust when they do. But even though the road lies clear and open before the white one-ton, the wind generated by our motion scorches our lungs as severely as any sun-baked silt, so we choose to seal ourselves against it and dream of an air-conditioned rental, or maybe just ice.

Blocking the road to the next site of the contract is a spruce green pickup bearing the logo of the Ministry of Natural Resources. Bob stops a foot off its fender and winds down his window to greet the woman in the matching green jacket.

"Dagmar. Didn't expect to be seeing you till the reefer." He shakes her hand. "The Cyclops blocks are about five clicks beyond this turnoff, right?"

"Road's closed."

"What's up?"

"Napalm drop."

Bob removes his sunglasses and raises a brow. "Really? It's a little dry for a prescribed burn ..."

"That's what I thought, too." She shuffles through the papers attached to her clipboard. "But a week of rain is in the forecast, and we've added another sprinkler line and a few extra bodies around the perimeter of the cut to contain the burn." Finally, she hands Bob a crisp site map that just smells of office. "Since Cyclops will be closed till the burn's declared dead, I was thinking you could get a head start on the chem-blocks up Calypso Creek. The reefer's waiting for you there."

Bob grits his teeth, tapping the eraser end of his pencil against his oversized incisors. "I was hoping we could save Calypso for overflow."

Dagmar pastes on a smile. "That's what the last two contractors said. And did. But hey," she pats his shoulder. "She might even be done with you before the contract's out. See you there when I'm finished here." She winks and returns to her truck.

Bob backs up the one-ton, turns up the left prong of the fork and radios the others to follow. His face is too expressionless to be trusted.

"What the hell was that all about?" I ask.

"They've set us up. They're sending us into the worst rockpile this side of Sudbury and it wasn't even the main piece on the bid."

"No — I mean that part about a napalm drop."

Walter emerges from the rear seat, yawns and grins. "I love the smell of napalm in the morning. Smells like forestry."

"What's she mean?"

"Exactly what it sounds like. The MNR's sending in the cavalry to firebomb a cutaway."

"What for?"

"Prescribed burn. Jack pine cones go off like popcorn in a fire, spewing their seed all over the warm, fertile ash. The chemical industry's answer to natural regen and the peace dividend."

Bob shifts in his seat as if he's got an itch that can't be scratched in public. "It's more likely the government and the logging companies' way of saving themselves the expense of paying s.o.b.'s like us to do a mass planting by hand."

"Same difference. The Pentagon wanted a cost-effective way of frying the Vietnamese and the MNR wants cost-efficient reforestation."

"Some similarity," Bob says. "Anyway, it wouldn't be the first time something developed for the military has been put to better use in a civilian application."

"I'll give you that." Walter leans over the seat back. "So, what did they *apply* to the chem-blocks this time, Bob? Round-up or Vision?"

"What's it matter to you?"

"Oh, I dunno — maybe that Vision does the same number on paradise as 2,4-D or Agent Orange."

"Agent Orange?" I turn to Bob. "He's shittin' me, right?"

"He's certainly full enough of it to be."

"Am I? You want the real dirt on Vision? Rather than killing a tree outright, it causes its leaf cells to grow out of control until they literally explode. Never mind what it might be doing to the birds and the bees and the frogs. I really shouldn't be scaring the greenhorns. Now don't you worry your head none, son," he winks at me. "Ranger Bob here is right: it doesn't matter what they're using, Round-Up or Vision. I can't say which'll make your testicles pop faster. You know, I haven't seen Vision for years, and I kinda miss it. A little douse and I could see for miles and miles ... far enough to round up every last critter for miles around. As long as I didn't get none in my eyes."

Bob slams on the brakes and turns to face Walter head-on. "So what are you saying, eh Westerley? You're finally hanging up your shovel because you're scared you'll end up carting your ever-growing balls around in a wheelbarrow? Fuck, after all the years of planting and smoking we've clocked, it's a little late to be worrying now."

"I'd just like to know what I'm going into for a change."

"He's right Bob," I say. "I'd like to know too."

"Vision. Aerial application. Spray date: two summers ago — way more than enough time for it to go inert and wash away."

"If it snows as much as it rains 'round here, there'd have been nothing to wash a car, let alone a cutaway."

"I'm telling you it's inert as a dead parrot. But if you want to know more about why we need Vision, the site prescription's in my trailer."

"See what I mean? The *prescription*," Walter says. "As if the whole forest's a sick patient. Well what are we curing it of? Poplar over-growth from being clear-cut?"

"If you'd rather be planting through fields of eye-high sticks, you can have all the spots the sprayer missed."

"Is this Vision stuff safe?" I ask.

Smirking, Bob lights a cigarette. "Safer than simizine, and they also used that to kill foot fungus in swimming pools."

Calypso Creek: if the loggers had named her in honour of her once-green luxuriance, of the life that had fucked and mated itself into an impassibly thick frenzy, now her name can only refer to the eon she'll let pass before she lets us go.

The ground is hard, fool's cream: a thin layer of sand over solid Shield. The only signs of her past life, left in the wake of the two summers and three winters that have passed since she was sprayed, are the residual patches of dense, matted brush that dot the gullies, and the thin, trickling sound of a dried-up creek that surfaces here and there from somewhere beneath the choke of slash.

The sun never slips behind a cloud, for no cloud ever strays into our eye of sky, and the wind is hot, but it's bugless enough to work topless. Across from where Aleron and I have been toiling, way atop an outcrop of rock, Cass and Mitra stop to apply another layer of Umbrelle. Mitra is a sun-worshipper in an age when the word is synonymous with death, but her dark olive skin isn't likely to burn readily. Despite her tanned face, Cass's body is so fair that I'm surprised to see her doffing her shirt. Mitra has barely finished slathering Cass's ivory back (spreading extra sunscreen over her bear scar as if it's a particularly vulnerable birthmark) when Buzzard crosses their flag line into the small patch of cream at the front of their piece.

"Hey!" Mitra yells. "Get back on your own side."

Buzzard doesn't even look up; he just keeps satelliting a line right along the furrow that demarcates glacial silt from Shield.

Mitra plants as quickly as she can toward him, her shovel pinging and clanging and ringing against the rock cap. "Hey creamer! Get the fuck off our land. Now!"

Cass doesn't say a word. She storms up along the crest of a furrow, climbs atop a boulder and stands tall, holding her planting spear in one hand and a rock in the other.

"Buzzard." She hisses through clenched teeth.

But he continues creaming them out as if the blowing sands of the past few days have filled his ears.

Squinting, Cass takes careful aim and launches her stone in a shallow parabolic curve, hitting the D-handle of Buzzard's shovel with a crack that knocks it right from his hand.

He looks at her, standing way up there on the boulder, bare-breasted, spear held ready for chucking, eyes blazing in the fierce heat of the one o' clock sun. "*You're stealing my tuition*," her eyes say. "*My food, my clothes, my shelter for this Fall.*"

Rattled, he picks up his shovel and hightails it back across the ribbon to his side.

Aleron and I bag out and break for lunch. Several planters from Lyndon's crew are sitting at the cache — Mitra on a log, Tim and Judd, whom I've barely spoken with all season, in the dust road —

drawing pictures in the sand with sticks, maybe hoping they'll petrify.

Going to Hell with Full Bags, Mitra writes below her drawing: a stick figure wearing seedling-packed bags and carrying a shovel. *I hate my 24 hour living girdle.* Smiling, Aleron sits down beside her and pulls a plum from his knapsack.

"Where's Cass and Buzzard?" I ask.

"Cass is way in the back of our piece," Mitra says. "Still a few trees from bagging. And Buzzard — I dunno, but last I saw of him he was heading for the van. Probably gone to lick his wounds in private."

"Joining us?" Judd asks.

"I'll be right back. I left my lunch at the other cache."

I stroll down the road to get my knapsack and refill my canteen from the ten-gallon jug in the back of the van.

"Noah. Over here." Buzzard's squatting on a roadside stump — the way Lyndon squats when he's spying on his planters to catch stashers — arms wrapped around his knees, so still I'd walked right by him.

"They're all drawing lotsa nice pictures, eh?" He nods in the direction of the other cache.

"Cartoons, jokes — graffiti, I guess."

"Cartoons and jokes. ... Any of me?"

"None that I could see."

"You know something? You make a very bad liar." He hops off his stump, selects a stick from a slash pile, steps up to Cass's pack, and starts carving large letters in the road, gouging deeper and deeper till, tapping into the earth's little remaining moisture, his word darkens to legibility: C-U-N-

Crossing the T, he looks me in the eye. "So ... what d'ya think the women would think of this?"

"Oh ..." I clear my throat. "You mean Cass. Why don't you ask her yourself? Or is she already too much for you at fifty paces?" I shoulder my knapsack and walk back to lunch with the others.

We pull into camp around dragonfly hour. We live for the moment when the sun has dropped enough to release the first sorties of dragonflies from their shady places of siesta. They fly in squadrons, breaking up somewhere overhead to dive down on the deerflies that have been cutting chunks of flesh from our bodies for the four to six runs that pass between the sun's daily equinox and late afternoon. Only sex and eating could be more satisfying than the plucking sensation of a deerfly being snapped from your arm or head. And the dragonflies know it: sometimes, after grabbing up their meal, they'll eat it in mid-air, hovering there at eye-level as if waiting to be thanked. Your predator; their prey.

But Clem pulled us off the hill early because the crew began dropping like flies from the forty-five degree heat and an outbreak of diarrhea and vomiting that's spreading through the camp and has so far spared me — knock on wood. As soon as Clem's taken my number, I spring from the Hendrix van and rush for the lake, leaving a trail of clothes behind me as I strip for my swim.

I dive into the piss-warm shallows, swim out for cooler water, backfloat offshore of the islet in its middle. Steve and Daniel had the runs so bad they went through a roll of toilet paper between them. Aleron spewed his cookies and plums, and Moira was so disoriented with sunstroke that Lyndon found her staggering around lost in a finger of land at the back of her piece and drove her home at two. Still, I wonder if it's really just too much sun, or the chem-blocks, breathing Calypso's sand and dust.

I swim back to shore, lie back in the hot sand of the dunes, shut my eyes, dream of a bigger eye closing: dark and heavy clouds circling in, the sudden drop in pressure, a breeze, the burst. Rain warm, then tepid, then cold. Scooping hailstones off the sagging big top and putting them in our drinks.

"That fucking bastard!" Cass's voice approaches from our tent.

I sit up. She practically rips off her basketball jersey and shorts, and when she kicks off her Birkenstocks, she sends one soaring into the lake.

"Watch out for the leeches," I say. "They're heat-seeking. They're probably lining the shore as you speak."

"You know what he did?" She sputters, wading in after her sandal. "You know what that stupid little worm did today?"

"Who?"

"All day long he's riding my ass about quality — as if he can tell every one of my trees from Mitra's. At noon he drags me way into the back of the block to plant a huge rock cap we'd skipped over, and by the time I get out of there, it's nearly quitting time. When I finally get back to the cache for lunch, I see he's left a love letter by my pack —" She squints into the water, bends down, plucks out her missing cork clog. "'cunt' is all it said. cunt in big capital letters, and he didn't even have the guts to admit to writing it. So I picked up a stick and wrote a word of my own, and drew an arrow between lower case *prick* and his feet, just so there'd be no mistake. Now he says he's going to get Bob to fire me."

I sit up, groaning. "There was a mistake. I can see why you'd think Lyndon's guilty — he's sure given you a hard time since his brush with that tree you didn't want him cutting. But it was Buzzard."

"How do you know?"

"I saw him. Actually, he called me over to watch."

"So what did you do?"

"I let him know I wasn't impressed 'n left him to stew in his own juices. Boy is he paranoid. He thinks the whole camp's out to get him. I think he was trying to test me."

Cass looks at me like I'm a stranger. "You? He was testing a lot more than you. He obviously wanted to get back at me for chasing him out of our cream."

"Well, you did chuck that rock at him, and being a biker, he's not gonna take that lying down."

"Unlike you, who won't even lift as much as a finger when someone harasses your girlfriend right in front of your nose."

"What?"

"Can't you see how much damage this has done? When Lyndon got his back up, I thought he was putting on an act, and now I've given him another excuse to hate me that much more. And what did you do? Turn on your heels and walk away — tail between your legs — when you could've prevented the whole thing."

My jaw drops open. "That's not at all true and you know it."

Cass whips the Birkenstock at my head — just missing — and storms past me toward our tent.

"Wait —"

"You could've erased the word. That would've spoken volumes and might've saved me the grief of duking it out with Lyn."

"Knowing Buzzard, kicking dirt over his word would've been as good as kicking sand in his eyes."

"What's wrong with that? You're a big enough boy. I'm sure you could've handled him easily in a toe-to-toe, maybe as easily as I did with a stone from the top of a hill."

"That's just it. You don't need any Sir Galahad. I wouldn't have been doing you any favours playing diplomat by covering up Buzzard's problem. I did the best thing I could think of — left him to chew on his own words."

She turns at the vestibule of her tent. "Baa-a-ba-a-baw-bawk," she glares back at me, bleating like a chicken, clucking like a sheep.

"No. He was the chicken. He left that word by your pack and Lyndon to take the blame, though I can't be sure Lyn doesn't deserve some of it for fostering that kind of attitude on your crew."

By the time I reach the tent, Cass is throwing my clothes, toiletries, creature comforts — everything — out through the flap.

"Hey!" I dive to catch my flying Walkman. "Can't we talk?"

"Talk? The only thing you did when Buzzard was spitting his venom all over the women of this camp was remain silent. That's what happened in the first camp I was in. "*Who is that Cass chick sleeping with?*" "*She isn't sleeping with me.*" "*She ain't sleeping with me neither.*" "*She won't sleep with any of us. We'll have to teach that bitch a lesson.*" Oh, there may have been the odd man who thought it was wrong, but he didn't come out and say it, so the rest of them assumed he was in with the pack. And now that I'm sleeping with a man I thought I could trust, I find out he's another one of those ostriches."

"There's plenty of sand around here for folks to be planting their heads in. That's obviously what you've done with yours if you think I handled Buzzard the wrong way just because I didn't handle him your way."

"Or the way Aleron would have."

"What in hell is that supposed to mean?"

"He stood up for a bear, but you can't even bring yourself to stand up for me."

"Aleron fled El Salvador. Does that make him an ostrich too? Or simply smart enough to know that you can't win a battle on your enemy's terms when he's carrying a big stick and you're not and big sticks are his terms?"

"Oh, come on. There's no comparison between facing death squads and —"

"And what? A biker who happens to have six inches on me and biceps as thick as my thigh? Sure there is. It's called intimidation. If you can be intimidated by a word, I can certainly be intimidated by a person. Had Aleron been in my shoes, I doubt he would have done much differently."

"Aleron's stopped running; you haven't."

"Yeah? And what about you? It sure as hell was easier for you to cut bait 'n run than it would've been to go to that hunting lodge in person with your beef."

"Easier for you to confront nameless campus security guards and policemen over an abstract cause than it was to stand up to Buzzard against a threat that's been very real and very much in my face all season."

"My cause was not an abstraction."

"Oh? It seems to me that it was as if, as your father suspected, you were simply trying to impress the *Birkenstock babes*."

"He said *hippy chicks*."

"*Flappers, beatniks, hippy chicks, granolas*. ... Same difference. He only needed to be updated by about a quarter of a century, but — you're right — the more it changes the more it looks the fucking same as it ever was."

"Cass, this is crazy. I don't understand where you're coming from or going with this anymore."

"I don't sleep with cowards."

"And I can't sleep with a censor who believes utopia can be achieved with the slash of a pen."

"Sleep with yourself then, if you can."

"Cass —"

"You've got two hands!"

She separates our sleeping bags; I separate our laundry. And now I'm left wondering how what started as a dispute over the felling of a tree has opened such a canyon between us.

CHAPTER TWENTY-SIX

THE NIGHT AIR is laden with the earth's release of weeks of sun, the expiration of the distant forest to our north — the final frontier stretching from here to the taiga, to the scrub barrens of the Hudson plains, where the treeline ends. It weighs down on the branches of the twin-trunked shivering aspen that looms over Cass's tent: a tree which, like us, was once two that have gradually grown together at the hip but farther apart at their crowns. This twin tree is the only tree left on this side of our small lake: there is a mixed pine and poplar stand on the northwest shore, and an island of trees in its shallow middle that will never be cut.

This night is not as insular as the cold nights of early May. The heavy, uneasy air sets in for a spell, warm winds belch up from the southwest, then are still; a brisk northern breeze fills the void of low pressure. This night breeds too many dreams — of confinement, of awakening; of never really sleeping for more than minutes at a time.

In the first, a lumber jack is hacking away at our twin tree with a rusty axe, girdling the bark around its trunk. Mitra leads the women in a cry of outrage. Aleron and Daniel are shouting. We all crowd in around him, our chants growing in fervour with the flow of sap. The lumberjack swings his axe across the sea of hands — splitting knuckles, lobbing off forearms (I lose my left hand at the wrist), but they keep growing back, as in a jungle but quicker. Cass presents me with my fishing knife: I step through the parting crowd, holding the blade out before me. The lumberjack laughs and laughs. But as he raises his axe over his head, my knife grows to the length of Aleron's machete, and with one clean downward swipe, I slit his side from lower rib to groin. He drops his axe behind him, and spine arched back, falls to his knees; his yells are drowned out by the crew as we tighten our circle around him again. When the circle opens, Mitra and Aleron are walking the lumberjack slowly counter-clockwise around the tree. It isn't until he emerges from his second time 'round that I notice his skin and innards are pinned to the trunk with his axe-head, his intestines fill the girdle with new blood, the skin peels right from his back, wrapping the wound he inflicted with a bark fine as paper. It isn't until his third time 'round that I see his face is my own.

In the second dream, I awaken, sweating, with a piss-on.

We're on fire-hours, so we have to rise in the dark of 4:30, eat, be on the hill by 6:00, be off the hill by 11:30 so we can be back at camp by noon. From noon to six, we're shut down, so we try to take a siesta after lunch. But the only place of shade besides the big top is our tents, and by late afternoon, the thermometer in Aleron's (my temporary home) reads one hundred and fifteen Fahrenheit.

"One hundred and twenty with you in here," he gripes. "You should make up with Cass. She is your girlfriend. At least her tent enjoys the shade of a poplar. Besides, people might start talking."

"Let them talk," I mumble through the wet cloth I've draped over my face. "I'm not apologizing for Buzzard's stupidity. I let him know how I felt about what he did. I even set things straight with Lyndon, who, thanks to my efforts, is trying to keep Buzzard as far away from

Cass as possible on the block. If that's not good enough for her ..."

"God you are stubborn. For what? If she were trapped in another country thousands of miles from here, like mine, you would not let such small matters come between you. You would do what you have to do to get her back."

"Like grovel? Christ, Aleron, taking another man's lumps with nothing to show for it isn't such a small matter to me."

"Then you have let the sun get to your head."

The dinner horn blares: five o'clock. We file into the mess behind the others. Gazpatcho, tabouli salad, hummus, falafel — desert food. But no one's really hungry. So we eat what little we can, pack away the leftovers for tomorrow's lunch, and mill about till six. Then each crew gathers in its half of the desert to plant the dunes till the sun sets in the slash around ten. For now, we don't have to drive the thirty minutes for the evening plant that we drive each morning. But this desert can't last us forever; we must plant especially fast in it, because the sand's so dry that it streams around our shovels, half filling our holes before we can flick in the long plugs of the oversized container stock.

"The sand disappears the hole," Aleron mutters as I puff up behind him.

Jaegs whistles a swinging, upbeat version of *In God's Country* — a U2 song he plucked from the *Joshua Tree* to seranade Rosemary, his *Desert Rose*. He plants to the tempo, in quick, jerky motions to beat the sand and always in his *kafiyah* and pitch black glasses now, even when it grows dark.

Buzzard gave up on the evening plant some days ago. He just sits outside the big top catching deerflies and tying hairs he's plucked from his mohawk around their legs until he's holding a bunch of furiously buzzing miniature kites between his toes.

At last light, Cass and I meet at the ribbon line between her crew and mine.

"Leaner," she points to my tree.

"You pull yours out. It's too close to mine and it was in the ground first."

"At least mine's planted straight."

I silently uproot my tree, walk past her for the lake and strip down for a quick dip. Silent, she follows.

We swim out to the island and back without exchanging a word. I emerge with several leeches stuck to my thighs. She has only one, but it has fastened onto her nipple. I give her the salt first.

"I don't know whether I should take this as a sign of remorse or something to rub into a fresh wound." She taps a few grains from the salt shaker onto the leech and watches as it shrinks and writhes and drops from her breast.

"That wound of yours is old, not new. I didn't inflict it and I'm sure I wasn't the first to reopen it, however unintentionally."

"Why can't you admit that you were wrong?"

"Because I wasn't. I just couldn't do right by you."

"No, you're never wrong, are you? Not even when you pulled up your tree back there."

"Look, Cass, you can't slam me for acting like I'm perfect then damn me for making a concession."

"One concession — one begrudging concession — is not the same as admitting you were wrong."

"Are you done with the salt?"

She eyes my thighs. "I think you should leave them on for a while to suck up some of that pride." She shoves the shaker into my hand, gathers her clothes and plods up the dunes to her tent under the twin-trunked poplar.

My leeches are as frosted as the lip of a tequila shot before they finally detach their sucker jaws from my thighs and drop to a death-by-sand.

CHAPTER TWENTY-SEVEN

WEEK 9, DAY 2 — Started my first run with the runs, and my day pretty much went downhill from there. Other symptoms: cold sweats, nausea, chills, the occasional bout of dizziness and an ever-bloating gut that, like the bladder on a bagpipe or bellows on an accordion, emits sounds when squeezed, which it was for each of the 2100 trees I bent to plant today. Thank you, Clem, for sparing me the embarrassment and others the agony of having to plant up behind me by giving me my own piece of turf.

Twice, I awoke looking up from the stony ground, crewmates huddled over me. The first time, I was found by Clem, who fortunately decided to throw a plot way at the back of a finger where I'd lain for God only knows how long, so hidden by poplar brush — a spot missed by the Vision — that he nearly planted his shovel into my chest.

"Catching forty in the furrows, Noah?" he said. In his Tilley Endurables whites, the high-noon rays blazing behind his head of golden hair, he looked very much like an angel.

Mouth agape, I summoned the strength to raise myself up on one arm just enough for his platinum melon to eclipse the sun. "Clem. ... What time is it?"

"One-thirty."

"Jesus, I'm behind."

"It's alright to have our off-days now and again. The way you've been working these past few weeks, you've certainly earned it. ... You look a bit pale around the gills. Maybe you've had a bit too much sun." He removed his canteen from his left hip and knelt down. "You know, in heat like this, you really should be packing some water on every bag-up."

For some inexplicable reason, the mere mention of water caused my gut to clench up. Another wave of nausea crashed over me, but I forced myself to swallow a couple of mouthfuls anyway, knowing that I was probably a bit dehydrated.

Clem wrinkled up his nose. "Say, have you come across any bear shit in your meanderings?"

"Not since the last contract."

"Something tells me you're bound to. ... Well, I'd better get back to my plots." He patted the can of cayenne pepper spray he packed in the flashlight holster on his right hip. "I'll be nearby for the next little while. Just holler if you see anything."

As soon as he'd disappeared from sight, I slipped my hand down the back of my pants. ... Dry, thank yahweh or whatever the hell put me here with such a cursed gut but at the very least spared me this one indignity.

Over the next two hours, I felt that I might be on the mend — so much better, in fact, that I made up substantially for my downtime. Bagging out my third tray since awakening and my seventh of the day, I jogged back to the cache to bag up for another run. But as I buckled the reloaded bags to my waist, my vision faded and my legs went to jelly. This time, mere minutes passed before Aleron and Jacques managed to shake me awake.

"I don't feel too good," I proclaimed, turning my cheek to the dirt to vomit.

Once I was emptied out, Aleron and Jacques each took an arm and raised me to my feet.

"You have had enough for the day, wanker," Aleron said. "We will take you to the crummy to sleep."

"It's the chem-blocks, isn't it?" I say, teeth chattering. "They're making us sick. Those banditos are fucking poisoning us."

"Could be," Jacques said. "Could also be gastro or stomach flu. Who knows for sure?"

"Wait ..." Bending one last time to pick up my shovel and day pack, my billows for bowels let rip with a blow that rattled the side doors of the Hendrix van.

Like synchronized swimmers, Aleron and Jacques turned their heads and cupped their hands round their noses. "Beaver fever," they groaned simultaneously.

"What? But you just said —"

"Remember, my friend, what I said that day we built the bridge? There is nothing that makes a fart so foul? I have had it before — trust me."

"Me as well." Jacques tapped his beaker. "The nose never forgets. The nose knows."

CHAPTER TWENTY-EIGHT

A HORN, FROM Therese's Suburban, echoes across the pillaged landscape. I glance over my shoulder but Aleron and Jacques have already
gone. Probably ran out of trees at the other end of the block, along
another catroad, or simply called it a day. So I turn back to the line
of trees I've been following, stick Aleron's spear into the red sand,
open a hole, and drawing the last Jack pine seedling from my side
as if it were an arrow, bend down and plug it into the ground. I smear
the sweat around on my face with my soil-caked hand: the dirt, the
iron-rich earth of a dried-up stream bed, feels cool and I notice it
has sealed a cut in the web of flesh between my thumb and index.
Somewhere under a higher sun, my blood dotted the land.

   At the cache, I stick the spear in a stump and hang my bags over
its staff handle. Dust rises in waves of heat off the catroad; rising with
it, a polyphony of old sounds, wave on wave, that the approaching
noise of the crummy (gravel crunching under tires, rough-running
engine) cannot drown out: a cacophony of songbirds, the screech
of an osprey, silence, then the sound of wind whirring through
the wings of a nighthawk tailspinning to earth, looping up at the last
possible second. I've never heard a nighthawk call. I wonder how
many other birds sing with wings only. Are its motions through the

air guided by what it has to say? Or are words a mere by-product of its actions: *I am hunting; I am looking for a place to nest; I am free.* Maybe those whirrs and wobbles are both: *I am hunting — stay away; I am looking for a place to nest; I am free — are you?*

My eyes focus through the haze. There are no nighthawks, no osprey, no other birds. But then there is no forest, not in the lowlands where the stump-stubbled dried-up sphagnum once bloomed red and orange and green beneath spruce boughs. And the highlands, where spruce would have given way to Jack and white pine, bear nothing but rock through eroding sands, and charred stumps standing bizarrely on exposed roots — floating like octopuses unaware the tide's gone out without them.

The Suburban pulls up, the converted RCMP truck Bob bought cheap from Rent-A-Ruin, which they'd probably purchased cheaper at a police auction. But instead of Therese, Lyndon's at the wheel.

"Get in," he says, a trucker's tan on the arm he's resting on the driver's door and a tailor-made hanging limply over his lower lip. I squeeze into the back with the other planters and their gear. Everyone is strangely silent, like trees before a squall-force wind sweeps through. No one as much as looks at me, and as I look from head to head, I see that no one else from my crew is among them.

"Hey Lyn," I say. "Where's Clem?"

"Took your crew home early. Guess you were missed."

"What's up?"

Lyndon snorts, Cass casts me a barbed glance, and suddenly all heads dart around; eyes burning into the space I occupy as if I shouldn't be here. All but Lyndon's, whose eyes move smoothly between the rear-view and the road.

"It's not my place to say," he says. "But I'm sure if you think about it hard enough, it'll come to you."

"Think about what?"

Buzzard grunts with disgust and shakes his head.

"Like I said," Lyndon says. "It's not for me to say."

I swallow, dust and sandflies but not much in the way of saliva. "Looks like you said enough already — to everyone here but me."

"And what's the significance of that?"

"Just cut the crap, alright? I don't need a fuckin' rear-view mirror to know when a bull's eye's been painted on my back."

"Some folks here seem to think you've painted that bull's eye on your own backside — only a little lower."

"Well, some folks oughta ask before they buy from a one-man rumour mill. That way they have a chance to separate the passable lumber from the shit — if you know what I mean."

Lyndon eyeballs me through the rear-view. "Believe me, the shit's gonna stick to those who shat it."

"Those? So I'm in shit and who else?"

"That's all your getting from me."

"Come on, you've already told me my crew's in shit for something. Either you're that easy to sucker punch or there's a part of you that really wants to let me know, after making me twist in the wind a little ..."

"He's mouthy for such a little cock, isn't he, Cass?"

Cass pins me with her eyes. "When it suits him."

My chest begins to pound, and I can feel my face flushing. I lean up over the back seat and fill the rear-view with a mask so ugly with anger that it surprises me. "If this is a cockfight to you, MacKerel, then have the balls to declare it. Tell me what your bull's eye's about or take it the fuck off my back!"

Lyndon slams on the breaks, and before I can get a grip I'm thrown over the bench and down between the bucket seats; my head just missing the stick shift. He grabs my hair in his fingers, swings the door open, and stepping out, hauls me up onto his seat, holding my face above his foot as if he's about to drop kick my head.

"You calling me a coward, huh?" He yanks. "Huh?"

My eyes tear with anger and pain. "Let go," I yell, swinging uselessly at his legs. "I'm warning you, MacKerel —"

"I don't take too kindly to being called a coward by fuckin' stashing scum like you. Bob'll probably just send you and your lot down the road without even having you charged, but if you were all mine I wouldn't think twice about lashing you buck naked to a tree and hangin' a bottle o' bug dope right in front of your nose for you to meditate on." He grabs the back of my collar with his free hand, drags me out a bit further and drops me onto the dusty road. Then he hops back into the driver's seat and slams the door.

"Wait —" I scramble to my feet.

"May as well get used to walking now 'cause you're gonna be sent down the road tomorrow and I've never known Bob to offer stashers a lift back into town."

"I didn't stash!" I shout, but I'm drowned out by the roar of approval rising up from behind Lyndon as he puts the crummy in gear and screeches off into the dust.

The road scorches my feet through the thinning soles of my boots and the all-around glare parches me inside out, churning up the gaseous by-products of the beaver-fever that's been bloating my belly for the past week. The bastard dumped me out an hour's walk from camp and didn't even give me a chance to fill my thermos. Delirious from the double dehydration of parasite and sun, I struggle to hold myself back from plunging into the stagnating water and gulping, as I round the western shore of our leech-infested lake.

Camp looks deserted. I stagger up to the big top, collapse under the water barrel, put my mouth to the tap, open the spigot wide. Warm, bleached water — my stomach cramps into a tighter knot. Groaning, I get up, stumble into the tent.

Rosemary's clearing away the remainders of lunch. Lyndon's crew is grouped at the tables around the centrepole, drinking beer, playing cards, shooting the shit, probably spreading rumours about my crew, which is nowhere to be seen; except for Daniel, who sits alone, slouched over a table by the mesh window, no one from my crew is here.

I clear my parched throat. "Clem around?"

Cass looks up from her watercolours. "Bob's trailer, getting his walking papers, no doubt. Speaking of walks, how was yours?"

"A breeze. But I don't think Clem will be taking the long walk you're hoping for, or anyone else from my crew either."

"Oh? You don't think the sixty thousand missing trees your crew claims to have planted isn't a good enough reason? At best, Clem's shown he can't keep on top of you, that none of you can be trusted. But maybe Bob will be merciful, give us the cream for the rest of the season and stick you in scuzz piles for a change."

"You know, I've been on Clem's crew for nearly four shifts now and I've seen little evidence of preferential treatment. But if we do get a little extra cream, it's because we work harder to get to it than the rest of you."

Lyndon enters. "If you can call diggin' big holes and planting fist-fuls of trees at a time working harder."

I glare. "There you go again, shootin' off your goddamn mouth without any proof."

"Sixty thousand fuckin' trees disappeared — that's proof. Aleron, a greener only weeks ago, planting thirty-six hundred a day in rock ..."

"Aleron planted beans to feed his family from the time he could walk, for Chrissake, and now that he's here he's pounding to bring what's left of it over from his homeland."

"All the more reason for him to cheat."

"Isn't that the same kinda trashy line that other planting companies use to turn down Natives, MacKerel? 'We don't hire Indians 'cause they all come from poor reserves and they drink so hard you can't trust 'em not to stash.' What about Jaegs and Kirsten — they've been planting with this company for years. Why would they start stashing only now?"

"Because some people refuse to accept that there are days, weeks or even whole contracts where the pickings are slim and they let their pride or greed get the better of them. And then there are foremen who turn a blind eye ..."

"You must be speaking from your extensive personal experience, then, because I've been planting shoulder to shoulder with the Hendrix crew for two shifts now and I can vouch for the integrity of every planter on it. As for Clem, he's the best foreman a highballer can have: does his job without unnecessarily interfering with mine."

"So now the Man from GLAD's a hero," Cass says.

I dart around. "Sure as hell looks like Lyndon's yours. Or maybe you're just hoping he'll give you the lioness's share of the cream you're starving for. But I doubt it. He's got everything to gain from this. He wants to be the highballer's foreman, don't you MacKerel? So you can sit in your goaddamn crummy all day without worrying about plots and production because you'll have the only maintenance-free, perpetual motion crew in the province." I turn back to Cass. "Don't think he'll be taking you to the Promised Land either, 'cause it's all in your head."

Lyndon drops his hand on my shoulder and swings me around. "I think you should apologize to your ex for being so rude."

"Go stuff a spade, MacKerel."

He grabs the wings of my collar in his fists, slams me up against the centrepole. "If you ever mouth off at me again, I'll be all over you. I'll be on your ass so hard you'll think I'm the whole fuckin' Comanche nation."

A dam inside me bursts. I clutch his neck, pushing my thumbs deep into the soft part under his jaw, then knee him in the stomach. Winded, he falls back. I swing him around the oil drum, knocking it over, and press him against the stove pipe so hard that it begins to crumple. "Get it straight, MacKerel. This isn't a fucking game of cowboys and Indians. You could be the Messiah for all I care, but no one lays a hand on my head without my fucking permission."

A fist catches me across the side of the mouth and I go down — Buzzard. Daniel leaps to his feet and blows a deafening blast on his bear-scare whistle. Buzzard draws back his leg, but before he has a chance to deliver his boot to my temple, Aleron bursts into the tent and tackles him to the dirt. The tables clear, and within seconds the big top looks more like an arena during a seventh game playoff final hockey brawl than the mess tent of a planting camp. Until the cold jets of water hit.

"Enough!" Therese yells, vigorously pumping the hose of her piss-pack like an exterminator dousing roaches. Our crews quickly part sides to their respective tables — everyone except me and Lyndon, still wrestling in the dirt. "Break it up! Now!" Therese blasts me in the ear. "Or I'm bringing in the firehose!"

Without warning, Bob steps in, the checker in tow. Lyndon and I freeze. Bob's face flushes.

"Looks like you're having some problems," Dagmar says. "Maybe I'd better come back in the morning."

Bob watches as she strolls, cool as cool, back to her pickup. As soon as she's far enough down the road to be out of earshot, he turns on us. "Abramson! MacKerel! In my trailer — now!"

Lyndon relaxes his grip, I relax mine, and pushing off each other, we stagger to our feet. Lyndon hurries after Bob but I stop in the entrance where Cass has been standing to avoid the fracas. I spit a mouthful of blood at her feet and look into her face. "I hope you got what you wanted out of this."

Cass glares back. "What did I want?"

Therese seizes the torn upper sleeve of my shirt and tugs sharply. "Let's go."

She drags me outside, shoves me up the trailer steps and shuts me in.

The trailer is hotter than the Kangas saunas, where we steamed our bones on that snowy early June day, and one look at Bob's face tells me we're headed for a meltdown.

"Where's Clem?" I ask.

"Packing," he says. "Si' down."

"I'd rather stand."

"See what I mean?" Lyndon says. "Never listens to a fuckin' thing he's told."

"I'm willing to listen to any reasonable proposition, but right now, sharing a bench with you sure as hell isn't."

Bob slams his fist on the forestry map taped to the table. "Sit!"

I sit on the far corner of the bench and cross my arms.

"Now listen up, Abramson, and listen good. I've been having enough trouble with your crew's missing tree problem without you making my operation look like some fuckin' reckless third-rate circus sideshow. I've a good mind to send you packin' along with Clem, even if I spare the rest."

"Me? What about him?"

"Lyndon's excusable under the circumstances. You're not."

"Dragging me out of the crummy and dumping me in the road an hour's walk from camp without any water is hardly what I'd call excusable. In fact, I'd call it reckless, and I'm sure the union steward will agree with me."

"What union?" Lyndon sneers. "This is an MNR job — government, non-union. That's why you're paying fifteen bucks a day in camp costs instead of a dollar seventy-five and getting less per tree."

"Don't give me that shit. The public employees' union provides some representation to workers subcontracted to government agencies as well. I can call them in to bitch about the checking, I can call them in to bitch about mistreatment — I can even call them in if I'm not averaging the hourly minimum that a planter directly employed by the Ministry would get, and many of us aren't. If you send me down the road without any evidence of wrongdoing other than the actions I took to defend myself against this goon, I can sue you for wrongful dismissal."

Bob pales. "Who told you that?"

"Therese."

"Bull."

"Ask her yourself if you don't believe me. It was Therese who told Cass her rights after she was forced to flee her last contractor."

"Fuckin' figures. Nobody around here's got any damned sense of loyalty, so why should I expect it from my partner?"

"You want faith, then show some in your workers." I stand up and open the door.

"Where the hell do you think you're going?"

"When you're ready to ask questions instead of painting us with tar 'n feathers, I'm sure we'll be happy to oblige. Send Clem or anyone else packing for no good reason and I promise you the rest of us will walk. I don't think you can afford to lose your highest production crew on a meat-grinder like this one, and I know you don't like unions." I step out, letting the door slam behind me.

After dinner, my crew gathers together in a circle outside Bob's trailer. We know he's inside, conferencing with Therese, making final decisions on what to do with us. So we let him know we're conferencing too, giving our versions of events loudly enough to attract a peek through the shabby curtain on their window, their silent listening.

"Hear the latest?" Daniel says, serving his hackey-sack to Jaegs. "The checker's levying a $10,000 fine against the company for the missing trees. Bob thinks we should pay."

Jaegs knees the sack into the air, eyes following it as it slows to the top of its rise, falls. "I wonder where that one came from?" He strikes it again with the inside of his ankle, popping it over to me.

"One of Lyndon's press leaks, no doubt." I catch the sack on the back of my heel. "Wouldn't surprise me if Bob leaked them through him deliberately to gauge camp opinion."

Kirsten smiles, toeing my pass into a high pop fly. The screen door opens and Bob steps down, grabbing the plummeting sack before Walter has a chance to kick it. "Complete your hack yet?" he asks, trying to diffuse the tension.

"We'll never complete a hackey again without Clem," Kirsten says.

Bob sits on the middle step, then we all sit, maintaining our circle.

"The air's as thick with rumours as it is with sand. I haven't made any final decisions yet. Clem's the least of my problems, but if he goes, a lot of the fault lies with this crew. Sixty thousand trees are unaccounted for, and they've gone missing from the Figure 8 area you were in four days ago. Dagmar thinks you're guilty of stashing, or a hell of a lot of over-cull."

Jacques shakes his head. "We haven't, Bob. We do a good job. Go out there and see. We have been very careful about the culling. Clem has been watching the cache like a hawk. Anyway, where would we hide sixty t'ousand culls? We'd be spending so much time stashing we would have no time to plant!"

"Then what's going on? Sixty thou's a lotta fuckin' trees to disappear into thin air. We're looking at a ten thousand dollar fuckin' fine. According to the contracts you all signed, you're fifty percent responsible for any penalties incurred. That's six or seven hundred each off your next cheques. So you'd all better start thinking."

There's a long pause, not of silence — that's not possible here — but of killdeers and blowing sands, grains grating over each other, buffeting against metal and canvas.

Jaegs chews his thumbnail, then breathing in sharply, raises his finger. "Could the trees have been spaced too tight?"

"They were a bit, as a matter of fact, but you'd've had to plant double density to account for all the missing stock."

Then it sets on me. "How many trees were prescribed for Figure 8?"

"Forty thou."

"Forty thousand?" Walter laughs. "No way. We planted eighty there, at least."

Bob pulls his crumpled, coffee-stained copy of the Ministry map from his shirt pocket, unfolds it across his knee, places a density grid transparency from his supervisor's binder overtop an area and starts counting, at first under his breath, then louder to hear himself over the wind buffeting sand against his trailer.

"... Forty-three, forty-four, forty-five. Forty-five thou' — and that's if you're being real charitable by counting all the dots that fall on the cutaway's boundaries."

"I don't understand it," Jaegs says. "Jacques is right."

"Can I take a look at that?" I ask.

Bob hands me the fraying, marked-up paper. I scan the black lines, the roads, the lakes, islands, muskegs, moraines that litter the page, looking for the shape I remember.

"Here." He points to a circular cut in the upper left-hand corner.

"That can't be it. There were a couple of corridors coming off the east end that opened up into another area at least as big as this one."

"You sure? You haven't had a lot of experience reading these things ..."

"My father's a cartographer, so I've seen just about every kind of map there is. Anyway, don't you think Figure 8 is a more appropriate name for a cutaway that bottlenecks in the middle, like an hourglass —" I pull the pen I use to record my numbers from my pocket. "Like this ...?"

Bob looks at the revised map, the faint blue line more than twinning the original area in size. "Go get Clem," he says. "We're heading back there now to take another look. You'd better be right about this, Noah."

"If you're right, tell your father these Ministry cartographers can't map a cutaway to scale for shit." Clem spits on the map, glaring at me, swearing for the first time all season, on the drive to Figure 8.

"If?" Lyndon says. "Didn't you view the area when you were throwing your plots?"

"I was tied up fighting Dag the Hag over the no-payment plots she'd thrown back in Calypso's rocks — your crew's and mine, remember? Besides, this other area wasn't on the map, and none of my people mentioned it, so I had no reason to go looking for it."

"I woulda seen it," Lyndon says. "I cruise the perimeters of every cutaway my crew's assigned. If Noah's right, asking him to bitch at his Dad won't do you no good 'cause he's drawn up forestry maps before, most recently the site plan for a cutaway to make way for a multi-level parking lot at Noah's *alma mater*. From what I've heard, Noah's Save the Trees campaign didn't go over too well with the folks who hired his old man, or with the police."

I feel my face grow hot, like it did before our fight. "Who told you that?"

"Oh, you know how things get around camp. You come here thinkin' you can pull a Grey Owl, but shit, turns out you can't keep anything secret — what your Mammy and your Pappy do, the colours of your gotch, who's tenting with who and who isn't, who's gettin' hairy palms instead ..."

"Like you?" I snipe back.

"Me? You're the one who was evicted from the tent of a lady with no last name."

"At least I was invited into one."

"How do you know I wasn't?"

"Alright, MacKerel, that's enough," Bob says. "If you're gonna air anyone's laundry, air your own.

"Yeah, MacKerel," I say. "What did your father do for you to turn out to be such a sweetheart?"

"Oh, Dad was one helluva feller."

"What did he do?"

"I just told you. He was a feller. Probably cut more coastal old growth than any man living."

I'm seized by a spasm of laughter. "That's why you decided to become a planter."

"No. I was a logger too. For a while we were a team. He'd top 'em and I'd fell 'em. I've got an old black-and-white of him standing way the fuck up on the growth rings of a Douglas fir he'd just topped, leaning on his axe. So high up he looks like a stick man. ... One day his harness broke. He had the choice of hanging on for a twelve storey slide down the trunk or free fall. He chose to hang on. By the time he reached the bottom, his gut was torn open and his intestines were spilling out. Died at my feet. That's when I swapped my saw for a planting spade. Figured it would balance my karma."

I can't shake the bloody dream from my head — of rebarking the pine he cut with his gut. But Lyndon had hinted at his father's death before I had that nightmare, the night he defended the skill in a game of chance: *father killed in a logging accident? Roll of the dice.* The skill in the game is not to confuse fortune with fate or take the hard knocks personally. That, and the bottle of whisky he keeps stashed under the seat of his crummy, the Conan, for his "bad tooth", is how he's kept his head. And though he quit logging, he wouldn't quit the forest.

Bob clears his throat to break the silence that has fallen over the cab. "That was the best career move you ever made," he says. "Another few years and you'd've been hitting spiked trees. Cut in half by your own flying saw chain — that's a shitty way to go."

"I dunno," Lyndon says. "I'm betting that the day Mac-Blo starts advertising their silvicultural efforts, planters will be next on the eco-terrorists' list."

"What can they do to us," Bob says. "Exploding culls? Shit — once upon a time, the worst thing you could be was a bastard or a whore ..."

We stop at the site and walk off the road and a ways into the field, following the furrows along the treeline to where the clear-cut curves in, appearing to close in a narrow bay. It isn't until we're at the very back that we see the furrowed skid trails.

Bob consults the map. "Well, well. Isn't even drawn in."

"Maybe this map was meant to indicate how the area was sup-posed to be cut," Clem says. "Maybe the logging crew found a stand too tempting to pass up."

"I doubt it," Bob says. "The maps are supposed to be drawn from aerial photos after the cut."

We follow the rows of seedlings through the bottleneck to the other area, an almost identical twin of the first.

Clem cracks a smile. "I'd say this piece just might hold sixty thou', wouldn't you Lyn?"

"Yeah, sure," Lyndon says. "But I wouldn't get too smug before that witchy checker has thrown her plots here. She's bound to pull something to cover her ass."

Bob moves his eyes between the map and the cutaway, and shakes his head. "How the hell did the Ministry miss this?"

"So I guess we're off the hook, then," Clem says.

"You're exonerated," Bob says. "I'm sorry it had to come to this."

I clear my throat. "Can we have that apology at breakfast?"

Bob nods. "And then some."

The ground rumbles. Our eyes are drawn to the sky: the hole that has exposed us and parched us for days on end is closing fast in an angry swirl of purple cloud.

"It's about bloody time," Lyndon says.

"Looks like we're in for a doorcrasher special," Bob says. "We'd better make tracks."

We pack into the one-ton and follow the road back, heading into the heart of the towering cloud that has blotted out the long light of summer. All along the advancing ridge, bolts are flying as if the cloud were a heavy woollen blanket being drawn over a bedsheet in a dry and thirsty house. But despite its flash and thunder, the storm remains curiously dry.

The air has fallen perfectly still. The pressure drops so swift it hurts my ears. A bolt licks down on the one seed tree the loggers have left to blow down in the next big wind — the old pine's crown bursting in a confusion of splintering wood and flaming sap. A great nest plummets, and in a flash of white and a thud, wings spread across the windshield, almost enveloping the cab.

Bob swerves and brakes, and the enormous raptor tumbles off somewhere over the roof.

"Think we killed it?" Clem says.

"Hey, it flew into us, alright?" Bob snipes.

Aleron leans over the seat back. "It may be alive. We should drive back and check."

"After taking a whack like that?" Lyndon says. "Who are you fucking kidding?"

"Dead or alive, I'd like to know what we hit," I say.

Cursing, Bob throws the truck into reverse.

Aleron winds down his window and pops his head out, looking back over the roadside slash. "Here," he points. "Here!"

We pour out into the heavy, gusty air and gather around the still, beige form. Wings still spread as if to brake for a landing, a great horned owl lies face down in a dune.

"Can't be alive," Lyndon says. "It hit the lights and then the windshield."

Aleron bends down, and taking the bird by its great shoulder, flips it onto its back.

The pupils in its large yellow eyes are shut tight as pinholes, as if they'll forever be flying into a blinding light. *Can't be alive, look at its eyes* — hoping they'll dilate.

Bob sparks up a smoke and squats down. "Not even a broken feather. Huh. Must've snapped its neck. ... Well, there's no sense in wasting it. I know a good taxidermist in town." He reaches for the bird, but Aleron grabs his wrist with a talon-like grip.

"Why you think it would be a waste to let the forest take it is a mystery to me, but it is your kill. You want it for your mantle? Fine — I only ask that you allow me to carry it."

"It may be my kill but I've got a clean conscience. It's not as if I shot it outta the sky."

"We would not have been here if not for that fucking map."

"I didn't draw it. So take your damned hand off my wrist before I take it off for you."

Aleron releases his grip. Shaking, he kneels to fold the great owl's wings, but the resistance of death is already setting in. "Too big for the cab," he says in a whisper, holding it up as if he's the crucifix against which its last breath was fixed. "I will have to ride in the back."

He staggers around to the rear of the cap, the owl growing heavier with every step.

"Want some company?" I ask.

He shakes his head.

"We've been having some bad luck around animals lately."

"No. The animals have been having bad luck with us."

I shut him into the box and take a seat in the back of the crew cab.

From time to time, I peer through the tiny window Bob has cut into the box for rear-view, and in hot strobing flashes — Aleron stroking an owl, Aleron clutching that owl to his shoulder — I watch mourning unfold.

CHAPTER TWENTY-NINE

I WATCH THE storm for hours after. I watch Bob try to outpace it as we swing east back toward camp. For a time, I watch it with the others, through the gauzy Egyptian cotton wall of the big top. Now I watch it alone, standing high on a dune, hands raised for a rain that won't come.

For the first time all season, I'm wearing my watch. I stopped wearing it to protect an heirloom from the wear and tear of working in the slash. I stopped winding it when time, gauged by anything other than the angles and lengths of shadows or the stretching of light toward solstice (now shortening) and the rising and setting of the sun and the moon, stopped making sense to my own internal clock. Now that I'm winding it again, it's all I'm wearing, and it's not to keep time.

I wait for something more than the sheet lightning that's been silently illuminating the advancing thunderheads since the one lightning bolt that struck the owl's pine when the system first closed in. I wait, finger poised over a tiny button, for the next clear bolt to pound the stretched skin of the earth. Finally a blanching flash: I click the button that activates the telemeter on my watch, wait for the thunder to roll to my ears and under my feet, click again, stop. In the dying beam of my maglite, I raise the dial to my face and squint. Less than 1k. That was close. "Close enough," Father would say were he watching with me, "to knock you to the middle of next week." I wish it could literally knock me back in time, only farther. To that day I could've kicked dirt over Buzzard's cunt, angrily scrawled in the sand, but didn't — figuring that Cass would be more persuasive than my fists could ever be. To that solstice night I snuck back into the arboretum with a sledgehammer and blowtorch to knock the teeth off the blade of a bulldozer, from which I and some tree-hugging granola chick I had the hots for had been bludgeoned by the cops. To the moment and the bend in the road just before the owl's pine. But in a flash the speed of light, hindsight's a luxury. By the time we've heard the thunder, the lightning's already struck.

CHAPTER THIRTY

THE CHOPPER ROARS in as we're finishing up breakfast, in the dim purple light of the smoke-stained dawn. Bob and Lyndon scramble from their table but are met in the door by four men in fluorescent orange jumpsuits: an advance attack team sent to extinguish the smouldering spot fires set by last night's dry electric storm, before the wind picks up and all hell breaks loose. A few words are exchanged. Bob shakes his head and frowns. Then he steps outside, leaving Lyndon in the entrance.

Buzzard springs up onto the oil drum. "Hear that?" he yells. "We're outta here!"

Suddenly, we're all on our feet, scraping our plates and stacking them for Jack. Mitra dumps her dishes in the wash bin and rushes for the exit but Lyndon stretches his arms across it and scowls. "Nobody better leave the mess," he says. "Nobody should get their hopes up either. For all we know we're about to be marshalled."

"Marshalled?" Jack laughs. "Most people here wouldn't have a clue how to wield a piss-pack, let alone a Wabax pump!"

"And you think that makes a good goddamn difference to them? There's a fire the size of Toronto burning up Red Lake just west of here and God knows how many others on our doorstep after that lightning show. Ten to one they'll put every last grunt among us through a crash course."

"If there's money in it, I'll go," Buzzard says. "Can't be any worse than the dog coin I make around here. Besides, I could use a little adventure."

"It ain't an armed forces' commercial," Walter says. "There's nothing romantic about sixteen-hour shifts cuttin' breaks 'n diggin' trenches in some hot 'n smoky fucking bunghole wondering if that chopper pilot's gonna be able to get you out before the damned wind shifts your way and the fire's jumpin' tops."

Jack nods. "Or fleeing across a flaming clear-cut, praying the pilot of the water bomber sees the tiny speck of you before he swoops down for the drop — praying again when you see your first prayer didn't work and you've got the shadow of a bitchin' bomber closing on your tail. Once saw a guy get doused. Couple tons of H_2O — squashed him like a fuckin' insect, knocked his head clean off."

"I've heard enough," Mitra says. "My contract says nothing about fighting fires."

"Your contract's got nothing to do with it," Lyndon says. "If you're marshalled, it's either fight or jail."

"Fine. They can put me in the slammer."

"All that shit you and Cass gave me for cutting that pine tree out front and now you're walking out on saving the forest." Lyndon spits. "Well, Ms. Environmentalist —"

"You can rant and rail till you're purple. I'm trained to plant trees, not to fight fires."

"Shut up and sit down," Bob shouts. "Everyone."

The big top falls so silent you can hear the grains of sand grating beneath his feet as he strides across the rippled desert floor. He stops at the centrepole. "As you've probably guessed from the smoke and ash that rolled through the woods this morning, the fire situation has worsened. The storm set off dozens of spot fires in our area, but the biggest threat is an older fire that surfaced sometime yesterday and flared up in last night's winds. It's currently about twenty k's from camp and we're right in its path. So we've been shut down and ordered to evacuate."

I stand and turn to the fire officers standing on the sidelines. "We've been on fire shifts for ten days straight, getting off the block before the last of the dew's dried up, and the smoking restrictions and campfire bans have been strictly enforced. What or who caused this 'older fire'? I mean, fires just don't 'surface' — as Bob here put it — outta nowhere. Somebody miss a spot fire set by a careless fisherman, or somethin'?"

The two men look at each other nervously. The taller one with the moustache clears his throat. "Actually, the fire we're concerned about is almost three weeks old."

"That's funny. Other than Red Lake Seven, which is hundreds of kilometres off, no one told us about any fires, and three weeks is almost as long as we've been here."

Silence.

I approach the fire officer, draw my Bic, click it right under his nose. "It's all because of this, isn't it?"

He flinches, stiffening his neck to keep his moustache from being singed. "Pardon?"

"The napalm your Ministry dropped on the Cyclops block. You thought it was out, and even though you can never be too sure it's dead out, you thought it would rain before any of the remaining hot spots could go underground."

The fire officer stands ill at ease. "In fact, the MNR did conduct a prescribed burn earlier in the spring as part of a Jack pine regen project. We had taken all the necessary precautions, and we thought the fire had burned itself out, but as it turned out, it was just sleeping somewhere, probably down in the roots of a stump." He clears his throat. "Evidently, the drought has awoken it."

"Evidently ..." I pocket my lighter. "Well, I guess we'd better start pulling up the stakes."

"We won't be taking the camp with us," Bob says quietly. "In fact, we won't be taking much of anything at all. The fire's closed the bridge at Calypso Creek, and it's heading up the road. We're being flown out."

"But Bob —" Mitra cuts in, worry furrowed into her brow. "Nearly everything I own is in my tent."

"Same here," Daniel says. "If I lose my guitar and all my gear, that's everything I've made at this fucking job, and the end of my busking career."

"I hear ya," Bob says, bowing his head to avoid even accidental eye contact. "Me and Therese put every last cent we had into this camp."

"You're insured," Mitra says bitterly.

"I'm sorry, but there's nothing I can do. There are so many fires burning across the north the MNR can only spare one chopper, and a jet ranger only seats five, including the pilot, so we're already looking at half a dozen trips to get everyone out."

"We'll be watching your camp closely," the moustached fire officer assures Mitra. "If the fire makes its way here, we'll do whatever we can to save it. In the meantime, I'll see if we can spare some cargo nets. If there's time and conditions permit, we'll sling your gear out. Otherwise, you'll each be allowed to stow one knapsack in the storage compartment, so pack wisely."

I hurry back to Aleron's tent to pack up my shit, unsure of what I'll take with me. If all I was allowed to take was what could be worn and pocketed, I would take my watch, and maybe my maglite. My knapsack could easily carry my journal, my mail, a change of clothes, a sweater, my raingear, a few pieces of fruit and a pack of cigarettes. Then there's my wallet. I imagine it burning — my birth certificate, my driver's licence, my bank card, my SIN card, my student ID, my entire plastic identity melting into one undefinable blob, and I'm no longer sure I want to take it and spoil what might be my only chance at a clean getaway. Then again, I'm not really sure I want to get away.

I reach Aleron's campsite. "Hey wanker!" I call. "Wake up! Calypso's on fire and we've got a free flight to town." But he doesn't answer. His tent is completely zipped up — not a single flap pulled aside for ventilation, which is strange, considering the heat and humidity. Maybe he's got a woman inside (I didn't see Josie at breakfast either) and they're too embarrassed to come out. I yank back the front-flap zipper in a quick, arcing motion, but he's not inside and his sleeping bag, foamie and day pack are gone. To Josie's tent?

I haven't seen Aleron since we pulled into camp last night, not since I opened the back door of the cap on the white one-ton and he stumbled out past me and shuffled off into the dark, still clutching that great horned owl to his chest. He'd been walking in the direction of his tent, but I'd had my own sanity to deal with, my own bloodstains to clean, and ended up falling asleep in the warm sand, wearing nothing but my watch, watching as the dry electric storm passing overhead threw down bolts of orange and blue and fireweed — almost praying to a god I don't believe in, for the gusts of wind to pick up enough to bury me as I slept. The night was practically biblical, and I awoke to see that I almost got my wish.

Perhaps Aleron went off into the woods to give the owl a proper burial — to let the forest take it, as he put it to Bob. I doubt he would have slept with anyone last night; he seemed so desperate to be alone. Or maybe I'm wrong, and he found the comfort of a woman's tent; after all, he sure could've used it.

I carefully pack what I must take with me into my knapsack, slipping my wallet into the map pouch for easy access just in case I change my mind and decide to ditch it before we leave. The rest I toss and stuff chaotically into my backpack and duffel bag, except for my pen and the postcards I've been steadily filling up without ever sending. To decide which story to send him, the contradictory man who fathered me, would be posting my fate. I don't know which story is more true, on either side of any postcard — the ones written by me or the ones written for me. I, who spat blood at the feet of a woman I love, but tilted at bulldozers for a complete stranger; he, who mapped to scale the "reduction" of the arboretum, but paid for my lawyer when I was charged for trying to stop it. Maybe the biggest difference between us is that he'd rather soar miles and miles above the earth, mapping and surveying the wrinkles and scars of mesas and canyons that I'd rather lose myself in. I just want him to understand me.

I scribble a note to Aleron on a blank, eliminating one possibility, and leave it on the milk crate he uses as a table, just in case he swings by his tent before he's had word of the evacuation. I duck out into the noonday sun and, for what might be the last time ever, lug my life to the big top.

The two sling nets choppered in for the evac are piled high with gear. The shelves, chairs, tables and oil-drum stove have been packed into the Prairie Schooner, which Therese has hitched to the one-ton to back into the lake's shallows, next to the Hendrix van and ATC already parked there. The plumbing has been disconnected from the pump, and a firehose attached in its place. Only the big top remains standing.

Rosemary, Kirsten and Daniel delicately peel away its colourfully patched Egyptian cotton wall, folding it up as they walk its reliable circle.

Steve and Mitra knock the two-by-fours out from under the edges of its big, round striped vinyl roof. I winch it down, hugging the centrepole to be born through the chimney hole as the top touches ground.

"Hey Noah," Lyndon calls from the Conan. "You seen Cass anywhere about?"

"No. Why?"

"Fuckin' figures. Just when she's supposed to be helping me fetch the piss-packs and fire-axes from our block, she's off fuckin' the dog somewhere."

"Now that I think of it, I didn't see her at breakfast. I'll check her tent. Maybe she slept in and got a late start."

"What tent? I went to drag her out of her bag right after the evac was announced and her shit was already packed up and gone."

I run down to the lake, my feet slipping in the rolling dunes, to the twin poplar where her tent once sat. The smell of smoke is everywhere, it's snowing ash and soot, and the sun is burning hot, even through the heavy haze. I look for a sign, a note hammered to the tree trunk, something she might have left behind, footprints in the sand. But the wind has erased everything, even the imprint where she had lain.

A wave of nausea rolls over me, chilling me through the heat of my fever. My legs go to jelly, I sink to my knees. Brightening behind the shifting plume of smoke, the stark sun cuts between the twin-trunked poplar, casting two shadows. I freeze. Lodged there in the tree's crotch is a large striped tail feather. I pluck it out by the quill, trembling with anger and aprehension and fear. Aleron spent the night here. He came to rope the owl up the tree so no animals could get at it and she invited him to stay.

"Back off," Bob snarls as he steps between the crush of sweaty, sooty planters and the jet ranger. "First flight's full."

I squeeze and elbow my way to the front. "Bob, I gotta talk to you."

"Did you hear me?"

"Aleron and Cass are missing. No one's seen either of them since last night. I was thinking that if you could get everyone in the camp to spread out and do a sweep —"

"No time for that. The pilot's on a thirty minute turnaround for each flight and it'll take seven trips to get everyone out. I'll be damned if I have to go tromping all over hell's half-acre to round up enough planters to make a load just because Cass and Aleron can't get their shit together in an emergency."

"But Bob —"

"It'll be three hours before last flight. They're bound to turn up by then."

Clem, Therese, Jack and Rosemary, laden with day packs, carry-ons, and in Therese's hand, Bob's brief case — jog toward the chopper, crouching as they near the sagging blades of the slow-sweeping propeller.

"Hey, why do they get to go first?" Buzzard gripes. "Aren't captains supposed to go down with their ships?"

"D'ya see me going anywhere? Eh?" Bob bellows, straining to be heard above the rising drone of the chopper revving for take-off, straining to be heard at all. "If I could have my way, I'd stay here and man the hose to keep all our shit from burning up."

"Then why are they going now?"

"To find a couple of vans to move the crew from the staging area to town and a motel where we can wait out the fire. With every bush-worker from here to Red Lake smoked out of the woods, the nearest accommodation may be in Thunder Bay."

"Who's next then?" Jaegs asks.

"How about ladies first?" Mitra suggests.

"Get lost," Lyndon says. "You gave up that privilege when you demanded to be treated like one of the boys. Welcome to the fucking club."

"I wish we were," Moira says. "Then maybe there'd be more than a handful of us in this camp — maybe enough to put it to a vote."

Lyndon pretends to ignore her, but I can tell by the way he cocked his jaw to one side, as if it's come unhinged, that he heard her loud and clear. "It should be done by the crew, and my crew should go first," he says. "They've been saddled with the shittiest ground all season. It's high time they got a break."

"The land's always greener on the other side of the slashpile, eh Lyndon?" Bartram says. "Considering the shit your crew slung at ours yesterday, maybe we should go first."

"Shut up!" Bob stammers. "Everyone! We're not evacuating by genitals or crew. We're spinning the shovel."

We spread out in the circle where the big top was only an hour ago. Bob stands where the centrepole once stood, holding Jaegs' cut-down speed spade halfway between its D-handle and the tip of its blade, slowly edging his hand closer to its steel shank until he finds its point of balance. He stretches his arm out from his body as far as he can and begins twirling the shovel — like a baton at first, and now, bending his wrist down, like a chopper prop. Now he releases the shovel, and it drops to the sand, its blade pointing to Mitra.

"Hey, girl," Moira calls out to her. "Looks like you got your wish after all."

Mitra doesn't say a word; she just steps back from the circle, and Josie and Moira close the gap.

The shovel is spun again — Judd — and again — Kirsten. Another spin: no man's land, the blade pointing to the tiny gap between Steve and me. Bob walks a straight line, foot before foot like a tightrope artist or a well-practised drunk, out from the tip of the spade.

"It's almost smack in the middle. ... But not quite. Good going, Noah," he declares, as if it's possible to credit anyone for chance. "You've got the last seat on the next flight out."

Bob continues spinning, letting the indifferent, muffled clang of a Sheffield steel blade decide what he won't. The original circle tightens and tightens, but those already chosen choose to form a new circle around it. "Buzzard," a collective nod, "Jaegs," silent smiles like twenty shovels pointing in his direction.

The shovel clangs against the earth one last time — "Josie" — denying Moira her spin. Dead last. I scan our circle, our site, the lake and distant treeline, but neither Cass nor Aleron are anywhere in sight.

"Moira can take my spot," I blurt. I wait for Buzzard to protest — if you give up your spot, then everyone should move up one in the line. But he doesn't, and no one else does either.

Finally, the jet ranger returns. Judd and Kirsten are off, running hunched and shielding their eyes against the whipped-up sand, as the chopper sets down. But Mitra hesitates.

"Go!" Bob screams. "This ain't the fucking ending of *Casablanca!*"

Moira shoulders her knapsack and turns to me. "You don't have to do this, you know."

"It's better this way. You and Mitra should fly together, or she'll worry."

"They'll turn up," she says, giving me a great big hug.

"I hope so."

"We'll book a double room in town for the three of you. Thanks for being such a *mensch.*"

The pilot shouts and gesticulates wildly. I think he's swearing.

Moira ducks under the blades, steps up into the last rear seat, buckles herself in and shuts the door behind her. She and Mitra wave and smile as the bird gently rises.

I should have asked her to reserve a single and a double, I think, as I blink back the tears.

CHAPTER THIRTY-ONE

FROM THE AIR I may have seen it, the flaming river, before it spilled out of the distant treeline and flooded across the clear-cut dunes in a tide of fire. From the air, with a little sun to cut the haze, I might have glimpsed the steely glint of the Grumman's keel, upturned on an island I'm now swimming to — the one place I never thought to look, till hours after the final flight left the ground, carrying only Bob, and smoke set in like dusk, probably forcing the pilot to scrub an aerial search. Or if the canoe has been hidden in the islet's green, from the sky, Father's distance, Aleron and Cass in night vision, drifting across a satellite's infrared eye, bush-beating it to a breezier shore, and fleeing like the invisible beasts splashing into the water behind me to swim that which drowns, to a haven where air is still possible.

Didn't they hear the clamour of chopper blades and camp coming down? Didn't they want to hear it?

Soon the lake will be engulfed in flame. The shallows will steam. Already the crack and flash of Jack pine cones exploding in anticipation of ash, and the leeches and mosquitoes seem that much hungrier — one last chance to eat and breed.

I splash up onto the sandbar beach, stumble to my feet, frantically slapping the dozen or more bloodsuckers that have latched onto my arms and legs and torso, as if I haven't already got enough parasites sucking on my gut. I throw off my knapsack and rifle through letters and toothpaste and identity cards and armpit grease. No salt. No bug dope.

Wincing, I grab the tail of the leech dangling from my navel and tear it off. The ones on my back? I'll roll in the sand, scrape off the tough fuckers with a stick. They're *so* dead if they're not here. But they have to be. The canoe's gone, and this is the only place they could've paddled it, other than in circles. They probably went round to the other side to get away from the smoke. One last chance to eat and breed. The fuckers!

I stand again and brush the sand from my body. A sudden gust chills my clammy skin, the fire breathing air, creating its own wind. I want to get into my civvies, to feel civilized again, but I'm not wearing my only change of clothes until my fever has cooled and my body has dried and I'm certain the canoe's here to paddle back.

I walk the beach to spare my naked feet the pricks and thorns of the short bush-crash to the west side. I walk the beach, gazing across the water, unable to pull my eyes away from the crummies crowding the shoreline, the Prairie Schooner still hitched to Bob's white one-ton as if we'd merely pulled up the stakes to move on to the next show. The wind shifts, the fire sucking air as it spills over the furrowed slash of the final dune before the twin-trunked oasis where Cass's tent had been. As I round the tip of the island, the sea of flame slips from view; ahead, another flame appears — the modest flicker of a candle or a distant campfire.

"Cass?" I call. "Aleron?" I fumble through my pack for the ziplock bag that holds my maglite. In a blink, I'm on my back, my body succumbing to the dark and sheer exhaustion. Overhead, the island's evergreen canopy is silhouetted against the salmon-orange sky.

I awoke before dawn and resumed my search as soon as the sun had burned off enough mist to tell land from water, but the morning brought me no closer to finding Cass and Aleron. The smoke rolled in so thick that, at times, I could hardly tell day from dusk. The island is much larger than the islet it first appeared to be. Now I realize that looking across to this speck of land from the camp road, which passes the lake's southern shore, is like gazing down the long shaft of a fishing hook from the eyelet end — a foreshortened view further truncated by a hill that conceals the bay nestled in its hooked end. If it had been Cass and Aleron's campfire I'd seen last night, and not the slash burning into view around the far shore of the lake, then they must've been camped way down on the barb of the hook — a narrow rock point that is now my destination.

Starting out, I thought that the way would be an easy stroll around a uniformly sandy shoreline, but the island turned out to be as wrinkled as a human brain — Precambrian shield ridges broken by dried-up gulleys that must have brimmed with water during the spring melt and runoff. With its irregular shoreline, ravines and crowded tree-stands, the twenty minutes I thought it would take to hike there stretched to almost two hours. Even then, I've only made it as far as the edge of the bay in the hook, where a rockslide has sheered off the cliff so steeply that I've decided to rest along a small strip of beach before attempting the next climb, which looks, in Bartram's lexicon, "chewy."

Voice raw from the burning smoke and calling out their names from atop every hill on the hike, weak from diarrhea, I close up my journal and slug back another mouthful of treated water from my canteen. I force back a couple of soda crackers, which don't do much to recharge my batteries but at least help to soak up some of the excess stomach acid from the beaver fever. I didn't expect to be out here looking for so long or I would've packed more with me, though I did at the last minute fold up my telescopic fishing pole and jam it into my knapsack before sealing all into the heavy duty kitchen bag for my swim out here. At this rate, it may come in handy. So far, I haven't seen a single sign that Cass and Aleron have been anywhere on the island — not one footprint on the entire stretch of beach leading up to the rockslide, no scalped or crushed lichens on the rock caps, no depressed or overturned moss. If the flame I'd seen last night on the hook-shaped point across the bay had been their camp-fire, it's now out, and they've pulled up the stakes and moved their tent — Cass's tent — and their gear elsewhere, possibly off the island, if they'd ever been on it in the first place. But they must be here: to have stayed anywhere on the land around the lake would've been suicide. The intense fire that blazed across it overnight still flares and rages in spots with abundant fuel, and smoulders everywhere else. Besides, they could've landed Bob's canoe on just about any rocky place in the bay, or around the back of the island, without leaving any hint of a disturbance. Perhaps they finally realized something serious was up and paddled or portaged the canoe to a spot that would be highly visible from the air — not that anyone seems to be looking for us yet. I haven't seen a Jet Ranger or water bomber all day, and the skies have been just as quiet. I can only assume that either the smoke's too heavy and low-lying for a search and rescue, or that the MNR's too tied up with the million hectare Red Lake 7 fire and evacuating imperiled reserves to spare another minute poking about for a couple of fuckheads, who somehow managed to miss the entire airlift, and their even dumber friend, who skipped it deliberately.

I reach into my knapsack for the ziplock bag that contains my pouch of Drum Light tobacco and rolling papers, a necessity now that it's been days since I've been able to keep down (or in) a single, square meal. How ironic. Of all the useless things I remembered to pack out here, I forgot my lighter, while several well-skipped stones across the lake to the mainland, I could light a smoke on just about any flaming stump or logging debris I could get near enough to without melting my face off. *Tabernac!* Right when I'm jonesing so bad for nicotine that I'd be willing to try lighting up a butt with a magnifying glass.

What am I thinking? In all this smoke, I'd be lucky if I could collect enough sun to overexpose a negative or melt a hailstone.

Shit! I can't believe I followed her out here — smack dab into the circle of hell, stinking like some mangy stray. For all this trouble, you'd think she was a royal or the number one model for Chanel No. 5. What have I come for? Try stringy hair and cracking skin on the soles of her feet. Try hairy pits and legs not shaven since who knows when. Try blackfly bites so thick she couldn't even open her swollen lids, let alone flutter them. Yet before her eyes could fully open, green irises flecked with autumn red and gold, I was already falling for Cass, whose disappearance with that one-time *amigo* and two-timing bandito is weighing heavier on my Neanderthal brow with every passing minute. "Who's tenting with who and who isn't, who's getting hairy palms instead," eh MacKerel? It sure as shit wasn't you, as hard as you tried and as much as you wanted me to think otherwise; half-blind as I am to the whims and mysteries of women's psyches — feminine mantle, feminist to the bone, sometimes vice-versa, etc. — I know Cass well enough to say without any doubt that she wouldn't have leaned-to you in your stinking lean-to if her life depended on it. No; you were talking about Aleron, which might explain why he stopped calling me wanker of late, seeing as that might come a little too close to the truth — of late. I suppose he quelled his conscience by assuring himself that, at the very least, he had the courtesy to leave me the use of his tent while he took my rightful place in hers. Fucker! By the time I'm done with you, you'll be the wanker again or I'll be flying to El Salvador and signing up for your girlfriend's bird courses in ornithology, if you get my intercontinental drift.

The solid mass of spindly spruces is packed to the water's edge of the pancake bay as tightly as the pines that hug the edge of the cliff. Even if I could summon the strength to scale it or bushwhack a trail back through the woods around it, I'd still have no clear casting spot. Besides, if the sandbars on the other side of the island are anything to go by, the lake might not drop off before I'm well out from its shoreline. I could always bush-crash my way across the island back to where I'd landed, swim back to camp to salvage any food the fire might have spared. But that would be counting on too many rolls of the dice: that bears, ravens and vultures haven't already scavenged it; that the flames miraculously skirted around the camp — or at least, the Prairie Schooner; that the fire passed over it hours ago and the ground has already cooled enough to set foot there. Without food, a good nosh if I can't stomach a big feed, another bloodletting swim after a bush-crash like that might be enough to finish me off.

Fuck you, Cass. Fuck you, Aleron. Couldn't you at least have had the fucking courtesy to park the canoe somewhere visible, you lousy, inconsiderate fucks? I'd tell you to go jump in the lake buck-fucking-naked if I were sure the storm hadn't sent you and the Grumman to the bottom already, leaving me alone and with no reason to be here instead of in an air-conditioned suite at the Ramada in Fort William, or is it the Port Arthur side of T-Bay? — chasing down my presciption with tequila, to kill ya beaver fever, and a jar of super garlicky kosher pickles. If you're just lost or happen to be able to make it back this way, I'm still in the circle of hell enclosed by the flaming clear-cut and, for extra security, ringed by a lake of leeches and other fine parasites — you know, the one where we once were in a circus together.

I stop and squint out over the bay: not fifty feet from where I sit, a tiny islet no bigger nor higher than a couple of side-by-side queen-size mattresses appears through the drifting fog. Against the smoky cloud retreating over the water, the lush green mass looks to be float-ing toward me. Perfect for my purpose. I check my knapsack yet again for the telescopic rod and reel (check) and ziplock bags of leaders (check), jelly grubs (check) and Cyclops and Red Devil spoons (check and check), filleting knife (check) and anything that needs to be sealed or resealed against the water — my tobacco, my flashlight, my watch, my Book of Numbers and my pen. Satisfied, I zip up all the pouches and slide the sack over my shoulders. Leaving my shoes on a shoreline boulder, I dash through the shallows where the worst of the leeches lie in waiting and wade out to my new fishing platform.

As I near the tiny islet, the sandbar that has kept the water waist-deep comes to an end; the lake bottom drops out of reach of my feet, forcing me to tread the rest of the way. Landfall ... I grab hold of a protruding root, haul and heave myself up over the matted pile of sticks that line the islet's edge and flop in exhaustion onto its lush bed of mosses. I need food, unable as I am to digest much of anything anymore. I don't even care that I can't find my lighter or any matches for a cooking fire — I'll eat the fillets of any fish I catch raw, stripping every last morsel of flesh from its bones. What I can't stomach uncooked I'll wrap up and swim to the mainland to char over the red hot coals of some burned out slashpile or molten slab of Precambrian rock, even if I have to flame broil myself in the process. While I'm sizzling in my own greasy juices, I'll be smoking a hand-rolled cigarette.

I try to rise, but my step's unsteady, as though the islet's sinking underfoot like a waterbed, displaced by my weight. I put my other foot forward and sink deep into the spongy ground, gases belching from the islet's edge, which is now undulating in sync with the lake's rolling waves. Looking up, I see the view has changed, that I'm no longer facing the mainland but back across the pancake bay to the island's impassably sheer cliff and the jumble of boulders below, and the view's still changing. This islet's adrift, a floating bog made up of a tangle of beaver sticks and logs — rotting driftwood — overgrown with mosses and stitched together by vines and the sucker shoots and roots of some poplar-like tree.

I find an edge where the moss seems extra firm and set up my fishing rod with a nice, shiny Cyclops No. 3, figuring it'll stand out from the lake's overabundant supply of leeches much better than a jelly-grubber twisty tail. Yum, yum. Whatever Piscean delicacies swim these waters are bound to find the steely blue flash of the spoon — designed to "mimic a wounded and flailing minnow/other baitfish" — a novel treat. Bracing my foot against a root embedded invisibly in the moss, I cast my line shoreward into the bay and start reeling. Even at this distance, I can make out the Cyclops, flashing its cisco eye just below the surface as I retrieve my line, and now a long, dark shape darting after it. I slow my uptake just enough to let him take it and — *bang!* — sink the hook. The fish — probably a northern pike three feet in length or longer — thrashes to the surface only once before diving and veering off to the right. I tighten up my drag, but instead of peeling metre after metre off my reel, he lets the line go slack, as if he's decided to just float there, tread on the spot for awhile, in no hurry for anyone's dinner plate. I take up a little slack, then some more, probing gingerly for that tension. But by the time I feel him, he's swimming right for my feet, faster than I can take up the loose line he leaves in his wake. Holding the rod high, I wait for him to turn sharply to the left or right, at which point I'll be able to regain the tension, but he continues on his course, right under the floating islet. My rod jerks down violently; I yank it back up with equal determination, reeling and tugging, till the line catches on something solid and I can't reel in anymore. Snagged. Damn! The fucking fish wrapped my line on one of the sticks or deadheads of which this islet is made. With a snap, my line is suddenly weightless and free — the Cyclops No.3 gone with him. Shit!

I tie on a heavier leader, attach a Red Devil to the snap and cast again, hurtling the lure with all the strength I can muster. I don't even wait for the Devil to flutter toward the bottom; as soon as it hits the water, I crank the reel and the bailer flips over to take up the line. Again, the long, sleek form of a pike follows, torpedo-like, and clamps onto the shimmering spoon. Not about to take any chances, I sink the hook hard, swinging the entire weight of my body to one side, and reel it in as fast as I can, keeping the tension constant.

Close to the islet's edge, the pike rolls its speckled body atop the gently rolling surface, and lashing its broad fanned tail, thrusts itself down steeply into the murk beneath my feet. Arching my back, I pull the fish up toward the light, praying the eight-pound test line weaving and cutting infinities in the water will hold long enough for me to land my meal in the moss. At last, its beak-snout pierces the surface. I hunch over, slide my fingers into its slimy gills; the pike is yanked down violently, its thrashing head and flailing tail caught in a tug-of-war, the water bubbling red. Leaning back with my full weight, I haul my catch up onto the moss, and with it, another pike that has latched his jaws onto its belly just above its anal fin, razor sharp teeth slicing through scales and into intestine, Cyclops No. 3 spoon lodged in his lip.

I don't know why I'm so disturbed by it. Maybe because I'm not used to killing, and killing the few fish I've caught until now was always quick and clean. Or it may be the sight of an animal cannibalizing, mauling and eating alive another of its kind. Perhaps it's the uncertainty that the pike I'd first hooked and lost is cannibalizing at all rather than trying with all his might to deny me a life I'd nearly taken from him, protecting his own at all costs.

I reach for my fillet knife, pull the sheath off in my teeth and plunge its point repeatedly through the top of the cannibal's head, almost severing it completely and losing the body. Even now that life has ebbed out of him, his huge jaw of razory hooked teeth remains clamped to the other's half-disembowelled, convulsing belly and the Cyclops No.3 spoon still embedded in his torn lower lip. My intended catch has inhaled the whole spoon and if I want it back, I'll probably have to cut him up completely. Cursing, I thrust the knife up through his lower jaw and between his eyes, dispatching him with a final twist.

The mauve haze hanging in the sky makes reading the sun almost impossible, but I'm guessing it's late afternoon. I should fillet these pike right away, before they've bled too much into their meat. I should eat what I can, swim the rest to shore and find a place to sleep before it gets dark. I force myself to rise and begin cleaning the fish.

Both have writhing bloodsuckers all up and down their lengths, and lesions from where others have attached themselves. Both have tumour-like growths — the first, behind its dorsal fin, the second over one of its gills. With the tip of the knife, I slice each pike along the spine and separate fillet from bone, trying to steady my hands, which are trembling with hunger. Pinning the tail end of each fillet with a stick, I run my knife between skin and meat to peel off the scales. After rinsing them, I slice off a piece of raw fillet and stick it in my mouth. The flesh is chewy and tastes like mud. Not even sushi rice, soya sauce and a daub of wasabi could redeem its swampy flavour. I cut off another chunk and dice it up into small pieces. The trick is to swallow without chewing, like those yuppie losers at the pickup bars who pay top dollar to knock back a few shucked oysters, scared of how they'll taste but hoping to get laid. Good practice for swallowing past the tastebuds when they finally do. I let another morsel of pike fillet slide down my throat, bypassing tongue and gag reflex with a sip of water. Reaching for a third, I see something spherical and white moving in a cavity in the meat, and now another in a piece right next to it. I grab one of the fillets and hold it up to where the sun would be, the wan light revealing an infestation of round worms too numerous to pick out with my knife. And the fish became flesh ...

Sick to my cramping stomach, sour taste filling my mouth, I hunch over the undulating edge of the floating islet and hurl into my gaunt, bearded reflection till I've heaved myself dry. Done tossing my cookies into the lake, I toss in the rest of the pike and, exhausted, collapse on the moss, not even trying to avoid the blood. If a c.o. were here to see what I just did, fire or no fire, I'd probably be charged with spoilage. And they say there's a god in heaven.

What, then, shall I eat in my time of dearth? Will it snow white lichens across these barrens as those showered on the Sinai in a mountain wind? When I close my eyes and my mouth falls open, will it be manna that I taste or ashes on my tongue?

CHAPTER THIRTY-TWO

WHEN I OPEN my eyes, there is only the acrid taste of smoke in my mouth and not much light left in the overcast sky. All around me, I can hear water breaking over rock, hissing in its retreat over sand. I can feel small waves gently lifting me but no longer sense that I'm floating. I raise myself up on one arm: while I slept, a breeze from the southeast beached my floating islet on the tip of the island's hook. I pack up my fishing gear. I shoulder my knapsack and step gingerly across the wet stones to the solid ridge of shield rock that is the hook end's backbone. Nestled in a circle of neatly arranged cobbles before it are the charred remnants of a campfire so recent that the fine greyish white ash within has hardly been stirred or dispersed beyond the pit. So they were here last night.

Following the ridge along its arc, my eyes are drawn like moths to the light of a live campfire in the back of the bay.

"Cass!" I call. "Aleron! Oh, thank God you're here."

I scramble up onto the ridge and sprint toward the flame, my voice cracking and breaking with fatigue and thirst.

"Ola Aleron! Ola Cass!"

No answer.

"Hey wanker," I call. "There's a fire ban on. Remember?"

I approach their fire ring. Aleron's sleeping bag, set well back from the heat of the stone circle, holds their imprint as snow holds the impression of wingless angels. Just beyond the grasp of the lake, the owl, frozen spread-eagled in the moment of death, has been laid out on a plywood sheet.

"Christ, Aleron, you really oughta bury the bird already. It's getting a little ripe." Something rustles in the underbrush. I squint into the blue haze shrouding the island's tree-stand. "Hey, you there somewhere? I don't suppose you could tell me if I was talking to myself ..."

Splashing in the shallows, too big for a fish. Cass pads up the beach, grabs her towel from a driftwood stump and pulls it around her shoulders like a shawl. "Stop it, Noah."

"Stop what?"

"Don't taunt him."

"Then who should I taunt — you? Or was all of it his dumb idea?"

"You have no idea what you're talking about."

"Let me guess. The plan was to have a sunrise burial for the owl, but distracted by more important matters, you lost track of the time."

"Instead of getting all snarky and sarcastic, why don't you just speak your mind? If you'd done more of that in the first place, I might've stuck with you. Yes, I slept with Aleron last night. I felt sorry for him. He looked so forlorn. I needed the company too."

"What you and Aleron did last night is your business. I'd just like to know what kind of stupid stunt you two are trying to pull? It's snowing ash and cinders, a chopper was flying in and out of here all day yesterday, and it never dawned on you that camp was being evacuated or that people would notice you're missing and would worry?"

"I shouldn't have to remind you why Aleron doesn't like the sound of choppers. You saw how he reacted to those fighter jets that flew over us that day."

"Well, he better get to like the chopper fast, 'cause it's the only way we're getting out of here alive."

"Are you listening? He won't go. And neither will I."

"What do you mean you're not going?"

"I'm sick to death of never feeling safe where I'm living. It's never-changing, no matter where I go. Bare-knuckled competition, jealousy, backstabbing, a pecker order. ... There's no point in going back to more of the same."

"At least there's more of something to go back to. Have you gone round to the other side lately? The whole damned place must've burned up by now and the wind's blowing northwest again! By morning, this island might be all that's left for miles around, and it can't hold you forever, even if the MNR lets you stay here."

"I don't mean forever. Maybe just till the fireweed comes up and blooms." She smiles. "Or I come up fireweeds. I have to know that it's possible, that all of this will heal over and come back more beautiful than before, that I can paint it and survive in it on my own in case I figure out somewhere down the road that I can't live in their society and decide to start my own."

"A society of one? Or is it two, plus however many score offspring the chosen pair can produce?"

"Noah, you're being irrational."

"*I'm* being irrational? Where's the canoe?"

"What's it matter to you? They're not coming back till it's light and the smoke's cleared."

"You've got the fever, damn it! You and Aleron both, and it's clearly messing up your judgement. Now where's the fucking canoe?"

Aleron steps out of the forest and stands in its drip line, straddling the edge of shadow and light. "The fever? Doctor — I am so relieved! I thought it was much more serious, but this explains everything. ... Nightmares and cold sweats? Just the fever. Heartburn? The bug breeding in your belly. Homesick for a woman? Beaver fever. Unable to keep anything down, not even feelings? This pill will cure everything. This pill is a miracle, doctor! Will it also clean the stains on souls? Can it mourn my father for me?"

I look to the owl, no longer all he's come to bury; another death of an innocent.

"I saw his murder — three years ago to this day — and I left. I did not even stay long enough to see him buried. You act like you could never lose anyone like that — in an instant! Since coming planting, have you phoned or written your father even once? I bet not. You don't even lift a finger to protect what you have right here. You refused to deal with Buzzard when he pissed all over Cass, and you wonder why she has quit you."

The hairs on the nape of my neck bristle up. "Is that really why you slept with her or does she remind you too much of your own?"

"You have it so easy it makes me sick."

"And since you didn't because you were facing a death squad, I'm to blame for not doing what you'd have done in my situation? I had other options."

"Bullshit. You wrap your cowardice in doves and olive branches and spit the blood of your failure at her as if she is to blame."

"Then you should've stayed home *because* they had guns. That's what I'd've done."

He raises his fists and lunges at me, his left hook smashing hard against the side of my face. The irony taste of blood fills my mouth. I force him back with a shove. "You want the other cheek too, Sanchez? Go ahead, but make it good, 'cause it's the last cheek I have to turn."

"Stop it!" Cass shrieks. "Both of you!"

But it's too late. He throws the punch that is my finger on the button.

We hit and hit one another, cutting flesh in the crush between knuckle and cheekbone, fist and jawbone. We hit and hit till we're past pain and Cass's screams and the drumming of her fists against our shoulder blades are washed out in the rush and hum of the adrenaline coursing through our veins. Eyes swelling shut, I stagger forward and pull him into a tenth-round embrace — so close that I can see the blood trickling from my chin down his back, too close for him to throw another punch.

Breaking the hug, he raises his trembling fists and uncurls them. Taking my face in his rough palms, he kisses me full on the lips.

I can't recall how we ended up in the lake. The next thing I remember, we were kneeling there in the shallows, daubing the blood from each other's faces and rinsing them with water squeezed from strips of cloth torn from Cass's towel.

"Jesus, those cuts are bad," Cass said. "What the hell were you two thinking? I can't find my soap. Either of you got any in your packs? I could always grab a clump of sphagnum. Lyndon says it's a natural disinfectant. Even with the drought, there should be a small patch here and there in the trees."

She started up the beach, but nearing the campfire, stopped and turned, as if she didn't want to be caught in its light.

"Oh God, I'm sorry," she said, and she began to weep.

"I shouldn't have spit blood at you," I said. "After that, I didn't think you'd ever speak with me again."

"I wouldn't have either, if your aim had been any good."

"I *was* aiming at your feet, you know. But I shouldn't have."

"No, and I shouldn't have spurred Lyndon on. He doesn't need any encouragement, as much as you might."

Our eyes met the way they used to before our blowout. She knelt in the shallows and drew me to her, kissing my cuts and then my lips. When she saw that Aleron was still trembling and lost and drifting farther off, she kissed his too.

"You were right to flee, Aleron," I said. "They'd already taken your father and brother. You'd've been next. The only way to help the people you love is to stay alive."

We hugged as three lovers desperately clinging to a life that, in a matter of hours, would be over. We kissed her and through her till we lost any sense of where our bodies began or ended. After, we flopped on the beach like salmon spent by the spawn.

When Aleron shook us awake, the sky was lit red, the fire spreading west along the north shore of the lake. He wanted to bury the bird.

On the plywood sheet he'd made into a raft, we stacked kindling in a triangle and stuffed the hollow with dead pine branches and cones. Aleron placed the owl on top, lit the pyre and set it adrift on the lake. Feathers flared, ashes winged, sun sank in the sand.

CHAPTER THIRTY-THREE

JULY 25, PRINCE George, B.C. — Left Thunder Bay about a week ago, after five days at the KOA, all expenses paid, waiting for the burn to be declared dead, and with it, the contract. Of course, Bob had known that the wait would be a formality from the morning of our rescue. Nearly a month's work and the last reefer of seedlings had already gone up in ash, but a wind had shifted the flames around camp central, sparing his caravan and clearing the smoke enough for a search. Cass, Aleron and I were drifting about in the canoe, slouched over in sleep, when the pilot spotted us. None of us has any memory of leaving the island, but at some point, the smoke must have forced us to paddle in search of a breeze.

When the chopper set down in Armstrong, Bob was visibly relieved to see us. He didn't even ask Aleron and Cass where they'd disappeared to or why. After all his years in the bush, perhaps he knew. All he could talk about on the drive to Thunder Bay was a summer contract Head Office had given him to run. Northwestern B.C. Ever seen the mountains? Glacial rivers and salmon-choked streams. Spear ground at twenty cents a tree. Mountains of green to be made. Cream. The Promised Land. Just a five-day drive cross-country — free. Cass signed up as soon as the Crew List was posted, dooming me to postpone my face-the-music return to Toronto.

After dropping us at the hospital in Thunder Bay to get tested and treated for giardia, Bob handed me the latest letter from my father. Another court date, based on those not-so-trumped-up charges, has been set for September 2nd. When I phoned him from the ER, he urged me to come home immediately to give my body some time to heal and prepare my defence. I told him there's no rush: a cold bunk in jail can wait; a warm sleeping bag must never.

Aleron signed up for the Smithers job too, but after the long drive cross the prairies, had a change of heart. I think seeing the Rockies looming up on the horizon reminded him of the true vastness of the distances he has to bridge. When we first saw them in the morning light, they appeared to be no more than an hour's drive farther west; five hours later, we still hadn't reached them. But it wasn't until this morning, when we stopped to gaze in awe at the ice-capped peak of Mount Robson, that Aleron announced his decision. The ground rumbled, the slow grind of two glaciers ever-merging on its back, but only touching as water.

We went our separate ways at Tête Jaune Cache, the T-junction where the highway through Jasper meets the Yellowhead. Aleron plans to thumb his way south to the Okanagan, where he might pick fruit for a few weeks before heading back to Vancouver. Anything to be closer to that connecting flight home. Cass will be planting till the end of summer, capturing the changes in scenery in paint, and I will be planting with her.

As we parted, Aleron gave Cass a birdcall he'd carved from a branch and he gave me his spear. Cass gave him her ever-changeable watercolour of an ever-changing island, and gave me a peninsula. I gave him the finished but unpolished lyrics of a song we'd started back in June, and gave her a quart of thimbleberries I'd picked on our crew's day hike partway up Mount Robson's Berg Lake trail.

Then he crossed from the TransCanada to the southbound lane of the Yellowhead and stuck out his thumb. He hitched it south and we headed north, our lives as open before us as an empty page and the open road.

CHAPTER THIRTY-FOUR

SOMEWHERE ON THE banks of the Suskwa River, Hazelton, B.C. —
The night before our day off, Cass and I went fishing in the river near
camp. It was good to get away from the thirty-five or forty-odd people we've been planting with, eating with, and sleeping in close
quarters with in the tent-crammed forest. It was good to look back
over my shoulder and see the red-, yellow-, and green-striped big top
recede behind the treeline: sitka spruce, red cedar, lodgepole pine, as
we rounded the bend in the dust road. Crummies full of drunken
planters gone to town.

I turned my head, rested my fiberglass fishing rod over my left
shoulder like a soldier packing a rifle and squeezed Cass around her
hips — into me.

"Don't," she said. "That tickles." Face as always when she's pretending to be mad: a serious smile. We kissed.

"Come on," I said. I pulled her along at a speedwalker's pace, the
lightfooted walk that a planter who's used to climbing slashpiles and
mountain overhangs walks when he finds himself on paved sidewalks
in the city or on a well-trodden trail. "The sun's sinking fast." Pale.

Pale-orange light brushed over the pastel green of the maple and
poplar, trickled through leaves the size of our outspread hands, and

needles, like the sound of river over rock, touching Cass's face. Orange light, pale on the grey-green of mountains, deepened each crevice with its shadows. Crevices where glaciers once, and still, bled icy streams down. Light that made the rock faces seem larger than they had been when planting on them in the high noon sun. But the large, unnaturally rectangular swaths left from clear-cutting — some so big that they rolled across the sloping faces of two or more mountains, and cut right up to the steep, barren grey — were small now. Up close, in them, was to be dwarfed by a mess of cut and unclaimed logs. Slashpiles ten feet high, in windrows left by unimaginably high machines, ran rabid as the dried-up brooks, but against the true shape of the land. If it hadn't been for the long, thin lines of trees — firebreaks — separating these strips, the logged hills would be one gigantic rolling naked obscenity. As vacant as the Bowron and Kapuskasing clear-cuts: visible to the nude eye, along with the Great Wall, from satellite.

The water got louder. We reached the bottom of the road where the dirt highway crossed and turned right. Spanning the rapids was a bridge, built like a wooden railway trestle; on the other side, a cliff so steep that it rose almost at right angles to the road that hugged it and the sky, where a mountain goat appeared to be heading, sending down a stream of small rocks and stones like a shower of cold meteorites.

We slid down the skree to the roar of the Suskwa River. The water white, the mist cool.

"Where we going to fish?" Cass said.

"Up over there, there's a deep pool — just below the point where the three streams meet." I pointed to where the water was no longer white but a dark green: the green of carved soapstone polished in seal oil.

"Is this where you and Bob saw the squatters?"

"No. They were trying their luck on the south side of the bridge. This is where we saw the Native woman pull up a giant steelhead. She didn't seem to want our company, though. When she spotted us coming, she clubbed it, grabbed her fishing pole and hurried off into the woods. God she was fast! Her catch musta weighed twenty pounds. Forgot her salmon roe, though. We used that for bait."

We walked up to where I'd pointed, over the rock-pierced sand-bank. I tied a fisherman's knot around my coho lure ("Five twists, one loop ... pull through, and through again the loop you've just made," Grandfather used to tell me. Grandfather knew his knots from having redesigned, refitted and converted looms to mass produce parachute parts in the Second World War: his machines made cords that wouldn't snap, harnesses that wouldn't cut a man in half under the stress of parachutes opening as the paratroopers plummeted toward the centre of the Earth. How delicate life was in his fingers, to be plucked out of a foreign sky by enemy fire, or pulled, alive, a fish out of water. He was also a great fisherman).

As I tightened up the knot, I thought about the young Native men — Gitksan or Wetsue'ten, I was too afraid to ask — we saw fishing the Skeena on our drive into camp the first day here. I remembered the long poles with gaffing hooks lashed to their ends laid out neatly along the rocks, the river roar, the sun, the smell of the blinding violet fireweed around us and the syrupy pine scent of a distant sawmill; young men my own age with tanned chests and veins standing in strong arms as they strained and grappled with their gaffing poles just to keep them from being ripped out of their hands by the current or undertow. Water white, like the head of a beer, to the bottom — if you could find it.

They couldn't see the salmon with their eyes: they felt for them rather like a blind man taps the sidewalk with his stick, only their pathway was unsolid. More uncertain. And when one could feel a soft scaly form graze over the top of his hook, he'd yank his pole up suddenly, then pull it in hand over hand to get a look at his catch. Sometimes he would come up with nothing — deceived by the will of the salmon to get back upriver to where it had been born and had given birth thousands of times over, to relieve its oxygen-starved body of its milt or its roe. But more often than not, the fisherman would clench his teeth in a half-smile as his fish broke the surface, the pole quivering as it flailed, and knees bent, swing it over to his left or his right, onto the rocks. Then he'd strike it once over the head with a small club on a leather thong and dump it, convulsing, into a glacier-cold pool alongside the rest of his catch: ten-pound, thirty-pound and fifty-pound salmon. The pool would redden, then settle back into its icy clarity — the blood sitting on the bottom. The clubbing of the sockeye brought to mind television replays of the seal hunt from the six o'clock news.

Before too long, the dead salmon would be cleaned of her guts and stripped of her roe. Bright orange roe heaped up like tapioca pudding in a separate pile. Fish bait. I remember Cass photographing all of these. *Clic-k.* A sockeye opening his beak-mouth, the bright red hump on its back, its gills broadening in the air like the opening of a flower, to swallow the sun. *Clic-k.* The fishermen posed in the back of a pickup, the hatchback down to display the catch headed for the reserve. *Sna-p.* Jack, his smile breaking the tips of his handlebar moustache, buying a fish for that night's dinner, though it's illegal for people with Indian status to sell any of their catch to tourists — even though theirs is a small and bruised fraction of the coastal fishermen's hauls.

Now, Cass and I were fishing the Suskwa, where three separate mountain streams, melted from lingering glaciers, empty into it — a river that, in its turn, feeds the seaward Skeena.

"Noah, you wanna give me a hand with this? I've never cast an open-face reel before."

"Sure. No problem."

Cass had borrowed Bob's gear — an old rod and reel that had been made before the Second World War.

"My father's," Bob had said, offering me the worn cork handle. "That's quite a watch."

"It's a stunning watch," Cass had said, seizing my wrist to hold its face up to hers. "Where on earth did this come from?"

"My father, and his." I'd looked from my watch to Bob's rod and reel and understood the depth of his attachment, and for the first time in my life, my own.

I positioned myself behind Cass, who held the fishing rod back and high. "Relax your forearm," I told her. "That's it. Now hold the line against the cork grip with your index. Pull back the bailer ... there, now you're all set."

"Where's the best place to cast?" She glanced over her shoulder, her green eyes as clear and bright as I'd seen them all season.

"I'd drop it just off that shelf there." I pointed to where the river's rocky bottom suddenly dropped into blackness — just below the opposite bank. There, where the three streams formed a basin, Bob and I had seen the long-haired woman fishing a few nights back.

I guided Cass's arm back a little farther.

"Remember to release the line just a split second before you've swung the rod forward all the way — when it's, say, at the 10 o'clock position from where you want to land the lure."

I let go, Cass snapped the pole out in front of her: the lure whizzed out diagonally over the water, dragging the line in a smooth arc. I was stooped over, about to pick up my rod, when Cass's line stopped in mid-air, ringing the lure violently like a miniature cowbell, before it plunged straight down, into the rapids.

"Shit!" Cass yelled. "The line's buggered up."

My eyes followed the slack, curling line, its tiny circles to its source. I groaned. The spool was the biggest nest of fluorescent yellow I'd ever seen. I straightened up and took Cass's rod.

"It'll be pitch black before I get this mess sorted out."

"Well don't look at me. That reel's half a century old. It's probably been due for a little Three-in-One for about the past decade or two."

I pulled out all the loose line and began working on the tangles: the kind of knots no fisherman could outdo, with nimble fingers or tongue.

Cass looked at her feet: her lips were pursed and she hid her soil-cracked hands in the front pockets of her jeans. I could tell she was unapologetic because she was too busy being mad at herself.

"It's chilly, it's starting to get dark. Why don't you use my rod? No sense in waiting around when there's a new lure to be baptized."

She looked at me with planter's eyes — fixed and brave from a distance; floating, nomadic, uncertain up close. "Well, alright. If you don't mind —"

I felt like a melting iceberg. I wondered if maybe my roughness wasn't because I was a rock or a block of ice or even a man, but because up close I sometimes wanted to flee also.

"No. It's not as bad as it looks. I'll be joining you soon."

By the time I began reeling in the slack line piled at my feet, everything was covered in a soft purple light. The no-see-ums were out in full force and reserve, and Cass was reeling in and tugging, reeling in and a-tugging: her own rhythms.

"The mountains look best like this. On a cloudless night when you can barely make out Jupiter coming up over the pines. You know?"

I nodded, silently smiling, and scratched my burning legs. I was wearing only my shorts and a T-shirt with the caricature of a lumberjack on the front and on the back, Lakehead U, where we'd slept the night before we left Thunder Bay.

"Cheshire," Cass said.

"Huh?"

"Your smile." She too had begun to scratch, and also smiled in spite of the bugs.

Taking up the rod again, I reeled in as fast as I could; passing the line between the index and thumb of my left hand. The spool had just about taken up all the slack when I felt the lure drag along the bottom for half a second before jamming fast.

"Damn it to hell," I cursed the sky.

"What now?"

"I'm snagged. If I lose this one, it'll be the second six-dollar spoon this week."

I tugged and jerked at the bent pole. The single-hook lure wasn't budging. So I decided to walk upstream — wade knee-deep into the river — to get on the other side of the snag. The lure must've been taken by strong undercurrents under a rock or ledge. If I pulled the line upstream rather than down, the spoon might come free.

I waded past the ringlets where the fishing line pierced the surface, reeling in a slow mechanical motion. Something was not right, though; something was defying the laws of physics: of what snags are supposed to do in a river — either stay put or loosen and drift downstream. At first, I said nothing until I was sure that Cass was certain that she noticed it too, and even then, neither of us said anything, not even as the snag passed my ankles and moved with sluggish deliberation upriver. Cass opened her mouth in a big wuh? I put my finger over my lips, then gripping the cork handle with both hands, leaned back in a full-bodied pull. The pool, a recess in the bank that broke the fast water, was rent in two as a fish took flight; propelled upwards by its flailing tail and fanned-out fins. But before the water had time to fold in on itself again, the fish dove straight back through its cleaved surface.

"See the size of it?" Cass said. "Quick! Get 'em ashore. I'll get the net."

"We don't have a net," I said. "Just get me something to club it with — fast."

I wasn't about to waste any time letting out line to play the fish, as the pros on the fishing shows insist you must do; I just reeled, became a reeling machine, as if that had been my soul occupation in some past life. I held fast to the quivering rod as it bent double to the brink of shattering. The light was almost gone and the moon hadn't come up yet. I could no longer see what was splashing me. All I know is this: once I had its tail a few inches above the water, I raised the rod high and swung the dark, dripping form over to a sandy patch of bank. The fish flopped and thudded across the white sand, then went still as a whale beached in a desert. The only thing I could make out in any detail was one of its eyes: a round-as-a-quarter, cooling eye that caught the last reflection of faded purple in the dusk sky and maybe a brightening planet.

I wedged the cork handle between two washed-up logs and waited. I heard a rustle in the leaves and twigs snapping under a light, fleet-footed step. A shape rushed toward me and I almost took heel like the Native woman had, when I realized it was Cass. She held out a piece of driftwood, a stubby knot in one end of it.

"Here. It's all I could find."

"Perfect." I grabbed the naturally-formed club and turned to the sandy bank. "Now where did that fish get to?"

"For Chrissake, Noah!" Cass pointed to the water. "It's getting away!"

I fumbled with the fish, which had flopped and edged its way over to the stream. If it hadn't been for the grit that clung to his slimy scales, he would've slid from my clutches, out of my element and into his. Lifting him at the middle, I felt something sharp and cold graze my skin, from my wrist to the joint in my thumb. Then a rush of warmth. His head angled up, the mass of his body sagging to the ground, I raised the driftwood club and, as Cass turned her head away, brought it down lightning-like over his back where his gills met his spine.

Aleron always said that fishing was best after the new moon. ... Too bad he wasn't here to join us for the feast. We would have to set an extra plate in his honour.

The hum and chugging of the pump and generator became louder: Jack was finishing up the dishes. From the road, we could see the glow of the big top; through the translucent Egyptian cotton, Jack wiping the tables. Buzzard was seated on a bench: its two-by-four seat sagging between two sections of tree stump. A Drum rollie hung from the side of his mouth, over his thick red beard. We walked triumphantly into the tent; Cass's fingers hooked through the fish's gills and out its mouth.

"Holy mackerel," Buzzard said. "That trout must weigh ten pound."

"Trout?" Jack bent forward and squinted. "Are you sure that's a steelhead?"

"No way this is a trout," I said. "Look at the beak on it. It's a salmon."

"It ain't no coho, that's for sure," Jack said. "No, I think Buzzard's right. It's gotta be a rainbow."

"Why don't you clean it now?" Cass said. "We all know what salmon fillets look like, right?"

Buzzard drew on his Backwoods cigar. "About the same colour as trout. They're from the same family."

Cass handed me the fish, and I took it around the back of the mess. I returned to borrow Jack's fishing knife and tear a piece of cardboard from a box of Okanagan peaches.

Cass held the flashlight for me as I slit the fish's belly from its anal fin to its gills. A large translucent sac, white with milt, spilled out onto the cardboard. I stripped out the mass of pink and liver-red organs — the stomach and intestines, the kidneys, the heart — made an incision along its spine, cut off its head and peeled its scaly body open into two orangey-pink halves.

"It's a salmon alright," I said. "Just look at the colour of those fillets!"

"The colour?" Cass said. "Look at the size! We're gonna eat well tomorrow morning."

"In the morning?"

"Queen Victoria herself used to have poached salmon at breakfast, until the Thames was so poisoned that the fish stopped running up her. Poached salmon ..." She smacked her lips. "Beats kippers 'n Billionaires by a long shot. Here —" she grabbed for the fish. "Let's show Jack and Buzzard."

"Not yet," I said. "First we have to take it down to the brook to wash it. I'm not at all interested in bringing a grizzly to breakfast, so I'm gonna throw these fish parts in the water."

"Okay. I'll get some saran wrap and foil, and make some space in the fridge."

I walked down the path, past Jack's tent; fillets in one hand, remains on cardboard in the other.

By the brook, the moon was almost blinding. Every night, I thought, I fall asleep to this tiny brook's steady gurgle, underlapped by the more distant roar of the river it feeds. I bent down on the rocks to wash. Scales stuck to my hands took on a strange lustre in the cool, milky light. As the icy water ran through my fingers, I noticed that the tear in my hand had clotted. The salmon sure was a fighter.

I rinsed the fillets and laid them out on a log. Then I picked up the piece of cardboard box, and tipping it slightly, ever so slightly, let the salmon's bones and skin and innards slide into the water; as if I were dedicating a body to the sea.

"Probably a spring salmon," Jack would say.

Cass would be wanting to get to bed. The last, bloated organ hit the water, was grabbed up by the current and pulled down. The cold brook, clear as glass, went white with milt, then cleared.

ACKNOWLEDGEMENTS

MY WARMEST THANKS go to Susan Swan, who encouraged me to use a short story I'd written for her class as the seed for this book and whose mentorship over the years has been essential to my development as a writer. I'd also like to thank my agent, Margaret Hart, for finding the right publisher; Marc Côté and Donya Peroff for their editorial insights on the final drafts; and Bianca Spence for getting word out. Last but not least, I greatly appreciate the support of the Canada Council for the Arts, which helped to get me started.